Jenelyn's Journey

The Werewolf of Wittlich

BOOK 1

Book Bubble Press

First published in Great Britain in 2021 by Book Bubble Press

www.bookbubblepress.com

A CIP record of this book is available from the British Library.
ISBN: 978-1-912494-80-4

Book Bubble Press

When you're safe at home, you wish you were having an adventure; when you're having an adventure, you wish you were safe at home.

- Thornton Wilder

May all who read this enjoy their life's adventure.

Acknowledgements

I would like to extend my utmost gratitude to Book Bubble Press for their commitment and effort in helping this book come to life. Also, to Scott Editorial for their painstaking work of tediously combing through each word to ensure the book reached the highest standard.

This book wouldn't exist without both these efforts, and for that, I'm forever grateful.

\- E. E. Byrnes

The Beginning

Chapter One

Jenelyn didn't hear the chaotic din of the city, the siren's plaintive wail, or the gang's aggressive shouting outside as she stood staring at her parents in the tiny living room. The amber glow of the late afternoon sun filled the windows, creating an orange tunnel of light that softly descended onto the faded blue sofa where her parents sat, looking at her with solemn pride. Her mother's almond-shaped brown eyes brimmed with tears.

'It's your time, Jenelyn,' she said, her voice quavering, 'you're eighteen; the Spirits are ready for you now.'

Her father laid a heavy, comforting hand on her mother's thin shoulder. Jenelyn didn't miss the twitch of a smile under his thick, black beard.

'This is part of our way of life,' he explained, his deep voice warm and patient. 'We don't choose our homes. The Spirits do, and we must honour them.'

Jenelyn nodded apprehensively, trying to grasp the meaning of her parents' words. She found her gaze sweeping over to the large painting that had been hanging above the sofa her whole life. It was an image of a group of Romani gypsies, dressed in traditional attire and playing musical instruments. The colours are vibrant, emulating perfectly the spirit of the flamboyant and jubilant people. Though her family wasn't from Romani heritage, her mother had always loved the painting, her bohemian spirit connecting with that freedom.

Along with this free way of thinking came a passionate, spiritual belief of higher powers that she called the Spirits. This bohemian culture had been the cornerstone of Jenelyn's upbringing, and for as long as she could remember, she had known this moment would come, but it did not prepare her for the shock when the time actually arrived. Her gaze focused briefly on the desk calendar stating the year '2008' before settling on her parents again. The year had seemed so far-off while growing up, but now it felt too much in the present.

'So, I must leave you forever?' she asked, her voice trembling with fear.

Her parents gave each other a quick glance and Jenelyn's stomach tightened. She recognised that look they always gave when trying to prevent her from being frightened.

'That isn't a guarantee,' her father reassured her. 'The Spirits may decide that Los Angeles is the best place for you, and you'll be back from your Journey soon. If not, you may earn enough money to visit us.'

Jenelyn snorted under her breath. She could never believe that. Her neighbourhood was in a dangerous part of central downtown, a ghetto filled with gangs who fought weekly over turf. She had loathed it her whole life. Surely, the Spirits understood this, although she knew other parts of the city were nicer. Perhaps the Spirits might bring her back to her parents under better circumstances. With this thought, she gathered a little bit of courage and pasted on a brave smile.

'When do I leave?' she asked, her heart fluttering with nerves.

'In two weeks,' her mother stated. 'Your father and I have already purchased your ticket to Germany. We know a nice couple in Wittlich who are willing to have you stay with them. Their names are Laszlo and Gretchen Weneseivers.'

Her mother rose and walked over to a small corner desk. She picked up an envelope and handed it to Jenelyn. Jenelyn stared at the online printout stating her ticket number, still in shock.

'This is a one-way ticket,' she said, alarmed.

Her parents nodded, her father still speaking in his gentle, comforting tone.

'Jenelyn, we provide the means to get there. The Spirits lead you the rest of the way. You must be self-sufficient during the Journey.'

Jenelyn gripped her jeans nervously, her hands squeezing the rough material in a panic. She bit her bottom lip and suddenly found it difficult to breathe. She had never lived away from home before. How could she survive all on her own in a strange country? Her mother saw the terror on her face and was quick to encourage her.

'I did this too when I was your age. My blood runs through you, and you have the same freedom of spirit that I have. You have the strength and courage to do this. I know you will succeed in finding your true home.'

'Why did you choose Germany? Is it because you know people there?' Jenelyn asked in a numb voice.

Her mother's full lips parted in a crooked grin as she explained. 'It's tradition that the first destination is always the country where your maternal great-grandfather was born. A woman I met on my Journey kept in touch with me, so it was convenient that we knew someone there. I've never shared with you the details of the Journey tradition. It wasn't time, but now you need to be prepared.'

She had settled back into the blue sofa and reached out a hand for Jenelyn to hold it and to come sit with her. Jenelyn tried taking a deep breath to still her racing heart. This was her family's tradition. She needed to focus through the nerves and pay attention.

Her mother continued. 'This tradition started with my great-grandmother. Her Journey was due to necessity since her family was killed during the Civil War. She was also not a religious woman but had strong spiritual beliefs. When she became orphaned at sixteen, the Spirits came to her. They told her where to go and continued to lead her until she found my grandfather and settled. She was so grateful to them that she raised her daughter to believe in them and wait for them to guide her life. The tradition has been followed ever since, with each generation successfully finding their true home. The rules of the Journey are simple. Always listen for the Spirits contacting you. They come in various ways, so you need to be observant. You'll feel them when they appear, just as you'll feel when they leave. And never settle until the Spirits let you know it's time.'

'And there's no way of knowing how long the Journey could be?' Jenelyn asked, biting her lip worriedly.

'Unfortunately not,' her mother said softly. 'Just have faith that they're guiding you in the right direction. I would give you some advice, but I think a lot has changed in thirty years.'

Jenelyn felt a tear escape and slide down her cheek. She didn't trust herself to speak without breaking into sobs. Her pale face and watery eyes, which were full of anguish, didn't escape her parent's notice. They stepped forward to hug her, and she basked in the warmth of their familial love.

That night, Jenelyn sat on her single-sized bed and looked outside her small apartment window. Neon lights flashed from the bars outside, and she heard loud voices calling each other, their cries boisterous and angry. Why the Spirits had chosen Los Angeles to be her mother's true home bewildered her, but she assumed it had something to do with her father. Her mother had followed the bohemian way of life from birth, and when her father had married her, he had chosen to practice the culture. They had met at the corner market, so Jenelyn couldn't be too disappointed in the Spirits' decision. Her parents adored each other, and had raised Jenelyn in a circle of love and support. However, she despised their neighbourhood. Her parents were too poor to go on holidays, and she had never been any further than an hour away from home.

She went to her window, straining to see the twinkling stars behind the towering skyscrapers. As much as it scared her, she wanted to leave this neighbourhood and travel the world. She wanted to see more sights than a gang fight on the street or drunken fools wandering past homeless people who had given up all hope that a better life existed. She yearned to see rolling hills and peaceful country towns.

She stared at the ticket lying on her bed between her much-loved childhood stuffed elephant and a tattered gold throw pillow with one consuming thought; her Journey. Wistfully, she picked up the stuffed elephant, running her finger down the golden tassel on the circus blanket it wore. It was the first stuffed animal her father had bought for her. She had been three when they'd gone to see the circus.

Despite their meagre livelihood, her parents always ensured she had everything she needed, and most importantly, their support and love. Her eyes shifted to the gold throw pillow, a relic of her early teenage years when she had wanted to make her room a little more mature. Even through those rebellious years, when she could have easily turned away from believing in the Spirits, her parents had gently guided her in the right direction. Yet throughout all that time, her parents had known they were going to lose her. It pained her to think that perhaps that's why they'd tried so hard to make her upbringing so comforting and secure. She held her stuffed elephant to her chest tightly, fear making her want to cling to her childhood for a moment longer.

She desperately asked the Stars*; do I have the wisdom and courage to do this*?

She often looked to the Stars for guidance, but tonight they twinkled silently back, and she wondered if she could have heard their answer if a car bursting with rap music hadn't been driving by. A soft knock rapped on her door, and she turned to see her mother smiling at her, her coal-black hair tinged with strands of grey. Jenelyn had watched that hair turn from shining black coal dust to a smoky-grey tinged with black highlights. It reminded her of how old her mother was, and made Jenelyn think about how many years she had prepared for this. Even then, it wasn't long enough.

'I've come to say good night and see how you're doing,' her mother said, her eyes warm and understanding.

Jenelyn shrugged and sat on her bed. Her mother sat next to her, wrapping her arm around Jenelyn's athletic shoulders, moulded from years of playing on her school's softball team. Feeling her mother's warm arm around her stifled the rising panic in her stomach.

'I suppose I'm alright,' Jenelyn said. 'But I'm scared. I don't know if I'm ready for this.'

Her mother shook her head, her tone rueful. 'I know I wasn't.'

Jenelyn looked at her in surprise, and her mother nodded.

'Oh yes, I was petrified when my mother told me,' she admitted. 'Nothing can prepare you for what's to come. But we can have faith that the Spirits will guide us in the right direction.'

Jenelyn frowned, serious doubt weighing on her as she wondered whether this path was the right choice for her. 'Do you feel that the Spirits chose the right home for you?'

Her mother listened to the chaos outside and seemed to know what Jenelyn meant. She pondered for a moment, and Jenelyn imagined she was thinking of the unknown possibilities that could have been her life.

'I agree that I would not have minded a quieter place,' she answered, 'but I can't second-guess them. I met your father, didn't I? And how would I have gotten my little miracle if I hadn't come here?'

Her mother gave her a tight hug, and stroked her hand through Jenelyn's raven-black hair. Jenelyn knew her mother was right, but she wished for a better life for her parents. She hated the thought of them growing old here. Or was it the thought for herself that scared her? Although it terrified her to leave her parents, deep in her heart she yearned for a life of her own and understood that the Journey could fulfil an unspoken promise of a happy future.

'I wish the Spirits would guide me to a place with green countryside for as far as the eye can see,' she said. 'It seems a little impossible, doesn't it?'

Her mother gave her a quizzical glance, and then raised her eyebrows, considering the possibility.

'Not impossible, but I wouldn't be too picky, Jenelyn,' she warned. 'There are so many wonderful sights to see in this world. It may surprise you what you end up loving. The Spirits know what is best for us all.'

Jenelyn knew her mother was right. She had to have faith, but that was easier said than done. Her mother got up from the bed and stretched her long graceful arms, reaching high. Jenelyn loved her mother's arms. They were a dancer's arms, and back in her day, her mother had been able to dance as elegantly as any professional had. Jenelyn wished she had inherited such grace, but unfortunately, she had only acquired two left feet.

'It's been a long day,' her mother yawned, 'I'll see you in the morning. Rest easy, Jenelyn. You still have another two weeks before you leave.'

Jenelyn smiled. 'I know, and I will. Good night, Mama, sleep well.'

'Good night, baby.'

'Hey hottie, why don't you come over here and give me some fries with that shake?'

Jenelyn glared at the tattooed gangster leaning on the chain-link fence. She was walking around the block to her friend's house, and catcalls always annoyed her. She knew the best thing to do was ignore them, but sometimes it was difficult. Keeping her head high, she walked faster. The voice came again, loud and vulgar.

'Aw, come on, sugar, don't leave me hangin'.'

Jenelyn couldn't take it anymore. She whirled around, her temper flaring out of her control.

'Oh go find a corner and beat it yourself.'

Instinct told her to run for it, and considering the murderous glare and curses the punk was shooting at her, she knew she couldn't run fast enough. She immediately took off, knowing the gangster would be on her heels. She looked behind her, not surprised to see his dark, hateful eyes and red face seconds behind her. But because of his drunken state, he tripped on the footpath and fell heavily. Jenelyn sprinted around the corner and didn't stop running until she got to her friend's apartment. Her heart was beating fast, and she shook with adrenaline.

Idiot! She was furious with herself for satisfying that hoodlum. When would she ever learn to keep her mouth shut? Usually, she was able to keep her temper in check, but sometimes she had the uncontrollable urge to snap back. So far, she had been lucky, but she knew one day she wouldn't be. Growing up in a rough neighbourhood had toughened her too much, and she hated it. Her friend answered the door on her first knock and grinned, though her smile dimmed at the sight of Jenelyn's flushed and flustered face.

'Hey, Jen, I'm glad to see you made it. Are you okay?'

Jenelyn's worried face relaxed as she hugged her best friend, Nicole, happy to see her familiar red curly hair and jade-green eyes. They had been friends since kindergarten, and they were as close as sisters were. It was going to be extremely difficult to tell her about the Journey.

'Sorry I'm late,' Jenelyn explained, her heart slowing from a racing gallop. 'My mom wanted me to go to the store before I came over, and then I got a little sidetracked.'

She raised her eyebrows pointedly and rolled her eyes. Nicole frowned, well aware that she lived on a gang's turf. Looking solemn, she walked to the phone, fully prepared to ring the police on speed dial.

'I can call the police and give them a heads up?'

Jenelyn shook her head, still remembering the creepy look on the hoodlum's face. She knew his vicious, beady eyes intently stalking her would haunt her dreams that night. Fortunately, she had learned long ago to try to shrug off these experiences quickly.

'No, I just did something stupid. This jerk catcalled me, and I snapped at him. I hate my temper sometimes.'

Nicole chuckled, leading Jenelyn to her bedroom through a tiny kitchen with peeling white linoleum and faded yellow cabinetry. Jenelyn noticed every detail, knowing it was the last time she would ever see it. The kitchen was as familiar to her as her own; a hard knot of sadness caught in her throat at the thought.

'I know what you mean,' Nicole was saying, laughing ruefully. 'It isn't hard to get you riled up, girl. I do it myself often enough.'

Jenelyn couldn't help but laugh at the honest statement. Like sisters, she and Nicole had often fought and squabbled over various events; they all seemed so petty and insignificant now. She always took comfort that she could be herself and Nicole would still love her. Telling her the news wasn't going to be easy.

Jenelyn gathered her courage and followed her friend into the bedroom.

'Nicole, I need to tell you something.'

'Alright, that doesn't sound good.' Nicole stiffened in worry.

Jenelyn shook her head and sat on Nicole's bed. She couldn't figure out the best way to do this. How do you tell a best friend, almost a sister, that you may never see them again? She looked around the tiny, cluttered bedroom and years of memories flooded through her. Countless Saturday night sleepovers where she and Nicole would binge on junk food and compete to stay awake the longest, the first time Nicole taught her how to paint her nails, and many afternoons where they helped each other with impossible algebra homework or long reports while gossiping about teachers and mutual friends. She choked back a sob as she spoke.

'You remember my eighteenth birthday party last week?'

It had been a small party, with just her parents, Nicole, and Nicole's parents, but it had been full of exuberant celebration, with her father playing his guitar, a table groaning with her favourite food, and the girls chattering nonstop about the enthralling concept of being an adult. Nicole nodded, her worried face lifting with eager excitement as she sat on the bed next to her, crossing her legs comfortably. Worry never sat with Nicole for long, since her upbeat and energetic demeanour always outweighed it.

'Heck yeah, I do! I can't wait until I turn eighteen next month. It's going to be great being able to vote, play the lottery, and gamble at Indian casinos.'

Jenelyn felt a sharp pain in her heart. She wouldn't even be here for her friend's eighteenth birthday. Tears formed in her eyes, and Nicole instantly hugged her, her eyes full of concern.

'Jen, what's the matter? You're acting like your family is moving or something.'

Jenelyn shook her head and managed to speak, the words falling through the air like lead weights. 'No, Nic. But I am.'

Nicole's face fell as she stammered a response. 'What? But why? How?'

'You know my family follows a bohemian culture, Nicole,' Jenelyn stated, knowing discussing the Journey would be tricky.

Jenelyn had never liked talking about it, and had only mentioned it in passing to Nicole several years ago when her mother had told her the story. But the girls had been too young to bother discussing it again. Until now.

'And when we turn eighteen, we have to go on the Journey,' she continued. 'I've told you about that before.'

Nicole nodded and twirled a string from her tattered quilt subconsciously, her thoughts racing. She and Jenelyn never really discussed Jenelyn's culture, so she had to recall faded conversations tucked away in a cobwebbed memory box.

'I remember, it's when the so-called Spirits guide you to your true home. Right? So, now you have to do that?' she asked matter-of-factly, suddenly connecting her faded memory with the news Jenelyn was giving her.

Jenelyn nodded and wiped her eyes, her voice muffled in her sleeve. 'I leave in two weeks for Germany.'

Nicole's eyes widened, and she leapt up from the bed angrily. 'Two weeks?' she yelped, 'But that's too soon! You're not even going to be here for my birthday! It's not fair.'

Her eyes became stubborn and challenging, the way Jenelyn knew they would. When Nicole got upset, she turned into a child. Jenelyn tried to explain calmly, knowing she needed to be patient.

'Nicole, it's not my decision. It's a tradition that I have to follow since it's our belief. Besides, though I'm scared, I look forward to finding a better home than this dirty city. I want you to be happy for me.'

Nicole's eyes softened, but her mouth was still pouting. Jenelyn knew she struggled between understanding and fighting the loathsome tradition that would take her best friend away from her. After a few moments, Nicole's cheek twitched up into a rueful smile and Jenelyn could tell that deep down, Nicole knew it wasn't Jenelyn's fault. Jenelyn knew Nicole almost as well as herself, and knew that as long as she was safe, Nicole would learn to be happy for her.

'Of course, I'm happy for you if you can get out of here, but I'm going to miss you so much!' she cried. 'When will I see you again?'

Jenelyn looked at her with distress and shook her head. 'That's the worst part. I don't know if you will.'

Impenetrable silence filled the room for so long that Jenelyn wondered if Nicole was ever going to answer. She squirmed awkwardly, waiting for her to reply.

'You may not live here, but you can always visit, right?' Nicole finally asked, her voice hollow.

Jenelyn shrugged. 'That depends on how much money I make. My mother never saw her family again. She settled here, and my parents never had the money to go visit her family in New England.'

'Well, what about writing or calling me? I know you don't like being on the internet with MySpace and everything, but you could manage to write a letter or pick up a phone, right?' Nicole persisted, refusing to relinquish this one hope of maintaining contact.

Jenelyn frowned, her eyes tearing up again at the most painful part. The bond of friendship that she and Nicole had grown over their lives was like a thick rope, strongly woven with laughter, tears, tantrums, and hugs.

'I'm not really allowed to contact anyone I know,' she explained, so softly that she hoped Nicole heard her. 'Part of the Journey is being alone.'

With those words, she could see in Nicole's eyes that she had cut their rope, leaving nothing but frayed edges.

Nicole erupted, her lips pursed tightly, her cheeks burning crimson, and her bouncy red curls flying as she paced the floor with fury. Her dangerous green eyes glittered when she looked back at Jenelyn.

'I can't believe it!' she hissed. 'I'm supposed to be happy about this? I have only two weeks left with you. Forever! How could you do this to me?'

Jenelyn shook her head, her eyes pleading as she tried to calm her friend. 'I'm not doing this to you. This is about me, not you. It's something that I *have* to do, whether I like it or not.'

Jenelyn was surprised at her friend's vehemence. She knew that Nicole would be sad, maybe even depressed, but angry with her? It hurt her to see how little Nicole understood what she wanted.

'Don't you see, Nicole?' she continued, desperate to make her understand. 'This is my only chance to make a new life for myself. I don't want to be stuck here forever. I'll miss you terribly, but this is a new beginning for me. Honestly, I'm scared beyond belief, but a part of me is excited too.'

Nicole took a deep, shaky breath and tried to calm down. She sat back down on the bed beside Jenelyn, and gathered what patience she owned. Her angry red cheeks softened back to their regular pink blush, and Jenelyn knew that meant her friend's outburst was over. To Jenelyn's relief, Nicole's voice was calm and collected when she next spoke, but her eyes were distant.

'I understand, but I hope it's for the best. How are you going to support yourself in Germany?'

Jenelyn shook her head and raised her hands helplessly. 'I have no idea! I don't even speak German, and I'm sure there are immigration laws about working that I don't even know. It's so daunting and intimidating I don't know if I can do it.'

Nicole studied her carefully. Jenelyn could see that Nicole didn't envy her, and for a moment, she wished they could trade places.

'Trust me, Jen, you'll be fine,' Nicole assured her. 'You've always been brave and smart. This is just going to put you to the test.'

Jenelyn grimaced. 'That's what I'm afraid of.'

Nicole hugged her, making Jenelyn's chocolate brown eyes widen with surprise at this sudden show of affection. She was grateful, though, and hugged her back fiercely as Nicole cried into her shoulder.

'Oh, Jenelyn Doe, I'm going to miss you so much!'

'Nicole,' Jenelyn laughed, her voice muffled in Nicole's red curls, 'it isn't like I'm dying. I will do everything I can to come back and visit. Or better yet, you could come and visit me when I settle.'

Nicole narrowed her eyes, suspicious. 'I would, but when are you going to settle?'

Jenelyn shrugged, knowing it could take years. 'I don't know. I have to keep going until the Spirits tell me to stop. I'm going to have to learn how to listen to them carefully.'

Nicole pursed her lips, her face heavy with resignation. 'Well, let me know. Then we'll see what we can do about finally meeting again.'

Two weeks later, Jenelyn's father was putting her bag in the boot of a cab outside of their apartment complex. The time had swiftly disappeared between being busy visiting Nicole as much as she could and going on final day trips with her parents. The entire time she felt as if these last moments with her friend and family weren't long enough. Nicole's anger had thawed, though there was a new distance between them that told Jenelyn their friendship had shifted slightly. No longer were they carefree girls bonding over school and childhood. Now they were two young women growing apart into their own lives. But her time with her parents had been the most bittersweet. They had spent their last moments together as a family visiting places they had enjoyed while she was young, such as having picnics on the beach and dancing to her mother's favourite music at home. These treasured moments had touched her deeply and made her wish she could turn back the clock to spend more time with them.

The final day had come now, and Jenelyn and her mother were hugging intensely, neither one wanting to be the first to let go.

'You be very careful, Jenelyn,' her mother sniffled, two streams of tears falling down her cheeks.

'I will, Mama,' Jenelyn assured her. 'But I can't believe you and Papa aren't coming to the airport with me.'

Her mother sadly shook her head. She grasped Jenelyn's hands tightly as she pulled away from their embrace and studied Jenelyn, seeming to memorise every line on her daughter's face, from her full lips to her milk chocolate eyes. Jenelyn watched her mother's eyes change from seeing her little girl to understanding the young woman she now was, and heard the heartbreak in her mother's voice as she said her final words.

'It's for the best, baby,' she murmured, a sob choking her voice, 'I can't stand goodbyes, especially at airports. Besides, it's good for you to be on your own from the moment you step away from home, and don't forget to watch for Laszlo and Gretchen when you get to Germany. They'll meet you at the airport and should be holding a sign with your name. Be safe, sweetie, and may the Spirits protect and guide you well.'

Her father came up behind Jenelyn and enveloped her in his strong arms, squeezing her tightly. For a brief second, Jenelyn wished he would hold her forever, and she could return to being his little girl who never had to leave his side.

'We never say goodbye, Jenelyn,' he explained firmly. 'It is *latcho drom*, good journey. I learned that from your mother, and it is a very wise saying.'

Jenelyn nodded quickly in agreement and tried to keep her tears from spilling. She wanted her parents to believe she was brave and capable so they would feel better about her leaving.

'Then *latcho drom*, Mama, Papa,' she said valiantly. 'I love you both, and I hope that the Spirits will allow us to meet again.

Her parents hugged her one last time, and Jenelyn couldn't keep her tears in check. Finally, she broke away and got into the cab before her parents could see her tear-stained face. Her voice was thick with sorrow but strong as she gave her orders to the cab driver.

'Take me to the airport, please.'

Chapter Two

Tears distorted Jenelyn's vision as she stared at the mass of people around her. How was she going to function if she couldn't stop crying for two minutes? She swallowed a sob and tried to find her airline's check-in counter. Her flight was leaving at four-fifteen this afternoon, she had two hours to check-in and go through security, and she needed to stop crying! Frustrated with herself, she inhaled deeply, wiped her eyes, and tried to focus. She had to be strong. She couldn't disappoint her parents.

Glancing around, she saw her airline queue. The clerk at the counter was smiling patiently as she assisted each passenger. Jenelyn saw that people were handing the clerk their printouts, and she was giving them their tickets. She took a deep breath and got into the long queue, praying that it wouldn't take so long that she would miss her flight. After an agonising thirty minutes, it was finally her turn, and she handed the woman her print-out and passport. The clerk greeted her, her expression cheerful and her tone cordial.

'How are you today? I see you're going to Munich, Germany. Do you only have the one carry-on?'

Jenelyn nodded, her lips frozen. She felt surreal. The woman smiled politely and told her to have a good flight. Jenelyn's heart stopped beating frantically, and slowed down to a steady gallop. Now that she knew her gate number, it was time to look for a directory. Finally, she managed to catch sight of one from the corner of her eye as she rushed past. She ran over to it, and saw that her gate was on the other side of the airport. At least she knew where she was going now. She breathed slowly, and her eyes started to dry, only to tear up again minutes later.

This is ridiculous! she snapped at herself. *You can do this*.

Unfortunately, she didn't believe herself at all. She didn't have any experience of travelling. What was she thinking even *trying* to do this? Despite her pessimistic thoughts, she kept walking, passing people by as if they were standing still. Jenelyn only vaguely noticed the onlookers watching her in surprise as she power-walked past, her bag bouncing against her thigh. The airport staff ushered her into the security queue, which was lengthy and tedious, though she was grateful she didn't have to talk to anyone. After another thirty minutes, she left security, arrived at her gate, out of breath, and terrified. Her long hair hung wildly around her shoulders in tangles, and her eyes were puffy and red from crying. She knew she had to look appalling. She stared at her ticket, biting her lip anxiously. She would arrive in Munich at twelve forty-five in the afternoon. It was her first plane ride, and it was an eleven-hour, twenty-minute nonstop, overnight flight! The length of it frightened her, especially knowing she would be in a confined space for so long. She had never liked enclosed spaces for long periods, and eleven hours seemed endless.

Her heart started beating uncontrollably again, and she began to tremble. What was she going to do for that amount of time? It hadn't even occurred to her to bring a book. When packing, she had been so panicked and depressed that she had simply brought her necessities: clothes, toiletries, and pictures of her parents and Nicole. She had figured that she wouldn't need anything else until she got to Germany, and then she could buy supplies after she found work. Now she wished that she had thought of a book.

The next hour passed all too fast, and soon the flight attendant was calling for her gate to board. Jenelyn watched everyone around her with wide, curious eyes. They all seemed very calm and organised, while she felt like she was one step away from running back home. She swallowed in fear and gave her ticket to the flight attendant with a trembling hand.

'Have a nice flight,' the woman said, her bright smile never diminishing.

Jenelyn nodded in thanks, and barely managed to form a grin in response. She walked haltingly down the grey terminal to the aeroplane, her mind frozen and barely noticing her surroundings. She felt overwhelmed when she looked at the sea of seats spreading out before her. It was a massive plane, with two aisles and three sections of seats. Her seat was near the rear, so she had to stand and wait for everyone in front of her to find their places before she could get to her own. Settling in her seat at last, she closed her eyes and wondered if she could simply sleep the whole way. She was so emotionally exhausted, her body drained of all strength and energy, that the narrow confines of the seat and sparse legroom didn't even bother her. She was finally sitting down, in the plane, after the chaos of the airport, and it was absolute bliss. After a long while, the doors closed, and a flight attendant was standing in the middle of the aisle, explaining all the emergency procedures. Feeling more refreshed, Jenelyn watched her in boredom, and was grateful when she said her closing speech.

'Thank you for flying Mapiya Airlines, and have a nice flight.'

Jenelyn looked at the back of the seat in front of her and was relieved to see a small television screen with a list of movies. She simply couldn't sit in one place for eleven hours without a distraction. Thank the Spirits they showed movies! She felt if she could keep her mind occupied, she wouldn't become nervous during the long flight. She stretched her arms to get comfortable and accidentally whacked her elbow into the person next to her.

'Oh, I'm so sorry!' she gasped.

The older woman turned to her and smiled dismissively, shaking her head. She was in her mid-sixties, with snow-white hair and pleasant wrinkles lining her face. Her blue eyes sparkled like two bright sapphires.

'Don't worry,' she said, her aged voice sounding as warm and soothing as melted butter, 'I'm used to cramped seating. I have a son who lives here, and I visit him often.'

Jenelyn's nerves from her mistake eased, and she was thankful that the woman wasn't going to get her kicked out of her seat. She wasn't used to meeting friendly people who were complete strangers. A brief flash of the punk's cold, hateful stare flashed through her mind, but she forced him out, focusing instead on the gentle woman sitting next to her.

'Well, sorry again,' Jenelyn said. 'I'm not used to this. This is my first flight.'

The older woman raised her eyebrows in surprise. 'Is it really? How old are you?'

'Eighteen,' Jenelyn replied, understanding the older woman's surprise. 'But my parents don't travel, so I never had the opportunity to travel on a plane before. I find it very nerve-wracking.'

The older woman chuckled. 'Oh, it is at first, that's for sure, but you grow accustomed to it. My name is Vicky. What's yours?'

'Jenelyn,' she said happily, glad to have someone to distract her.

Vicky's face glowed pleasantly. She also seemed happy for the company. 'That's a very beautiful name and so unique. So, Jenelyn, why are you going to Munich?'

Jenelyn hesitated a moment before answering. Vicky seemed lovely and certainly not a person to be afraid of, but she was a stranger, and as naïve as she was, she didn't want to say too much.

'My parents are sending me to see old family friends,' she explained cautiously. 'They wanted me to have a vacation.'

If only that were the truth, she thought miserably. A vacation sounded nice and fun; relaxing, interesting, even pleasurable. She was doing exactly the opposite, but she didn't want to tell Vicky about her Journey. People could sometimes be wary of her family's way of life, thinking they were crazy and peculiar. There were times Jenelyn couldn't blame them. Being the only one who believed in Spirits and different traditions had made her cautious.

'My goodness, that's very nice of your parents!' Vicky exclaimed. 'I'm sure you'll have a good time. Germany is gorgeous this time of year.'

Jenelyn's ears perked up. 'It is?' she asked, feeling the first pangs of hope. Visions of sweeping meadows and cloudless blue skies filled her mind. She even optimistically added a glittering stream and majestic mountains in the background.

'Oh yes,' Vicky chirped happily. 'I love May in Germany. The snow is still melting, and the warm air is such a relief. I always enjoy preparing for my gardening about this time. I love to garden and have many different roses and such.'

Jenelyn was curious about Vicky, who was obviously American. Yet, she spoke of Germany as if it had always been her home. As Vicky continued to ramble on about her rose garden and topsoil, one word stood out to Jenelyn. Snow? Her bright vision faded somewhat. It never snowed in Los Angeles. If it was already May and the snow was *still* melting, then Germany must be very cold. Her sparkling stream froze in her mind, and a chill wind swept away her cheerful meadow and covered her mountains with a white blanket. Her hope vanished.

'That sounds very nice,' Jenelyn mumbled, catching up with Vicky's explanation of her marigolds, and then ventured to ask. 'How long does the snow last?'

'Oh, the snow will only last a couple of more weeks during spring, and soon we'll be right into summer,' Vicky continued, not noticing Jenelyn's downcast expression or the fact that she had missed most of the gardening story.

The mention of summer cheered Jenelyn up a bit. She had never liked the cold, instead preferring warmer weather. Summer sounded more promising.

'I'm sure I'll enjoy seeing everything,' she stated, deciding to have a better attitude.

This was an adventure, and quite possibly the only adventure she would ever have. It was time to start enjoying it. They had taken off by this time, and Jenelyn's stomach was still somewhere up in her chest, trying to get down.

'It's pretty intense when we lift-off, isn't it?' she asked, releasing her clasping fingers from her armrest.

'Yes, but I love the feeling,' Vicky sighed wistfully. 'It always reminds me of home.'

'How often do you come to Los Angeles?' Jenelyn asked, hoping Vicky wouldn't mind her curiosity.

'Oh, I visit my son at least two or three times a year. I only have one son, so I try to go as often as I can. I would move here, but I love my Germany so much.'

Jenelyn thought it was nice that Vicky had the money to visit her son as much as she did. She knew that airline tickets from Los Angeles to Munich couldn't be cheap. Her parents had saved her whole life to send her to her first destination.

'Have you always lived in Germany?' Jenelyn wondered aloud. 'You don't have a very strong accent.'

Vicky shook her head patiently. 'No, I was born in Missouri and married my husband there. He belonged to the Air Force, and they transferred him to Germany when my son was three, and we lived there until he turned twenty. Then my son decided he wanted to live in California. We missed him very much, and when my husband died of leukaemia, I found that I couldn't bear to be away from my son all year. But nothing could ever take me away from the country I learned to love and the established friendships I've made.'

It sounded as if Vicky had found her true home. Jenelyn couldn't wait for that to happen to her, though she felt sorry for the widow's husband passing.

'When did your husband pass away?' she asked gently, wondering if she was starting to offend Vicky with all of her questions, but the older woman seemed delighted to talk to someone.

'Five years ago,' Vicky said reflectively. 'It doesn't feel like it at all. Jerry was a good man, and I miss him dearly. But it's a joy seeing my son turning out just like him.'

Jenelyn knew her parents would feel the same way about her. And that made this Journey all the more important. She simply couldn't disappoint them.

'Oh,' Vicky said after a few moments of contented silence. She had been combing through the selection of movies on her screen, 'this is a good movie. I hope you don't mind. I always watch them.'

Jenelyn assured her she didn't and found the same movie on her screen. Vicky put her headphones on, and Jenelyn followed her example. It was a comedy, and she found it a light relief from her worries.

The second movie Jenelyn chose was a drama, and she was crying halfway through it when she felt the overwhelming need to nap. She was far too emotional to handle anything heavy. She set aside her headphones and snuggled her head into the seat, trying to find a comfortable place on the small airline pillow. Closing her eyes, she savoured the silence from the movie. The hum of the plane was like calm white noise, and she drifted off quickly. After an hour, Vicky woke her, telling her that they were serving dinner. Jenelyn was groggy from sleep, but extremely hungry. She hadn't eaten since she had lunch before the airport. To her surprise, the food was in sealed packaging, but it was surprisingly good. She inhaled the green beans, potatoes, and small slice of turkey. She had ordered a soda to drink and decided not to take the risk of pouring the can into her glass of ice. Her tray rattled as they hit an air pocket, suddenly causing her fork to leap off the tray. Jenelyn barely caught it and looked around, nervous that the plane was bucking beneath her. Vicky saw her expression and laid a placating hand on her arm.

'Don't worry, this happens all the time,' she soothed.

Jenelyn managed to calm down and keep eating, though it was difficult to keep her heart from racing around her, and her bouncing stomach still, as the turbulence continued. After a half-hour, she chose an action movie, knowing the loud noises and active pace would match the frantic tempo of her heart that the turbulence had caused. Nestling into her seat, she put on her headphones for another two hours.

Three and a half hours later, Jenelyn looked out her window into another world. She was used to the skyscrapers of Los Angeles, yet this city was a vast landscape of greenery and old buildings. Jenelyn couldn't stop staring below her in fascination. A trickle of excitement snaked its way through her stomach as the plane descended gradually, and she started to see tiny black dots racing each other around the buildings. She realised they were cars, and a knot of anxiety formed in her throat. This was it! Her Journey was officially beginning. There was no turning back now.

The plane landed with a hard jolt, and Jenelyn relaxed for the first time in eleven hours, relieved to be on the ground again. Unfortunately, she didn't stay relaxed for long. Vicky was busy grabbing her carry-on and smiled at Jenelyn before she left with a cheery wave.

'I hope you have a wonderful time here in Germany, Jenelyn. Be safe!'

Jenelyn waved back, and a fist tightened around her heart. She walked down the long tunnel to the airport and shivered at the cold. When she entered, she noticed signs pointing her towards Immigration that directed people towards either a European queue or a non-European queue. Her heart pounded even harder. She had forgotten that she would need to pass through immigration. She timidly followed a group of people toward the non-European queue. There was a large crowd in the line already, and she wondered how long it would take. She also worried about what she was going to say. No one had warned her that she would need to tell someone why she was here, though she should have thought of it. She supposed all she could do was tell the truth. Far too quickly, even though the better part of an hour had passed, it was her turn. The uniformed officer sitting behind the window was horribly intimidating, and it didn't help that he never smiled.

'Hello,' he said curtly in English. 'May I have your passport?'

Jenelyn immediately handed it to him, her mouth so dry with fear that she wasn't sure how she would speak. He glanced up at her.

'How long are you in Germany for, and for what reason?'

His deep voice was direct, demanding an immediate answer. Jenelyn took a deep breath and answered, her voice shaking.

'I'm here to visit family friends,' she explained. 'I'm not sure for how long.'

At this, he narrowed his eyes and pursed his lips.

'Since you are from the US, you are not required to have a Schengen visa,' he explained firmly. 'However, you are only allowed to stay here for up to 90 days. If you stay longer, you must apply for a resident permit.'

Jenelyn nodded fervently. 'I understand,' she assured him quickly.

'Are you planning to work while you're here?' he asked.

'I will have to if I'm here long enough,' she explained, nerves coiling inside her stomach. She hoped her pale face didn't make her look like a scared rabbit.

The officer stared at her for a brief moment, and grunted. She couldn't judge what he was thinking, but he didn't seem very happy.

'To work here, you must apply for a work permit,' he explained, his tone short and stern, 'But you will need a residence permit first. You need to go to the German Aliens Authority in the town you're staying and apply there. This needs to be done immediately.'

He put heavy emphasis on the last word and stared hard at her, his dark eyes boring into her own in warning. Jenelyn nodded seriously.

'Yes, sir,' she said sincerely, 'I will go there first thing.'

'Gut,' he said, clipping the word through his teeth, his tone final. 'Then that is all. Have a good day.'

He handed her back her passport, and Jenelyn walked quickly past the window. She was sure she left her stomach and heart pounding on the floor in front of him. Her body felt empty and cold. Fear had overtaken her once again, but she knew she wouldn't forget one word that officer had told her. Taking a deep breath, she looked around the busy airport. What now? Well, somehow, she needed to try to find Laszlo and Gretchen and a big sign with her name on it. She clutched her bag and stepped out into the arrivals area. Searching frantically, all she saw were hundreds of strangers.

So far, the Munich airport didn't look too different from the one in Los Angeles. Of course, the layout was different, and the design, but the atmosphere was the same. Passengers rushing back and forth, people waiting, people wandering, everywhere people. Jenelyn had no idea how busy it would be. For some reason, she didn't expect Germany to be as populated as Los Angeles. She frantically found a place to sit down, panic consuming her. Since there had been signs and queues to follow off the plane, she hadn't had time to feel lost or alone. Now in arrivals, she felt truly alone for the first time. She was in a foreign country, and as far as she knew, the people she was meeting had no idea what she looked like.

Breathe, breathe, she commanded herself firmly.

When she felt the terror subside, Jenelyn stood up again and took charge of her senses. She was intelligent; she simply had to use her common sense. The logical step would be to search the immediate area in arrivals and see if that's where they were.

This should be where Laszlo and Gretchen are, she thought, and looked around, worried that she might not be in arrivals.

She searched the wide-area for what seemed like an agonising eternity, checking every seat and walking past every couple. Finally, she saw an older couple standing next to an escalator but somewhat hidden behind a fake plant. The man was holding a large, white sheet of paper with her name typed in an elegant, but clear font. Her name was spelt wrong, with the 'y' replaced with an 'i', but she didn't care as the rush of pure relief washed over her. Jenelyn ran to them ecstatically, her bag clunking against her leg. She was no longer completely alone!

'Are you Laszlo and Gretchen Weneseivers?'

The man and woman nodded, their eyes sparkling. They were a well-built couple who appeared to be in their mid-fifties. Laszlo was tall, broad-shouldered, with curly brown hair, and deep blue eyes. Gretchen was a little shorter but still a very tall woman, with golden-brown hair that rolled in waves down to her shoulders and light brown eyes. She flashed a bright, excited smile of white teeth and ruby-red lips that captivated Jenelyn.

'Hallo!' Laszlo greeted and gave Jenelyn a big hug. 'I'm glad to see you have arrived safely. Gretchen and I were starting to worry you might have gotten lost.'

Surprised by their warm greeting, Jenelyn was pleasantly surprised to find that they spoke English, even if their accents were incredibly thick.

'I'm glad to see you, too! I was worried I wouldn't find you.'

Gretchen nodded sympathetically, her amber eyes gentle and warm, similar to the way her own mother looked at her. Jenelyn felt a maternal love coming from her.

'Kommen sie, you've had a long flight,' she reassured her, placing her arm across Jenelyn's shoulders and guiding her towards the exit doors. 'It's understandable to be a little flustered.'

Laszlo started leading them out to the car. The road they had to cross was busy with traffic. Like in Los Angeles, though, Laszlo and Gretchen crossed at the pedestrian crosswalk, then walked for a little way down a road to a large car park. Jenelyn curiously ran her eyes over multiple signs in German, wondering what they meant. A strong smell of petrol wafted on the chilly wind, and as her arms shivered through her thin windbreaker, she wished she had worn a warmer coat.

'I would like to thank you both for allowing me to stay at your home,' she said gratefully. 'I truly appreciate it. And if I can get a good enough job, I might be able to afford my own place.'

Gretchen squeezed Jenelyn's shoulders, her arm still wrapped around them. This unnerved Jenelyn a bit, but she was too polite to say so. She wasn't used to strangers touching her.

'Now, don't worry. We are more than excited to have you with us. Laszlo and I have been lonely for a very long time.'

She gave her husband a meaningful glance, and he acknowledged her with a tight smile, though neither indulged. Jenelyn was curious at the silent exchange but didn't want to pry. They arrived at the car, and she was shocked at how small it was. It seemed small enough to easily be run over on the road, and she could imagine it being crushed in an accident. Feeling a little nervous for her safety, she folded herself in the back seat next to her bag. It was a tight fit, but she figured if Laszlo and Gretchen could do it, so could she. Laszlo turned to her, his face apologetic.

'I'm sorry, but since it's usually only Gretchen and me, we only needed a small car for the two of us. I hope you are still comfortable.'

'Oh yes,' Jenelyn assured him, not wanting to complain about her knees almost reaching her chest. 'I'm quite comfortable. How far is it to Wittlich?'

Laszlo chuckled matter-of-factly. 'Five hours,' he said, giving a low whistle at the thought. 'I wish your parents had chosen a closer airport, but they had purchased the ticket before contacting us. Now, because of the long drive in such a confined space, I was hoping we would make a few stops. I want to show you some of the cities we'll pass on the way to Wittlich and give you a nice feel for Germany.'

Jenelyn thought that sounded perfect, though she was beginning to wonder if she would be able to stay awake. Her eyes felt heavy, and laying her head down on her bag was painfully tempting. The jet lag from the nine-hour time difference wasn't helping either, but she didn't want to be rude.

'That sounds very interesting, Laszlo,' she said politely. 'I think it's a great idea to help break up the five hours.'

Gretchen turned to her, her eyebrows raised in genuine agreement. 'Me too!' she exclaimed. Jenelyn watched Laszlo put the car in gear, and they zoomed out onto the autobahn.

Chapter Three

Laszlo and Gretchen kept up a steady conversation, but Jenelyn had difficulty staying focused on what they were saying. She was intrigued with the cars speeding past them and the lack of speed signs on the autobahn. Sitting in the tiny car felt remarkably unsafe, and she was sure that any second other cars would crash into them. Laszlo didn't seem to be driving nearly as fast as the people around him.

'Are there any speed laws at all?' she interrupted Laszlo and Gretchen. 'I don't see any signs for them. Couldn't that be really dangerous?'

Laszlo laughed and looked at her in his rear-view mirror. 'I wouldn't worry too much, Jenelyn. Speed signs aren't always posted, but there are general rules. The recommended maximum speed on the autobahn is 130 kilometres per hour, but there is technically no legal speed limit. Inside urban areas, the average speed is 50 kilometres per hour and outside them is 100 kilometres.'

Jenelyn wasn't sure if she ever wanted to drive in Germany. It sounded very intimidating. Gretchen seemed to be reading her mind and quickly reassured her. 'You don't have to learn to drive right away. Spend some time settling in first.'

Jenelyn nodded in relief. She had gone through her driver's education courses and had even gotten her driver's permit, but since her parents couldn't afford to buy her a car, she had never bothered to acquire her actual driver's licence. Driving was a luxury in the city for those who could afford it. She had relied solely on public transportation along with her parents, so she wasn't upset in the slightest by not being able to drive.

'Where are we going?' she asked Laszlo, hoping that the next city was close. They had been driving for a little less than a half-hour, and Jenelyn's folded legs were already beginning to ache.

'Augsburg, which is about 88 kilometres northwest of here,' he responded. 'It'll take us about an hour to get there. I wanted to get some distance between us and the airport before we stopped.'

Gretchen turned to Jenelyn, her face shining with excitement. 'We haven't been there in years since Laszlo and I don't get out very much. We're so excited to have you stay with us.'

Jenelyn was starting to like Gretchen a lot. She was so cheerful and sweet, and she genuinely seemed to enjoy having Jenelyn with them.

'I'm happy that you don't mind me staying with you,' Jenelyn admitted. 'I was a little nervous about being a nuisance.'

'Oh, you're not a nuisance at all!' Laszlo assured her. 'Gretchen and I needed some company.'

Jenelyn was getting a little suspicious that it was the third mention of him and Gretchen needing and wanting company. The couple seemed very happy together, but she sometimes noticed an underlying message of sideways glances between them that she couldn't fully read. Jenelyn decided not to worry too much about it. She would be staying with them for a while, and would surely learn all there was to know in due time. This was not the moment to pry.

'Well, I'm happy to be of service,' Jenelyn said. 'How long has it been since you've gone to Augsburg?'

Gretchen counted in her head. 'Meine güte,' she replied in surprise, 'it has to have been at least twenty-five years ago! Lately, Laszlo and I haven't been into travelling. But now that you're here, perhaps that can change.'

Jenelyn noticed Laszlo's lips tighten at this, but Gretchen smiled warmly at her. Jenelyn returned it with her own, but she was curious. Her family never travelled either, but that was because they didn't have any money. She knew this could be Laszlo and Gretchen's reason as well, but the subtle actions from Laszlo and Gretchen made her doubt it. They didn't seem to think she was watching them, but their glances and tight faces had not gone unnoticed. Jenelyn pushed down her suspicious thoughts. She was overthinking the situation. She looked out the window and watched the cars whizzing past them. It was time to change the subject.

'What autobahn are we on?' she asked Laszlo, saying aloud the first question that came to her mind.

'We're on autobahn A8,' he replied. 'We'll take this all the way to Augsburg.'

They were silent for a while, and she enjoyed watching the scenery pass by. There were small patches of snow next to the road, the icy white softly melting into the brown earth and eroding away into mud puddles. Vicky had been right.

It may be warm enough to melt the snow, she thought dismally, *but it's still cold.*

Jenelyn wasn't used to snow. In fact, she had only seen it once, when a friend of her father's had invited them up to Big Bear to stay at their family's cabin. Big Bear was a mountainous region near San Diego, and one of the rare places in southern California that snowed. She hadn't liked it then, and she didn't like it now.

She cuddled closer to her bag, trying to get warm. Laszlo had turned on the heater, but it wasn't quite hot enough for her. She yearned for the scorching heat of California. Her parents used to tease her that she must be cold-blooded and needed a heat rock since it could never get hot enough for her. She didn't know how she was going to cope with snow. After a long time, they turned off the autobahn and travelled through a large city of colourful old buildings with grand architecture that still managed to be quaint. Jenelyn was impressed with its size and loved how charming the buildings were, unlike the cold glass and steel skyscrapers in Los Angeles.

'Is this Augsburg?' she asked, excited.

Laszlo nodded, amused at her excitement. 'Ja, it is. It's quite sizeable, actually. Augsburg is the largest city of the Swabia region.'

Jenelyn stared at the ancient, tall buildings, her eyes inhaling every detail. Each one of them had a different colour and design, from being bright yellow covered with ivy, to a line of grey, green, and blue buildings with faces of windows. All of them seemed to have individual personalities, and were much older than the ones in Los Angeles, at least by two hundred years.

'What are we going to see first?' she asked, her tone eager. 'All of these buildings are so beautiful!'

Gretchen chuckled. 'I'm glad to see you're excited. The first thing to see is the Augsburger Rathaus, the town hall of Augsburg. It was built in 1620, and it's quite impressive. Laszlo, why don't we find a place to park?'

'That's what I'm trying to do,' he answered, his words clipped and lips tight with concentration.

Gretchen grinned and rolled her eyes at Jenelyn. 'He takes parking very seriously.'

Laszlo finally found a place to park on the side of a narrow street. Jenelyn couldn't wait to stretch her tired legs. She didn't have long to stretch though, because Gretchen immediately set off at a fast pace, with Laszlo right beside her. She struggled to keep up. They certainly liked to walk fast!

'How far is it to the Town Hall?' she asked, breathless, and her legs screaming.

'Only a couple of kilometres,' Gretchen replied easily, her long legs swallowing up the ground with incredible speed.

People were everywhere as they walked down the streets. Tall buildings towered over them, and cars rumbled loudly beside them. Jenelyn soaked it all in like a sponge and heard the guttural sounds of peoples' conversations. German certainly wasn't the prettiest language, but it was interesting to listen to. She couldn't imagine how she was going to learn such a complicated dialect. At the pace they were walking, it didn't take them long to get to the Town Hall. She stopped in amazement. It was six stories high, with two enormous towers on either side with roofs shaped like dewdrops. There were two balconies underneath the towers, and Jenelyn hoped that she could stand on one. From there, she was sure she could see all of Augsburg. She turned to Gretchen and Laszlo, awestruck.

'It's absolutely magnificent!' she cried.

'This hall was built in the Renaissance style. Notice the unusual tops of the towers,' Laszlo explained.

Jenelyn nodded in eager agreement. 'Can we go inside?'

Gretchen gave her a wide grin, her eyes shining. 'Ja, you will need to see the Goldene Saal on the second floor. It was a meeting hall. We'll also show you Mozarthaus, which is the house where Mozart's father Leopold was born. You do know who Mozart is, don't you?'

Jenelyn racked her brains as they walked inside the Town Hall, knowing the name sounded familiar and that she should know it. It was embarrassing, but she couldn't remember who he was.

'I'm sorry,' she apologised, feeling completely uneducated, 'I know I *should* know him, but I'm afraid that I can't quite place him.'

Laszlo looked shocked, but Gretchen answered before he had a chance.

'Das ist in ordnung,' she assured her quickly. 'Mozart was a very famous composer back in the eighteenth century. He wrote many compositions and operas. If you listened to any of his songs, you would recognise them.'

'I'm sure I would,' Jenelyn mumbled, though uncertain.

In truth, she had never been one to listen to classical music very much, preferring mainly new age and rock, but she didn't want to embarrass herself again in front of Laszlo and Gretchen. It was obvious that they were much more cultured than she was. Finally, they arrived on the second floor and arrived at the hall that Gretchen had mentioned, the Goldene Saal. Jenelyn immediately understood why Gretchen had seemed so eager to show her. It was much more elegant than the Town Hall, with ornate statues sculpted in dramatic and artistic poses of emotion. She could see why the name of this hall meant 'golden.' Gold moulding and sculptures dripped from the walls, and all of the accents of the décor were a gleaming gold. At first glance, the sculptures seemed to be simply of normal people or creatures, but on closer look, she noticed some of their faces were twisted in agony or their eyes were wide with fear. She cocked an eyebrow and looked away.

Jenelyn wasn't quite as impressed with this hall since it was a bit too ornate for her taste. She preferred the grand, but simple design of the Renaissance style.

'This has always been an exquisite building,' Laszlo began, 'but never one of my favourites. It has too much gold for me.'

'I'll remind you, Laszlo,' Gretchen continued, 'that this hall is the most important room in the Town

Hall. It was one of the most famous monuments rebuilt during the German Renaissance.'

'I stand corrected. Let's keep going,' Laszlo chuckled. 'I don't want to get home too late.'

Jenelyn agreed with him. She was tired and hungry but didn't want to sound like she was complaining. It was already nearing two o'clock that afternoon, and they wouldn't be eating dinner for four or five hours.

It will take that long just to get home, she thought dismally.

She hoped that maybe Gretchen would say she was hungry, but until then, she simply had to wait. They walked for another few kilometres, searching for the Mozarthaus. Finally, they arrived at a line of houses, which were all narrow and two-story. Each house was the same, with flat faces, tiny windows, and very dull colours, aside from one. To Jenelyn's shock, this one was a very poignant pink. Gretchen immediately pointed out the golden letters over the door that said *Mozarthaus*.

'It's a very unique little house, isn't it?' she asked.

Jenelyn nodded slowly. She had never seen a pink house before, and it seemed all the more vivid because of its brown and tan neighbours.

'Was it always pink?' Jenelyn asked incredulously.

'Oh, I'm not sure, but I doubt it,' Laszlo explained. 'You see, this house had massive extensions and re-designing in the last few decades. They may have stuck with the original colour, but I'm not sure. It's been here since the seventeenth century.'

Jenelyn studied the building for a while, fascinated by its history and age.

'It's a very interesting design,' she said, thinking it looked odd with the second and third story windows in the middle protruding further out, 'Did Mozart ever live in this house?'

'Nein, he never lived here,' Laszlo answered, 'But he visited several times when his father lived here for a short period.'

Jenelyn wished she knew more about this Mozart. Laszlo and Gretchen were well educated in his history. They looked at the odd house a while longer, and then Laszlo began walking away.

'We need to keep going,' he said. 'We still have two more cities to see before we get home.'

Jenelyn and Gretchen agreed and followed Laszlo to the car. A cool wind was picking up, and Jenelyn wrapped her arms around herself.

'Is it always so cold here?' she asked Gretchen.

Gretchen grinned and shook her head. 'Nein, it gets warmer when we get into summer. We've actually had a pretty mild spring too.'

Jenelyn was relieved to hear this and felt summer couldn't arrive soon enough. They arrived at their car at last, and she grimaced at the thought of having to squeeze back into the tight little back seat. Gretchen saw her face and gave her an apologetic smile.

'Es tut mir leid,' she consoled. 'I really hate to see you so restricted. Stuttgart isn't terribly far, only an hour and a half from here.'

Jenelyn forced a polite smile and accepted Gretchen's apology; however, inside she was screaming. Her legs were already preparing to fall asleep, and she was hungry. The spicy smells of meat and onions wafting on the streets as they walked past restaurants hadn't helped, but she enjoyed Laszlo and Gretchen's company and sightseeing, so she wasn't about to complain. The car roared to life, and soon they were back on the autobahn heading to Stuttgart. Augsburg had already impressed her with the architectural design of the buildings in Germany and she couldn't wait to see more.

Chapter Four

Pressing a hand to her grumbling stomach, Jenelyn looked out the car window. They were approaching more forests, and the landscape was becoming a lush green, despite the patches of snow still covering it.

'It's beautiful,' she said in admiration.

Laszlo nodded, happy to show off his country. 'We have to drive through these vineyards and forests to get to the city. The vineyards and forests surround Stuttgart, and the city is close to the River Neckar. It's very rustic here, and what I love is there aren't very many tourists.'

'Laszlo,' she suggested, 'We should really eat. It's already nearing four o'clock, and poor Jenelyn hasn't eaten since her plane ride. She must be starving.'

Gretchen gave Jenelyn an understanding look, making Jenelyn nod in appreciation.

'I am a bit hungry,' she admitted.

'Bestimmt,' Laszlo agreed jovially. 'Not a problem. I knew we would have to eat before we got home anyway. Stuttgart is a great choice. They're known for their wine and their stew, which is their famous dish. Do you like wein, Jenelyn?'

Laszlo looked at her curiously in his rear-view mirror again. Jenelyn didn't want to sound rude, but she had never tried it. She quickly explained how a person had to be twenty-one years old to legally drink alcohol in the United States. Laszlo looked surprised but shrugged good-naturedly.

'Well, being eighteen, you're allowed to drink here, so you'll be able to try it!'

Jenelyn felt a rush of goose bumps prickle across her in nervous excitement about trying her first alcoholic drink. She looked out the window, picturing Nicole's green eyes widen with surprise and her pert mouth pouting with childish jealousy.

Imagine what Nicole would think, she smiled to herself, *she would be green with envy that I can drink now! I sure miss her.*

A heavy melancholy wrapped around her, warming the excited goose bumps and dampening her nerves. Nicole seemed very far away now, and it saddened her to know she wouldn't be able to share this momentous memory with her. Shaking her head to clear her thoughts away from her friend, Jenelyn turned back to watching the road and scenery around her.

They were nearing Stuttgart, and Jenelyn's eyes widened. They were going over the crest of a hill into the city, and the bird's eye vista was breathtaking. Stuttgart appeared much larger than Augsburg had been, spread out like a patchwork quilt of old buildings and greenery that was nestled between emerald hills. Laszlo drove carefully off the autobahn and into the city, finally parking on the side of a busy street. Once inside the city, Jenelyn could have a closer look at the aged buildings and noticed they were of the same style and colours as the ones in Augsburg. She loved how quaint and elegant these buildings were here compared to Los Angeles, and was happy to see that they continued to be the same in each city. Jenelyn jumped out of the car the moment it stopped, stretching blissfully. Her legs were tingling and painful, but she was standing. She stared at the bustling activity around her and grinned. It was wonderful being out of the cramped car and in the fresh air again! Laszlo and Gretchen joined her.

'Well, I think the first thing we need to do is eat,' Gretchen commanded.

Laszlo and Jenelyn agreed, so they set off to find the nearest restaurant. The footpaths were busy with well-dressed day shoppers and business executives similar to Augsburg, but not crowded, and Jenelyn found them to be a nice change from the rough crowd from her neighbourhood back home. These people seemed sophisticated and friendly, adding a general pleasantness to the city itself.

'So, what else is Stuttgart famous for?' Jenelyn asked, hoping that Gretchen and Laszlo would know.

Laszlo looked at Gretchen in question, his voice uncertain.

'Ich bin mir nicht sicher. What do you think, Gretchen?'

Gretchen raised her eyebrows in surprise and laughed.

'You mean you don't know?' She teased her husband, poking him playfully, 'Stuttgart is called the 'cradle of the automobile'. That's because the motorbike and the four-wheel automobile were invented here in 1887. They even have the Mercedes-Benz Museum here. I can't believe you, Laszlo. You remember Mozart in Augsburg, but you couldn't remember the automobile in Stuttgart?'

Laszlo gave her a wry look.

'I'm not a walking encyclopedia, Gretchen,' he said dryly. 'Now, let's get to a restaurant and eat before we all collapse with hunger.'

Jenelyn agreed full-heartedly. They walked further into the city centre and finally came to a small café called Grand Café Planie. It seemed large and was a bright yellow with dark blue awnings stretching over iron dining tables and wicker chairs for outside seating. Laszlo opened the door for them and they went inside. It was quite busy, but Jenelyn liked the atmosphere. It was an interesting mix of industrial and cosy at once, with farm-style dining sets and large industrial iron pipes that reached high into the vaulted ceiling. Low-hanging black lights hung over them as they sat down at a small table and waited for the server to arrive. Jenelyn hoped she didn't look too conspicuous as she looked around wide-eyed, but she had never gone out to eat very often and felt self-conscious. Her face must have shown some uneasiness since Laszlo leaned over to her and grinned.

'When the waitress comes, say you want to order the Gaisburger Marsch. That's the famous stew I was telling you about.'

'Will she understand me?' Jenelyn asked, concerned. She wasn't sure if everyone in Germany spoke English.

'She should, but if not, we'll take over,' Gretchen assured her.

When the waitress came over, Jenelyn swallowed nervously. The waitress looked at her first, smiling.

'I would like the Graisburger Marsch and water, please,' Jenelyn ordered, feeling very uncertain and stumbling over the foreign words.

A slight frown crossed the woman's face and she looked at Laszlo and Gretchen in confusion.

'Was hat sie gesagt?'

Gretchen patted Jenelyn's hand in reassurance.

'Don't worry, we'll order for you.'

Jenelyn breathed with relief and sat back in her chair. Laszlo took over the order.

'Wir würden drei glas weine, und drei eintöpfe bitte mögen.'

The waitress nodded and walked away, jotting down their order.

'What did you say?' Jenelyn asked Laszlo, 'I didn't hear you say Graisburger Marsch.'

'I told her we would like three glasses of wine and three stews,' Laszlo explained, 'I figured she would know what stew I wanted. They are famous for it, you know.

And you're lucky to be having their famous wine as your first!'

'Very true,' Jenelyn said, feeling like an adult for the first time.

It was hard to believe she was sitting in a foreign country with strangers and about to have her first alcoholic drink. She felt sophisticated and grown-up, which made her sit a little taller and smooth her napkin on her lap. She suddenly felt prepared to handle being with strangers and so out of place. But really, she was very fond of both Gretchen and Laszlo. They weren't quite strangers anymore. She knew she was fortunate that her parents had known such kind people here. When the waitress returned with their orders, she set down their plates and gave them a friendly smile. Jenelyn immediately picked up her spoon to start eating, but the waitress's cocked eyebrow of disapproval stopped her.

'Guten Appetit,' she said pointedly, and Laszlo and Gretchen smiled back at her gratefully.

Gretchen turned to Jenelyn in explanation. 'It's the etiquette here that we wait for the host to say Guten Appetit before we begin eating.'

Jenelyn nodded, feeling a little sheepish and murmured an apology, which Gretchen quickly dismissed as unnecessary. That awkward embarrassment over with, she looked at the bowl of stew greedily. She found that it consisted of some sort of noodle, pieces of potatoes, beef, vegetables, meat broth, and roasted onions. It looked very strange to her, but she was so hungry she didn't care. Taking her first bite, she relished the pungent spiciness and beefy depth that exploded in her mouth.

‘What do you think?’ Gretchen asked, watching as Jenelyn savoured the bite and was eagerly reaching for more.

‘Oh, it’s very good,’ Jenelyn exclaimed. ‘What is this noodle? I’ve never had anything like it.’

‘It’s called spätzle,’ Gretchen answered. ‘It’s a staple here in Germany. It’s not really a noodle; it only comes out looking like one.’

Jenelyn had fallen in love with the stew, but she also noticed that Gretchen and Laszlo were enjoying their glasses of wine very much. She was curious about the wine, since she didn’t really know a lot about it. She stared at the ruby liquid in her glass, admiring how pretty it was.

‘It’s made with Trollinger grapes, which are only grown in this region. It’s delicious, have a sip,’ Laszlo encouraged, lifting his own glass and tipping it towards her, ‘Zum Wohl!’

Gretchen repeated the cheer and sipped her wine. Jenelyn repeated him, lifted her glass, and took a small sip. The taste was strong, slightly bitter, but there was a hint of fruitiness in the flavour. Still, it made her tongue feel somewhat heavy and she knew it was going to take awhile to get used to.

‘I’m sure it’s an outstanding wine,’ she assured Laszlo, ‘but I’ll need more time to appreciate it.’

Laszlo chuckled, understanding. They finished their meal, and Jenelyn felt a lot better. She was more energetic and felt like she was finally awake. Gretchen noticed her bright eyes and chuckled.

'I knew we just needed to get some food into you,' she said, poking Jenelyn in the ribs. Jenelyn was starting to notice that Gretchen had quite a fondness for poking.

'So, what do we want to see first?' Gretchen asked, looking around.

'Zuerst?' Laszlo asked, 'I think we should only see one place today, Gretchen. It's getting rather late, and I don't want to get home at midnight.'

Gretchen looked disappointed but agreed with Laszlo. They still had quite a way to go before arriving in Wittlich.

'You're right,' she conceded.

Jenelyn held up her hands and shook her head. 'Anything we see will interest me.'

Laszlo seemed to be thinking deeply. 'It is four-thirty right now,' he mused. 'How much longer do we have before dark?'

Gretchen looked at the sun hanging in the middle of the sky and shrugged. 'I would guess another two hours.'

'If we have another two hours before dark,' Laszlo explained, 'then I suggest we go to the Fernsehturm. It's a wunderbar day, so it should be quite clear.'

Gretchen agreed and turned to Jenelyn. 'That's a good choice,' she said enthusiastically. 'You can see everything from the Fernsehturm, and it's breathtaking.'

Laszlo and Gretchen took off before Jenelyn could ask them what they were talking about. They jumped on a bus and travelled for several miles. Finally, they arrived at a tall tower, but unfortunately, Jenelyn still had no idea what it was. A narrow metal pole loomed in front of them, and Jenelyn could see that there was a sight-seeing place at the very top. The top of the pole was striped red and white, and underneath was a round, glass-paned circle as a viewing point for people to gaze out. They were standing beside the doors to the restaurant at the foot of the pole called the Ristorante Primafila, and she could see it was an elegant place filled with gleaming wooden tables set with sparkling cutlery, wine glasses, and fine-linen napkins. Gretchen looked at Jenelyn in excitement.

'Isn't it wunderbar?' she asked, her eyes shining with excitement.

Jenelyn nodded but was a little confused. She honestly couldn't see what was so remarkable about this...structure.

'It is pretty impressive,' she began, hesitant to sound ignorant. 'But, what is it?'

Laszlo laughed.

'I forgot we never explained that to you.' He chuckled. 'It's a television tower and was built in 1956. We're very proud of it because it's the original model for all television towers around the world.'

'Really?' Jenelyn asked in amazement. 'That is impressive. Can we go up and look around?'

Gretchen nodded and started to walk towards a small door at the bottom. 'Ja, but I can't guarantee that there will be a guide to talk about it. We're a little late since it's five o'clock.'

That was alright with Jenelyn. She was genuinely amazed at the tower's importance and height since the tallest building she had ever seen was the U.S. Bank Tower in downtown Los Angeles, which was around 73 stories high. This radio tower seemed taller, though she wondered if perhaps that was due to faulty memory or the fact that being a pole made it look higher.

'How tall is this tower?' she asked Laszlo, hoping he would know.

'It's 368 meters tall,' he stated. 'A guide could give you more information about it.'

Unfortunately, this was lost on Jenelyn since she didn't understand the metric system. Before she could think of how to admit this, they crowded into a tiny elevator and started to go up. Elevators had always made Jenelyn a bit nervous since she was afraid of them stalling and wasn't too comfortable in small, enclosed spaces. To her dismay, this elevator ride was quite long since it was one way up without any stops, and there were several stories! She tightened her lips grimly and tried not to panic as images of the elevator breaking and them plummeting to their deaths flashed through her mind. Finally, after what seemed like hours, the elevator arrived at the top, and they got out. Jenelyn couldn't believe her eyes. They were as high as birds! Her eyes widened as she walked up to the glass window and looked out. Tidy squares of lush forests and vineyards sat before the horizon while an indigo river threaded its way through them. In the far distance, she could see vague mountain summits surrounded by misty clouds. It was the most breathtaking sight she had ever seen. Gretchen smiled at her, enjoying the pure admiration in Jenelyn's eyes.

'It's fantastisch, isn't it?' she murmured, taking in the beautiful panoramic view herself.

'Yes,' breathed Jenelyn, understanding what Gretchen said even though it was in German. Her sentiment had been clear at such obvious beauty. 'It's the most beautiful sight I've ever seen. What are those mountains over there?'

Gretchen looked at the shadowed summits in the distance, and turned to Laszlo. 'I can't remember, Laszlo; what are those mountains again?'

Laszlo put his arm around his wife. 'Those are the German, Austrian, and Swiss Alps,' he explained. 'You can't see them every day of the year, so we're actually quite lucky to get the view that we have. Some days it's clear, and others, it's like this or worse.'

Jenelyn soaked in the landscape greedily. It was as picturesque as a postcard! She turned to Laszlo again, her brown eyes swimming with curiosity.

'So, what are we looking at exactly?' she asked, excited. 'I know it's the city and everything, but how much can we actually see?'

Laszlo smiled. 'Well, obviously, the city is Stuttgart, and then the vineyards are the Neckar Valley. All the forest is the Black Forest, and then the rest of the land up to the Alps is Swabian land.'

They stood for a while in silence, simply enjoying the beautiful land in front of them, and watching the sun set gracefully behind the mountains. Gretchen sighed in contentment as if waking from a dream and began walking to the elevator.

'Well, we had better be going,' she said. 'It's going to get dark soon and we still have quite a way to go.'

Laszlo and Jenelyn reluctantly agreed, not wanting to leave the beautiful sight. But they knew that soon the tower would be closing as well. Jenelyn wasn't quite as nervous in the elevator this time since she kept picturing Stuttgart. For the first time since she had left home, she felt like she might enjoy her Journey. After all, if she hadn't left, she never would have dreamed that there could be a place so lovely. Laszlo glanced at his watch when they got to the car and frowned.

'It's already five-thirty,' he grumbled, 'and we still have another two-hour drive to Kaiserslautern. That means it'll be seven-thirty by the time we get there!'

Gretchen patted his arm, consoling him. 'Now, Laszlo, you knew that this trip wouldn't be short and we would get home late. Don't worry about it so much.'

Laszlo gave a short grunt of reluctant acceptance and then sat in the car, followed by Gretchen and Jenelyn. Jenelyn folded her legs tightly and nestled against her bag. She knew she wouldn't be able to stay awake for the next two hours. Though she wasn't hungry anymore, she was definitely losing energy.

Good thing I'm young, she thought drowsily.

The car started with a loud rumble, and soon they were back on the autobahn. Jenelyn vaguely noticed Gretchen turn to see her resting peacefully on her bag through her half-closed eyes. As she slowly drifted off, she could hear Laszlo and Gretchen's hushed conversation.

'I'm glad that we agreed to have Jenelyn stay with us. She's a nice girl,' Gretchen said, and Jenelyn could hear the happy contentment in her voice and the soft rustling of her hand being placed on Laszlo's thigh.

'Ja and it will be nice to have company again.'

The soft catch in Laszlo's voice as he said this made Jenelyn's ears perk up curiously, but she was too tired to fully awake. All she could manage was to squint one eye open just enough to see Gretchen nod, a tiny prick of light making her certain that Gretchen had tears in her eyes. As she closed her eyes again, the sun fell from the sky and wrapped the travelling car in the dusky blue of evening.

Chapter Five

Jenelyn peered out the car window with bleary, sleep-filled eyes. The sun had disappeared, leaving the scenery outside in opaque darkness. She yawned, stretching her arms, and focused on the two people sitting in the front.

'Where are we?' she asked groggily, a bit disoriented from not being able to see outside.

Laszlo's eyes beamed at her in the rear-view mirror. 'Well, hallo to you! Have a good nap?'

Jenelyn nodded and tried to look out her window again. She could see vague silhouettes clustered together and knew they were passing through dark forests, but she could only imagine how beautiful it was.

'We're just outside Kaiserslautern,' Gretchen went on, 'It's in the middle of the Palantine Forest, a natural preserve. It's very picturesque, Jenelyn. I think you would like it.'

Jenelyn agreed, knowing she would. 'I've liked everything about Germany so far,' she said happily. 'I can't wait to see your home.'

Gretchen shrugged modestly. 'Well, I hope you don't expect too much,' she chuckled, 'But we like it well enough.'

'Unfortunately, we won't be able to see Kaiserslautern today, Jenelyn,' Laszlo apologised, 'It's already seven-thirty, so we're only going to stop there to change drivers. I'm going to let Gretchen drive the rest of the way.'

Gretchen gave Laszlo a withering look at this and he smiled at her teasingly. Jenelyn didn't mind. Even though she was able to nap, she was still tired, so she could only imagine how exhausted Laszlo and Gretchen were. The car took an exit, and Jenelyn stared at the tall buildings surrounding her. The city indeed lay in the middle of a forest. It was a large city, but the forest and gardens surrounding it took away from the demanding presence of the buildings. They stopped the car beside a small park and got out to stretch their legs. Laszlo gave a huge yawn and leaned tiredly against the car's hood.

'I'm erschöpft,' he said, staring vacantly ahead for a moment, blinking hard.

Gretchen laid a comforting hand on his arm. 'Laszlo, Liebling, that's why I'm going to drive the rest of the way,' she assured him. 'I would like to see Jenelyn get to our house safely so we can call her parents.'

Jenelyn looked at Gretchen, her eyes wide with excitement. 'You're going to call my parents?' she asked eagerly.

Gretchen looked surprised but then frowned. 'Ja, but you know you can't talk to them,' she apologised, patting her shoulder. 'It isn't allowed for your Journey. I only want them to know you're safe. In our times now, at least the parents can be assured their children survived the first step. Back in the past, they couldn't even know that.'

Jenelyn was severely disappointed she couldn't talk to her parents and tell them about everything she had seen, from the colourful old buildings to the amazing radio tower. She wouldn't even be able to tell them that she had tasted her first wine! Nevertheless, she understood the point of the Journey. She had to grow accustomed to being without them. Laszlo noticed her distraught face and squeezed Jenelyn's shoulder in comfort.

'Kommen sie, schätzchen,' he said lightly, trying to lift Jenelyn's spirits, 'Let's go home.'

Jenelyn gave him a grateful smile. She could see that Gretchen and Laszlo really wanted to help her, and she appreciated that. As wonderful as she knew this Journey was going to be for her, she also knew that it would challenge her in many ways. She was appreciative that she had such benevolent people watching over her in the beginning.

'Jenelyn,' Gretchen whispered, shaking her shoulder, 'Wake up, schätzchen, wir sind zuhause!'

Jenelyn squinted sleepily and looked up into Gretchen's sweet, tired face. 'Are we there?' she mumbled, sitting up and rubbing her eyes.

'Ja, we are,' Gretchen said, 'I just woke up Laszlo and he's unlocking the door. Don't forget to get your bag out of the car.'

Jenelyn looked at the bag beside her on the seat. Gretchen spoke as Jenelyn lifted it out. 'I'm surprised you only have the one. What made you travel so light for your Journey? You have no idea how long it will be.'

'That's why,' Jenelyn explained. 'Since I didn't know how long I had to pack for, I decided to pack only the necessities. I plan to work this whole time, so I can buy clothes and things as I go along. I thought it would make travelling much easier.'

'I can't argue with that,' Gretchen chuckled.

Jenelyn looked around her for a moment before walking to the door. The house was nothing like she had imagined it, though admittedly, she hadn't known what to expect. The paved driveway sat to the left and was lined by manicured, round hedges. Two tall evergreens towered over the left side of the house like sentries. The house was white, with two storeys and a pointed roof. On each storey, flower boxes were lining the balconies, making it very homely. A light orange awning hung down in front of the door, and large windows covered the house. Though the large front lawn was blanketed in snow, Jenelyn could see it was well maintained. She was taken aback at the house's size. Gretchen had said it wasn't much, but compared to the tiny apartment Jenelyn had been raised in, it was a palace! It had to be the most gorgeous house Jenelyn had ever seen. At that moment, all her fears vanished, and she knew that she would adore living here.

'Gretchen, it's absolutely perfect,' she said, her voice dripping with admiration.

Gretchen blushed and shrugged modestly. 'Oh, really, Jenelyn, it isn't much,' she said.

Laszlo came out to them and grabbed Jenelyn's bag for her. He laughed when he saw her face. 'You look star struck!' he chuckled. 'Let's get inside so you can settle in.'

Jenelyn couldn't have been more excited. If the house looked this amazing at night, she knew she would love it even more the next morning. Laszlo led both of them into the living room, which made Jenelyn squeal with delight.

It was the happiest room she had ever seen. The walls were white, except for the back wall which was painted a bright, cheerful yellow. In front of it sat a small, light wooden entertainment centre with a television. On top were two, dark brown candleholders with cream-coloured tapers and three framed photographs. On the wall behind it was an artistic painting of large, bright flowers and to the left was a tall, fern-like plant, which sat cosily next to a large window. To the right of the entertainment centre was a small door that led into the next room. It took all of Jenelyn's willpower not to march right through it.

Laszlo placed Jenelyn's bag down beside one of the sofas. There were two of them, facing each other in front of the entertainment centre.

They're very classy, Jenelyn thought, impressed.

The sofas were white and cream and made of an exquisite brocade pattern. Red pillows with artistic designs sat in the sofa corners, matching the very bright red sideboard that stood behind the sofa placed in front of the right wall. The sideboard was filled with tropical-coloured plates and glasses. The other sofa sat in front of the window by the plant. Between the two sofas was a small, narrow, cherry wood coffee table with a light pink runner over it and a vase of flowers in the middle. Jenelyn couldn't think of what to say about such a vibrant room. Gretchen and Laszlo stared at her expectantly. She finally took a deep breath and shook her head, smiling.

'It's amazing,' she stammered. 'I can't believe how bright it is!'

Gretchen gave a deep laugh, her shoulders shaking with mirth, and sat down on one of the sofas.

'Es ist hysterisch that you should say that,' she said chuckling. 'Laszlo can't stand how bright this room is. I love bright, cheerful colours, but he complains that by the time he's old, he'll be blind. This is the only brightly painted room I'm allowed to have.'

Jenelyn walked around, noticing that there weren't any wall decorations. The only pictures in the room other than the large flowers were the three framed photographs on the entertainment centre. From where she stood, she thought one of them was of a small child, but as she walked closer to get a better look, Laszlo called over to her.

'Kommen sie, Jenelyn,' he said, 'I'll show you to your room. We have a three-bedroom house. There's the master bedroom, which is our room, a second bedroom, and an office. We have an en suite in the master bedroom, so the second bathroom is yours.'

Jenelyn followed him up a narrow flight of stairs that led from the front door, with Gretchen following behind. She scanned the narrow hallway as they passed through. There were two doors on the right and two to her left. She noticed, oddly, that it was barely decorated with any pictures as well. Back in Los Angeles, her house was full of photos of their family, as she knew most homes were. All of the doors were closed, which made her curiosity rise. Laszlo opened the door on the far left and waved her in.

'This is your room,' he said matter-of-factly, with a strange underlying tone that made Jenelyn look at him. He didn't look back at her but simply stared into the room.

Jenelyn looked inside, immediately exclaiming, 'It's lovely!'

She wasn't surprised at all that it was the cosiest bedroom she could ask for. In fact, it was simply made for a girl. The ceiling was lined with honey-oak wood beams, with a small, elegant light fixture in the middle. The far wall pretty much consisted of a large window with floral drapes adorning the sides that the warm, cream-coloured walls complimented. In the middle of the room was a queen-size bed, much larger than the tiny single Jenelyn had slept on at home. The headboard and footboard were silver iron with stylish criss-crossing designs in the middle with a plush white comforter that made Jenelyn yearn to lie in it. There were four pillows, two large, and two decorative. The two large pillows were a simple white, and the decorative pillows were a light gold. A white chest and yellow and pink flowered quilt folded neatly were at the foot of the bed. On either side were two, dark wooden nightstands that had small, white-shaded lamps with curvy stands set in the middle of each. Jenelyn walked in and noticed that there wasn't a closet. She turned to Laszlo and Gretchen.

'Don't you have closets?' she asked in surprise.

Gretchen nodded, and Jenelyn noticed in surprise that her eyes were misty. 'Ja, we do,' she said softly, 'but this room doesn't. You can put your clothes inside the chest.'

Jenelyn frowned and looked over at Gretchen with concern. 'Is something wrong?' she asked worriedly.

Gretchen shook her head and her lips trembled into a watery smile. Before she could reply, Laszlo spoke for her.

'She's fine, Jenelyn. It's been a long time since we've had someone stay with us. We enjoy company a lot.'

There he went about liking company again. Jenelyn's suspicious thoughts were about to escape, but before she could respond, Gretchen seemed to collect herself again and spoke cheerfully.

'Well, your bathroom is the room right next to yours. I think it's time for all of us to get to bed. I'll give you the tour of the house tomorrow, Jenelyn.'

Jenelyn politely swallowed her words and said goodnight. She closed her door as Laszlo and Gretchen left, and looked around her room as she turned on the bedside lamps. They sent a warm, yellow glow throughout the room, and a comforting cosiness flooded through her.

This house seems so happy, she thought wonderingly, *yet Laszlo and Gretchen seem so sad at times.*

She unpacked her clothes and laid them in the cedar-lined chest. At least she didn't have to worry about moths eating her clothes like she did at home. It was too dark to see what was outside her window, but Jenelyn enjoyed the view of the starry sky, and mostly, the calm silence. For the first time in her life, she wouldn't have to fall asleep to her neighbourhood's lullaby of angry fighting, wailing sirens, or blasting rap music. She changed into her pyjamas, pulled back the cotton sheets and thick comforter, and nestled into the soft, warm bed. She lay awake for a bit, staring at the beautiful honey-oak beams on her ceiling. She had assumed the peacefulness would help her fall asleep instantly, but instead, the quiet allowed her mind to race too fast to be able to fall asleep.

She found her thoughts meandering back to Laszlo and Gretchen. Though she didn't want to pry into their private lives, she couldn't stifle the nagging curiosity of why they were so sad. She wasn't sure how long she would be able to live with them without knowing. But since she was a stranger now, she would simply have to wait until she got to know them better. With this plan in mind, her eyes drifted shut, and she was able to put her curious thoughts to sleep.

Chapter Six

A dazzling stream of sunshine woke Jenelyn the following day. She grumbled softly, and tried putting her pillow over her face, but the warm light stubbornly peeked through. The day before had exhausted her, and she found it difficult to believe she had left the States that previous morning. It felt like she had been in Germany for days, not hours. She opened her eyes a crack and stared at her surroundings. Sure enough, the room was as cheerful as it had looked the night before, and had an airy, welcoming feel to it. Her curious thoughts had awakened with her, and Jenelyn had the suspicious feeling that this welcoming room had been lonely for quite some time, despite its neat and clean appearance.

In time, she reminded herself, *get to know them first.*

Yawning, she stumbled out of bed and grabbed her toiletry bag. It was time to take a peek at her bathroom. She'd never had her own, and she was looking forward to the extra space and freedom. She opened her bedroom door quietly, not wanting to disturb Laszlo and Gretchen in case they were still asleep. Unfortunately, her room didn't have a clock, so she had no idea what time it was. The sun wasn't telling her much. Tiptoeing across the white-carpeted hallway, she reached the door beside her room. It seemed the whole house had white carpets. She wondered how on earth Gretchen kept it clean.

Not having animals helps, she mused.

Jenelyn was a little disappointed about this, since she had always wanted a pet. A small part of her had hoped that perhaps Laszlo and Gretchen had owned a dog so she could experience having one. If she had been able to choose a pet, she would have loved a giant, scruffy dog, but growing up in an apartment building and with parents who could barely afford to feed themselves, it had been an impossible dream.

Opening the bathroom door, she was blinded by a shining whiteness. A small window filled with bright sunlight overlooked a gleaming white claw-foot bathtub with an elegantly attached showerhead standing on a floor made of bleached wooden boards and surrounded by walls freshly painted with whitewash. Lining the windowsill were small glass jars of oils, soaps, cotton balls, and Q-tips, and the glittering rays of sunlight reflected through them onto a narrow, iron stand to the left with a potted plant. Above that, on a little ledge cut into the wall, was a mirror with curly-cue edges. Underneath an old-fashioned, light-green scale and a pale yellow metal bin sat beside a white pedestal sink with another mirror above it, and a white porcelain toilet beside it. The bathroom was clean and small, but it appeared larger since it was so bright.

She set her bag down on the toilet and noticed again how impersonal the room was. There weren't any pictures, the same as her bedroom and the hallway. Shrugging off her persistent curiosity, Jenelyn stripped off her pyjamas and set her mind to figuring out how to work the shower.

An hour later, she wandered down to the kitchen to see about breakfast. So far, she hadn't seen a clock anywhere, but she assumed it had to be at least eight o'clock. She hadn't heard any sounds coming from Laszlo and Gretchen's room, and she hoped that she wouldn't wake or anger them by prowling around the house without them. But at this point, Jenelyn was fully awake and couldn't bear the thought of sitting in her room waiting. As she had expected, the living room greeted her with a burst of energetic happiness. The vivid colours absolutely radiated in the sunshine, and as she squinted at the yellow wall, she understood what Laszlo had meant about going blind by the time he was old.

She assumed that the little door in the corner of the living room led to the kitchen, and sure enough, it did. And who was there to greet her, but Gretchen, dressed very casually in slacks and a white blouse. Her golden-brown hair rippled across her shoulders as she stood over the stove, humming happily. Jenelyn quickly glanced around the spacious kitchen before announcing herself. The cabinets and lower cupboards were all honey-oak, as well as the solid island in the middle. There were three sections of windows, each with square, yellow curtains hanging on the sides like banners. The sun poured through the windows like golden syrup, creating such a cosy warmth that Jenelyn wanted to bask in it all day. Two potted cacti were adorning each windowsill, and three old clay pots decorated the corner. There was a small step down into the kitchen, and as she looked down to watch her feet, she noticed the floor had white tiles. Jenelyn started to suspect that though Gretchen loved bright colours, she loved white floors just as much. It also started occurring to her that Laszlo must make a great deal of money.

'Oh, Guten Morgen, Jenelyn,' Gretchen greeted, turning around and smiling.

'Good morning, Gretchen,' she replied happily, instinctively knowing what Gretchen was saying.

She started looking around for a place to sit. Finding none, she leaned against the marble counter, admiring the red bowl brimming with apples, oranges, and bananas sitting on the counter next to her.

'Did you have a nice sleep?' Gretchen asked, pouring a fresh cup of coffee for herself.

Jenelyn nodded, her gaze sweeping over the miscellaneous baskets that lined the tops of the cupboards.

'Yes, very well. Did you?'

'Oh ja, we slept very deeply,' Gretchen said with satisfaction, 'What do you want for frühstück? I have bread, butter, and jam, or some cold-cuts if you like? I might have some yoghurt here too if you prefer a light breakfast. Of course, tea or coffee if you want.'

Jenelyn listened to her growling stomach and yearned for the eggs and pancakes her mother occasionally made for her. After a day like yesterday, she felt like she needed a real meal. Yoghurt and bread weren't going to cut it, and meat in the morning didn't entice her.

'Um, do you have any eggs?' she asked timidly, not wanting to be a bother.

Gretchen looked at her curiously and nodded. 'Ja, sometimes we have a hard-boiled egg in the morning if you would prefer that instead?'

'Alright,' she said happily. 'I'll have an egg and some toast with jam, and I'll try the yoghurt too. I can help you if you want?'

Gretchen seemed a little surprised but shrugged good-naturedly. 'You Americans must eat much larger breakfasts than we do here,' she commented, plopping an egg into a boiling pot.

'Yes, I think we do,' Jenelyn agreed. 'Do you have pancakes here?'

Gretchen thought for a moment, seeming to be at a loss. 'I think some restaurants serve them here for the tourists, but I have no idea how to make them.'

Jenelyn was surprised but then had a brilliant idea. 'Well, then one day soon, I'll make you and Laszlo a traditional American breakfast,' she stated cheerfully, glad that she could give something back to the people who were doing such a big favour for her.

'That would be wunderbar.' Gretchen beamed.

Jenelyn smiled at Gretchen's strong accent and occasional use of German. She knew that after a while, she would have to learn the language. She couldn't get a job without it. The egg was soon ready, and Jenelyn buttered a slice of toast, spread it with orange marmalade, and set this beside a small bowl of yoghurt on a plate for herself. It would be an awfully light breakfast, and she hoped that she could survive until lunch. Due to an overachieving metabolism, she had a hearty appetite despite her slender frame.

'Why don't we take all this into the dining room and talk?' Gretchen said, picking up her own plate and coffee.

Jenelyn agreed and followed Gretchen to an adjoining room to the right. Right before they got there, though, Jenelyn snapped her fingers.

'Oh, I forgot to get something to drink,' she said. 'Do you have any milk, or juice?'

Gretchen looked surprised. 'Do you not like coffee or tea?'

'I can't stand coffee, and I'm not a real fan of tea,' Jenelyn said dubiously. 'Orange juice would be fine though, or milk.'

Gretchen shook her head critically. 'You can find some orange juice in the refrigerator, but I must warn you. Now that you live here, it would help you to learn to like tea or coffee. They can be very beneficial.'

Jenelyn grimaced at the thought while she poured herself a glass of orange juice. She couldn't even stomach the smell of coffee, so she knew if she were to give anything a chance it would have to be tea. Though she wondered why it was so important to have to learn to like it. She walked to join Gretchen in the dining room, and was met with another charming room. Gretchen had a real sense of style, though it was a bit eclectic at times. Jenelyn could tell that she loved her house very much.

The dining room was small but not crowded. Like the living room, one wall was painted a bright yellow, with two paintings framed in heavy, ornate gold, while the other walls were white. An oak wood cabinet with baskets cluttered on top stood to the left. The far wall was entirely made up of a large window framed with goldenrod drapes that hung heavily to the floor. A tall, potted plant stood in the far right corner and in the middle of the room stood a small honey-oak wood table with four chairs. In its centre was a red glass vase with bright red flowers fanning out dramatically. The table stood on a rug patterned with squares and flowers of different colours in each square. The rest of the floor was white carpet. Despite its bright colours, it was a pleasant but understated room, without the brilliance and flash of the living room.

'Such a cute room,' Jenelyn commented, setting her breakfast down on the table. 'I've noticed already that you have a wonderful decorating style.'

'Danke, Jenelyn,' Gretchen replied. 'I enjoy decorating my house, and I take much pride in it.'

Jenelyn took a sip of her orange juice and almost gagged. It was full of pulp! She hadn't considered that it might not be smooth. Gretchen didn't seem to notice, and Jenelyn decided not to mention it. She took a bite of her toast quickly.

'Where's Laszlo?' she asked, swallowing her bite before she spoke.

'Oh, he went to work,' Gretchen explained as she heaped a surprising amount of jam on her bread, 'He has to be there around seven in the morning. Poor man was so tired after the trip yesterday.'

'I bet he was tired,' Jenelyn agreed in surprise. 'Couldn't he have taken today off?'

Gretchen shook her head. 'He has the time, but Laszlo is what we call an arbeitssüchtiger, someone who loves to work all the time. I don't know what Americans call it.'

Jenelyn thought for a moment, and then her face brightened when she figured it out.

'Oh, you mean a workaholic,' she said. 'Well, it obviously keeps you both living well.'

From the moment the words left her mouth, Jenelyn was mortified at blurting out something so tacky. She was about to apologise, but Gretchen noticed her discomfort and shook her head.

'Nein, don't be embarrassed,' she assured Jenelyn, 'I know we live comfortably. Your parents knew this too and were very happy that we agreed to have you. They wanted you to experience another way of living. That reminds me, I need to call them.'

Jenelyn's heart pounded eagerly at the mention of her parents. She already missed them dreadfully, and she hadn't even been gone for two days! Being alienated in a strange country made it much more difficult. As Gretchen left the room, Jenelyn felt very alone. She nibbled on her toast and stared out the window, where the two evergreens swayed gently in the breeze. It was a beautiful day outside, and though she felt lonely and slightly scared, she also felt curious. She wanted to see the neighbourhood and surrounding area.

Suddenly, she heard Gretchen's voice from the kitchen.

So that's where the phone is, she thought. *I wonder if there's a clock in there, too.*

'Ja, she's fine,' Jenelyn heard Gretchen say. 'We're eating breakfast right now. Oh, she loves Germany so far, but she misses you both. She was disappointed she couldn't hear your voices. Ja, I'll tell her and give her a hug for you, auf wiedersehen.'

It didn't take long for Gretchen to come back into the dining room, where Jenelyn was still nibbling on her food, her deep sadness over her parents making her lose her appetite. They were so close, and yet also incredibly far away.

'Are you not hungry?' Gretchen asked in surprise, looking at the nearly full plate in front of Jenelyn.

'No, I am, but I started getting a little homesick. I miss my parents,' she admitted, feeling like a little girl.

Gretchen gave Jenelyn's shoulder a maternal squeeze, her face soft with understanding. 'Well, I'll try to help you as best I can. I know this Journey is hard. I remember your mom struggling with it as well. But, in the end, it's all for the best. By the way, your mom wanted me to tell you that they love you and hope you're doing well.'

Jenelyn nodded appreciatively and turned back to her food. She promised herself that during her time here she would show Laszlo and Gretchen how grateful she was for them. If there were any chores or assistance they needed, she would be there. She simply needed to stop thinking about home, and the busier she kept herself, the easier that would be. Gretchen sat down across from her with a cup of coffee and relaxed.

'So,' she started amiably, 'what did you want to do today? I thought I would give you a tour of the neighbourhood. You have pretty much seen the house.'

'I would like that,' Jenelyn answered, though a prick of responsibility reminded her of the officer at the airport, 'but I don't want too much time to pass before I need to go to the German Aliens Authority office here. The immigration officer made it very clear that I needed to do that since I want to work. I also need to start learning German.'

She pondered for a moment as she said this. She had only arrived the previous day and had barely settled in. Seeing more of the neighbourhood and having fun with Gretchen was a lot more appealing. Did she want to start dealing with paperwork immediately?

Yes, she thought firmly, *the sooner I do this, the less difficult it will be for me later.*

Gretchen nodded in understanding and thought for a moment. 'Well, we can start working on your German immediately. I can teach you myself. That will take a bit of time, however. I can take you to the Ausländerbehörde today if you'd like? That's the German Aliens Authority office.'

'Perfect,' Jenelyn said quickly, before she changed her mind.

Although it was intimidating, picturing German officers knocking on Laszlo and Gretchen's door was worse. She could just imagine them taking her away and locking her in a cell before deporting her. Then she would have the embarrassment of admitting to her parents that she failed her Journey simply because she had wanted to explore a neighbourhood! Blood drained from her face as she imagined these scenes, and her rising panic was only ebbed by Gretchen's sweet voice. Gretchen seemed to understand how she felt and reassured her as they left the dining room.

'Don't worry, Jenelyn,' she said, smiling proudly, 'it will be fine. And it's very mature of you to handle all of this so soon.'

Jenelyn nodded and took a deep breath, forcing her overactive imagination to stop. She could do this; she knew she could. She glanced over at Gretchen in the kitchen dressed in slacks and a nice blouse and had a horrible thought.

'Am I dressed alright?' she asked insecurely, looking down at her casual attire, 'You're dressed so nice this morning.'

Gretchen studied her thoughtfully for a moment, taking in Jenelyn's faded jeans and poet-sleeved cotton shirt.

'Wahr,' she mused, nodding in agreement. 'You'll be fine for now, but we'll need to take you shopping before you find work. Go grab your passport and we can leave now.'

Jenelyn nodded, looking forward to when she wouldn't look so conspicuous and could blend in with everyone. She bolted to her room, grabbed her passport, and ran back down to meet Gretchen at the car. Settling into the passenger seat, Jenelyn stretched her legs to their full length happily. It was much more comfortable than it had been in the back seat! Up here, she had plenty of room.

'So, how far is the German Aliens Authority office?' she asked casually, studying the tree-lined street they drove down. The neighbourhood was neat and clean, every lawn manicured and not one piece of litter on the ground. She couldn't help but compare it with her grungy, gang-infested neighbourhood in Los Angeles.

It's like being in a dream world, she thought, *I wish Nicole could see this.*

'Not too far,' Gretchen replied, 'I would say about ten minutes. Remember, Wittlich is a tiny town.'

Sure enough, it didn't take long for them to arrive at a very simple brown building. Jenelyn looked around curiously at the tiny town around them. The streets were narrow, and the shops lining them were small, but everything was tidy and quaint with an old-world charm. It made Jenelyn wonder how many tourists this small town got since it seemed so charming. Gretchen opened the glass door for her as they walked inside. A long counter loomed before them with uniformed official clerks bustling behind it. Jenelyn's heart pounded nervously. She always felt intimidated in offices, having never done any legal paperwork except for when she got her driver's permit. Gretchen walked up to the counter and smiled at the trim, tall man that stood behind it. He smiled back at her politely, though Jenelyn didn't miss the brief flash of surprise in his eyes when he saw Gretchen. It lasted only a second, and when he spoke his voice was cordial.

'Wie kann ich Ihnen helfen?'

Gretchen motioned for Jenelyn to come join her and turned back to the man.

'Mein Freund besucht von Amerika und wird für wenigstens sechs Monate bleiben. Sie braucht eine Arbeitserlaubnis und Wohnsitz zulassen.'

Jenelyn nodded at the man optimistically when he looked at her, ignorant to what had been said, but hoping that what Gretchen had told him was possible. He frowned thoughtfully for a moment, then motioned for her to wait and went to talk to one of his co-workers. Jenelyn instantly turned to Gretchen.

'What did you say? What did he say?' she asked, impatient at not understanding the stream of babble that had poured out in front of her.

'I told him that you were visiting from America and that you need a work permit and residence permit,' Gretchen explained patiently. 'He's going to find someone to help us.'

Jenelyn's head swirled in surprise at everything that had been said. All she had heard was guttural noises and chopped words. How on earth was she going to learn German well enough to work? After a while, a different man walked up to them with a welcoming, professional smile.

'My name is Frederick,' he stated, his tone measured but friendly. Jenelyn didn't miss how he gave Gretchen a quick, careful glance before settling his gaze on her. 'My co-worker told me that this young lady is visiting us from America. He thought that it would be easier for you if you were assisted by someone who could speak English.'

Jenelyn instantly felt more at ease once she could understand someone.

'Thank you,' she said gratefully. 'I just want to know what I need to do.'

Frederick took a deep breath and picked up some forms, all in German. 'Since you are staying here for over six months, I will start with getting you a standard residence permit. You'll need to show me a valid passport, proof of where you'll be living, and proof that you can support yourself.'

Jenelyn's mouth dropped open. 'All of that?' she asked in dismay. 'But how can I show you proof that I can support myself without being able to work? Wouldn't that mean I would need to get the work permit first?'

Frederick looked at her patiently. 'You cannot get a work permit before you show proof that you are a resident. If you have funds in a bank account that you transferred here, that could be provided as proof.'

Jenelyn shook her head. She fumbled in her pocket for her passport and put it on the counter.

'I don't have a bank account, but there's my passport, and I'm living with Gretchen,' she said, pointing to Gretchen beside her.

Frederick looked at Gretchen with his brow raised in question and evident surprise. 'Is this true?' he asked, not being able to hide the astonishment in his voice.

Gretchen nodded, pulling out her identification so he could write down her address.

'I can vouch for her,' she stated, eyeing him firmly. 'She'll be staying with us the entire time, and we'll be supporting her financially until she can find work.'

Jenelyn wasn't sure why this was such a shock to the man, but she could tell his reaction hadn't been missed by Gretchen. Despite this, Gretchen remained nonchalant, her expression smooth and impassive. Frederick nodded as he filled out all the information on the form. He sat back for a moment, thinking. Then he looked up at Gretchen again.

'If you could fill out and sign an affidavit stating that you are supporting her, then I can use that as proof of residence and financial support,' he explained, his tone professional once more.

Gretchen nodded politely. 'Of course, I can fill that out now.'

He handed her the form, and she filled it out quickly. Jenelyn was relieved to know that there was a way Gretchen could help her. She was also fascinated by the obscure, tense interaction between Gretchen and Frederick that was underlying the entire conversation.

'Alright, that should work,' Frederick said, stamping in Jenelyn's passport, 'you have a standard residence permit, which is good for a limited period and can be extended when needed. If you want to stay permanently, you need to apply for a permanent residence permit. Now, let's see what we can do for your work permit. To get a work permit, I will need to see a certificate from an employer stating that they're willing to hire you.'

Jenelyn and Gretchen looked at each other worriedly. Gretchen answered for her.

'But, Jenelyn hasn't had a chance to seek employment yet,' she told Frederick, 'Is it possible for her to apply without a work permit?'

Frederick shook his head.

'No, but there are some cases where non-Germans can find someone willing to hire them and wait for them to get a work permit.'

Gretchen looked over at Jenelyn, and spoke with a comforting tone.

'Perhaps Laszlo can help find you a job in his office, and then we can come back,' she assured her.

Jenelyn hated to inconvenience Laszlo but she also couldn't see another way she could find work. They said goodbye to Frederick and left the office. Jenelyn kept her head down, choosing to watch her feet instead of meeting Gretchen's eyes. Guilt consumed her as she thought of how much these people had to go through to take care of her.

'I hate to bother Laszlo with this.' She groaned, looking down at the resident stamp in her passport as she settled in the car, 'It feels wrong that I can't take care of this on my own and have to inconvenience you both.'

Gretchen shook her head and started driving down the road.

'Don't be silly, you are hardly an inconvenience,' she admonished with a scoff, 'I will talk to Laszlo tonight and see what he thinks about you working for his company. I'm sure he won't mind in the least.'

Jenelyn hoped Gretchen was right. She found the courage to look at her again as she heard the reassurance in Gretchen's tone. As they drove back through the town, she looked outside her window and exhaled in relief. The hard part was done, she was halfway there. Once she could work, she could start focusing on learning to live here.

Chapter Seven

Gretchen and Jenelyn pulled into the paved driveway of the house. All of her anxiety from the trip to the authority office evaporated as Jenelyn saw the beautiful house awaiting them. The orange awnings gleamed in the sunshine, and the sentry trees swayed gently, their soft pine needles grazing across her bedroom window. It had looked comforting at night, but the daylight displayed all the beautiful details the darkness concealed. Gretchen paused for a moment, reflecting contentedly as she looked at the house with Jenelyn, and then turned to her with a smile.

'We only live about two hundred meters from some very nice forest trails,' she explained. 'Would you like to go for a walk?'

Jenelyn immediately nodded, yet she was slightly worried about being cold. Even though the sun was out, the temperature was low.

'Sure, that sounds great! It must be nice living so close to trails,' she said.

Gretchen nodded, getting out of the car.

'Oh, ja,' she agreed. 'While Laszlo is at work, I stay at home and take care of the house. But on pretty days, it's nice to get outside.'

Jenelyn ran inside to put her passport away, and then she and Gretchen took off down the street.

'So, how far exactly is two hundred meters?' Jenelyn asked curiously, swinging along beside Gretchen, who was nearly power walking.

'Don't worry, it's not even a mile,' she assured Jenelyn. 'I forget that you don't know the metric system. We'll have to work on that.'

Jenelyn silently groaned at everything she needed to learn. As interesting as it all was, she had no doubt it would be a difficult transition. She looked around the neighbourhood, still impressed how every house was maintained immaculately. Gretchen and Laszlo lived in a beautiful part of Wittlich, and it reminded her that she still didn't know what Laszlo did for a living.

'By the way, I hope you don't mind me asking, but what does Laszlo do?' she asked Gretchen, who seemed pensive. Her expression was far away, as if dreaming instead of acknowledging the world around her. Jenelyn would have thought she was simply peaceful, but a tiny downward tick at the corner of Gretchen's mouth told her otherwise. It only lasted a moment though, since her voice broke Gretchen's reverie.

Gretchen turned to her and chuckled.

'I don't mind you asking,' she replied, amused. 'I know that you have been wondering ever since you saw our house. Laszlo works for a private company called Heller Funke Europa. He's one of their engineers.'

'An engineer!' exclaimed Jenelyn. 'No wonder you live in such a nice house.' She blushed, wondering if Gretchen would find her outburst tactless. Instead, Gretchen laughed out loud, her eyes shining.

'You are so easily impressed,' she chortled, 'it amuses me. What do your parents do?'

Jenelyn was almost embarrassed to answer. Compared to what Laszlo did for a living, Gretchen would think her parents weren't very educated. She also couldn't help but be surprised.

'You don't know?' she asked. 'I thought you were friends with my parents.'

'We are,' Gretchen replied, 'but we knew each other many years ago. I met your mother when I was in college, and she was on her Journey, earning money by dancing on the streets. I grew up in Wittlich, and we met at the market where she was busking outside. We were friends the entire time she stayed, which was a year, and then her Spirits took her elsewhere. For a long time, we tried to keep in touch, but of course, I got married to Laszlo and she fell in love with your father. After that, we didn't write much, and I was surprised to hear from her when she asked me if you could stay with us. Of course, I immediately accepted, but we didn't get much of a chance to talk since it was a long-distance call for her.'

Jenelyn soaked in this information, fascinated at the story of her mother's time here. Her mother had never mentioned her Journey much, only sharing bits and pieces of her memories. Though Jenelyn had known she used to dance, she hadn't known that it had been to earn money on the streets! She couldn't help but voice this amazement to Gretchen, who laughed.

'It was a very different time back then,' she chortled. 'Your mother wasn't doing anything different than many of the hippies of the time were doing. She was a lovely dancer.'

Jenelyn genuinely hoped that Gretchen didn't think less of her mother for not having a good job after all these years.

'My mom works in retail, and my dad is a waiter, so we don't have much money,' she said hesitantly, the words wrenched from her mouth.

Gretchen seemed to sense this and gave her a soft smile.

'Don't feel bad about that, Jenelyn,' she said in a comforting tone. 'Your parents are doing what needs to be done, and are trying very hard. Your mother explained why it was difficult for her to go to college. She said the Spirits always moved her on the Journey. As long as they raised you in love, kept a roof over your head, and made sure you were well-fed, they are good parents, and you have every right to be proud.'

Jenelyn knew Gretchen was right and appreciated that she didn't judge them. Not long after, they reached the trailhead to the forest, and Jenelyn gasped. She had never seen a forest before. The shadowed path and walls of trees set her imagination on fire. Visions of deer, bears, and all kinds of creatures flashed across her eyes as she pictured what kinds of lives they led behind the secretive screen of the forest. The wind stirred around her feet, playfully tossing pine needles over her shoes.

'Oh, it's lovely!' she cried, staring at the canopy of leaves above her head, and the thick, dense pine trees that were surrounding them. Their feet were soundless as they walked along the dirt trail. Gretchen's mouth lifted in a brief smile, but her eyes seemed far away as if she were thinking back on another time.

'How big is this forest?' Jenelyn asked, too preoccupied listening to the distant cries of birds, and watching the squirrels scattering from tree to tree around them to question Gretchen's withdrawn demeanour.

Gretchen snapped back out of her daydream and noticed Jenelyn again.

'What?' she asked.

Jenelyn frowned a little and gave Gretchen a careful look.

'I was wondering how big this forest is,' she repeated. 'Are you alright? You seem distracted.'

Gretchen waved her hand at Jenelyn in reassurance.

'Don't worry about me,' she replied, and then her tone sobered. 'This forest isn't terribly large, only one thousand square kilometres. There are hundreds of trails here. It's very easy to get lost, so you must be careful if you ever come alone.'

Jenelyn couldn't mistake the warning in Gretchen's voice, and wondered what experience Gretchen had been through here.

'I'll be sure to remember,' she answered seriously, wanting to assure Gretchen that she would listen to her.

Gretchen immediately relaxed, the worried lines around her eyes melting into a peaceful grin. 'Despite that,

I love it here,' she said softly, once again seeming to be thinking of something else.

Jenelyn was frustrated at hearing these odd tones and seeing these far-off gazes of Gretchen's. Her curiosity was getting the better of her. She stopped mid-step, put her hands on her hips, and narrowed her eyes in a suspicious glare.

'What happened to you here?' she asked, figuring being blunt was quicker than beating around the bush.

Gretchen looked at her in shock and stopped.

'What?' she asked, her eyes wide with amazement, though her lips puckered and she couldn't quite meet Jenelyn's eyes.

'It's not hard to guess that you've had some sort of experience here,' Jenelyn answered evenly, keeping her eyes on Gretchen's uncertain face.

'Well,' Gretchen started hesitantly, looking at Jenelyn as if wondering if she could trust her, 'I'll tell you, but you must promise not to overreact.'

Jenelyn raised her eyebrows sceptically but grinned.

'I promise,' she said.

Gretchen began walking again, seeming to gather her thoughts.

'Alright,' she began, 'I'm going to tell you a story that's very famous here in Wittlich, though no one speaks of it anymore. They should, to warn everyone, but nothing has happened in so long----'

'What happened?' Jenelyn interrupted, not being able to contain her eagerness for quenching some of her curiosity at last.

Gretchen cut her a sharp look, and she immediately felt sheepish.

'Don't interrupt me, bitte,' Gretchen snapped, her tone stern. 'This story is not to be taken lightly, despite what many say. Now listen carefully, and perhaps you can stay out of trouble.'

She stopped walking for a moment, closing her eyes and thinking as if carefully remembering. Her eyes seemed older and she began to walk again slowly as she recited the ancient legend.

'The town of Wittlich is said to be the last place in Germany where a werewolf was killed. Thomas Johannes Baptist Schwytzer, a deserter from Napoleon's Army and a veteran of the catastrophe at Moscow, was fleeing to his homeland in Alsace. There were a group of Russians with him, also deserters. While passing by Wittlich, the hungry soldiers saw a farmhouse and decided to take what they wanted. During their raid, they were discovered by the farmer, whom they promptly murdered along with his sons. The farmer's wife, seeing this, let out a wail and cursed Schwytzer.

'Let the full moon show the world the wild animal you truly are!' she'd screamed in her anguish.

'Schwytzer ended her suffering by crushing her skull. But the curse worked. Gradually a change came over Schwytzer. He became colder and lost all conscience. He robbed, raped, and murdered at his pleasure. He soon left his comrades who had grown tired of him and took up with bandits and highwaymen. Even those ruffians were appalled at Schwytzer's behaviour, so the ex-soldier fled to the sanctuary of these forests. They're deep and vast, perfect for disappearing into. There became tales of a wolf that walked like a man that spread throughout this countryside. At night men and cattle were brutally slaughtered by the beast. One night, while at his campfire in the woods, a group of villagers discovered Schwytzer. They gave chase and cornered him near the centre of town. Promptly killing Schwytzer, the villagers buried him at a crossing in this forest. There is a shrine erected here where a candle will burn continuously. As long as the candle is lit, so the legend goes, the werewolf will not return.'

At this point, Gretchen stopped talking, her face becoming pinched and sad. She stayed silent for so long that Jenelyn assumed the story was over and was about to speak. But before she could, Gretchen went on haltingly in a soft voice.

'That is until 1988. One evening a group of U.S. Air Force personnel from Spangdahlem Air Base travelled through Wittlich on their way back to the base. Passing the old shrine, they noticed the candle was blown out. They began to laugh and joke about it since all had heard of the legend of the werewolf.

Later that night, at the base, automatic sirens started wailing. Someone or something had activated the perimeter fence sensors. While investigating, a security guard spied a large creature similar to a wolf, standing on its hind legs. It gazed at the soldier for a moment and then fled, clearing a three-meter fence with ease. A police dog was brought to track the beast, but upon arriving at the spot where the werewolf was seen, the dog trembled and howled, refusing to go further. Some say the security guard made up the story, but some disagree. No matter what anyone said, however, the candle was relit, and no one has seen signs of a werewolf since.'

Gretchen finally looked over at Jenelyn, who was staring at her in amazement.

'I take it that you believe this?' Jenelyn asked, not really sure what to think.

'Ja,' Gretchen replied shortly, 'I have reason to believe. I will show you the shrine before we leave so that you may know where to go if anything happens.'

Jenelyn couldn't help but chuckle.

'Do you really think something will happen?' she asked incredulously, thinking it was just an old legend.

Gretchen snapped her head towards her sharply, her brown eyes glittering with angry passion. It was the first time Jenelyn had ever seen the mild-tempered woman upset, and she cast her eyes down immediately with guilt.

'I can assure you, Jenelyn,' she hissed, enunciating each word carefully, 'if no one had lit that candle, the town of Wittlich would have been rampaged again like it had been in Schwytzer's time. Some teenage pranksters would no doubt think it funny to blow out that flame. If you ever see it blown out, light it immediately, no matter what you believe.'

Jenelyn nodded carefully, her face serious. Gretchen took a deep breath, calming herself. Now it was her turn to look sheepish.

'I'm sorry for snapping at you,' she apologised smoothly, 'but it means a lot to me. Now, follow me.'

Jenelyn followed in silence, her thoughts racing.

What on earth had happened to Gretchen to make her have reason to believe? she thought, bewildered.

She knew Gretchen wasn't going to tell her, but she sincerely hoped she would find out one day. After around a half-hour of walking deeper into the forest, the trail split into two different directions. In the middle of the split was a huge granite headstone about six-feet tall with carvings on its face. Sitting high on top was an extremely thick maroon candle, its flame flickering lazily, and a small fence of tiny iron spikes surrounding it. Half-moon shaped light plastic pieces had been placed behind the iron fencing in an obvious attempt to thwart the weather from blowing out the candle. But it didn't cover the candle completely. People had thrown flowers and letters at the base of the shrine. Jenelyn stared at it, becoming sober. It was obvious this shrine was taken seriously. She felt the wind tickle her neck, and she sensed that it carried something along with it. As she focused on the candle, the hairs rose on Jenelyn's neck and she shivered into her windbreaker. Gretchen walked closer to the shrine and knelt reverently beside the boulder, touching the flowers gently.

'So many have lost loved ones,' she whispered. 'Even if it was centuries ago. We still honour the long dead that were killed by the werewolf. Hopefully, these flowers and letters will be reminders to the people who have stopped believing.'

Jenelyn walked closer and stood beside Gretchen, who was reading the faded out, carved writing on the stone face, knowing Jenelyn would be unable since it was in German.

'Burial site of Thomas Johannes Baptist Schwytzer,' she murmured. 'May All Remember to Keep the Light Burning.'

Jenelyn stared at the headstone a while longer and then shook her head sadly.

'It's such a sad story,' she told Gretchen, who had finally gotten up off her knees and seemed ready to leave. 'He was only a man. He was evil, but surely there must have been some goodness in him.'

Gretchen's face remained solemn, and she motioned to Jenelyn to follow her.

'Even the best of people can be overtaken by darkness,' she said, her voice gentle. 'The candle is a symbol of the light that Schwytzer lost inside. He was cursed, but even before that, he was a monster.'

They walked in companionable silence for a while longer, each lost in their own thoughts. The story and seeing the fresh flowers at the headstone had shaken Jenelyn a little. For such an old legend, it was obviously still active in people's minds. So why was Gretchen so convinced that people still didn't believe in it? It also didn't help that her imagination was running away with her again. Every tree seemed to be hiding a dark shadow behind it, and the slight breeze whistling through the branches were the soft, padded steps of a wolf. Suddenly, an arm wrapped around Jenelyn, making her jump. But it was only Gretchen, and Jenelyn blushed slightly.

'I guess that story has me a bit spooked,' Jenelyn admitted. 'It's easy to imagine anything in these dark woods.'

Gretchen nodded but kept smiling.

'Ja, it is,' she agreed, her tone much lighter, 'but as long as the candle is burning, no dark creatures can enter. If we remember that, this forest can be beautiful.'

Jenelyn still felt there was more to the story that had affected Gretchen personally, but she sensed that Gretchen didn't want to tell her. It didn't take too long for them to reach the trailhead again, and Jenelyn heard her stomach grumble. That light breakfast had finally been digested. She looked over at Gretchen.

'On a lighter note,' she said. 'Are you hungry? Lunch sounds awfully good to me right now.'

Gretchen said lightly, 'Oh, I'm sure I can fix something for us. I'm hungry too. Lunch is the main meal of the day here in Germany.'

It surprised Jenelyn that three hours had already passed since breakfast. So much had happened in that time, it didn't feel possible. She was grateful that it didn't take them long to reach home again. Soon, they were settled in the kitchen, with Gretchen gathering ingredients from the cupboards and Jenelyn leaning against the counter wondering how she could help. Gretchen seemed so organised.

'So, what do you usually have for lunch?' she asked, her tone nonchalant. She tried not to sound too hopeful.

Gretchen piled a bunch of potatoes on the island and reached inside the refrigerator for a packet of steak. Jenelyn couldn't believe her eyes.

'Well, since it's our main meal, we have some sort of meat and kartoffeln,' Gretchen explained, holding up a small potato to demonstrate what she meant, 'It's the heaviest meal of the day. I know that in America, your dinners are the heaviest meals, but we prefer to sleep on a light stomach.'

Jenelyn's eyebrows rose in surprise at this. Meat had been a rarity in her house since it was expensive, only reserved for special occasions and holidays, aside from ground beef. Jenelyn admired Gretchen's organisation and easy way of cooking as she floated effortlessly from chopping to boiling.

'You do everything so easily,' she said, impressed, 'I never really learned to cook well.'

'Oh you're young yet,' Gretchen chuckled. 'You'll have years to learn as I have.'

After a few minutes, she started feeling a little guilty standing there and asked what she could do. Gretchen looked at her in surprise and thought for a moment.

'That's a difficult question,' she said, thoughtful, 'I usually do this alone, so I'm used to it. I suppose you could wash the broccoli and start chopping it. It's in the refrigerator. You do like broccoli, don't you?'

Jenelyn nodded and grabbed the green stalk from the refrigerator.

'Oh yes,' she said, 'It's one of the rare vegetables I like. I'm not used to eating vegetables, to be honest. My family mainly ate pasta dishes, but when we did have vegetables, it was always corn and broccoli.'

Gretchen nodded, stirring the potatoes in the pot.

'Well, you'll start eating them here,' she said firmly, sounding nothing short of a clucking mother hen to her chick. 'Gut vegetables are essential to our health, you know, and we're sure to have them every day.'

Jenelyn chuckled underneath her breath. She loved Gretchen's maternal demeanour. It reminded her of being with her mother. If she closed her eyes, she could picture standing with her mother in this gorgeous kitchen, her mother commenting on how beautiful it was and enjoying cooking together. As Gretchen taught her how to peel the potatoes, Jenelyn smiled warmly, feeling secure with such a loving woman watching over her. She only wished she knew the story behind Gretchen's sad eyes.

Chapter Eight

It was nearing five o'clock before Laszlo came home from work, dressed in a smart business suit and carrying a briefcase. Jenelyn had never lived with a professional businessman before, and was quite impressed. She remembered her father coming home in his stained restaurant uniform, smelling of grease, food, and sweat, completely different to the fresh scent of aftershave wafting from Laszlo. Of course, Laszlo didn't break into a sweat sitting at a desk all day. Like Laszlo did now, her father had always come home with a smile to greet his wife and daughter. Laszlo gave Gretchen a small kiss and greeted Jenelyn with a warm smile.

'So, what did you think of your first day in your new home?' he asked curiously, setting his briefcase down in the small entry hall. 'I'm sorry for not being here this morning, but I couldn't take the time. I hope you and Gretchen had fun together.'

Jenelyn nodded and looked over at Gretchen, sitting across from her on one of the sofas in the living room. They had been there for a couple of hours, relaxing after the busy morning, and enjoying getting more acquainted. Jenelyn could now understand why Gretchen was so happy for the company. She imagined how lonely the house would feel being alone all day.

'I had a great day,' Jenelyn replied, 'Gretchen and I went to the German Aliens Authority office to get my residence and work permits, and then we went for a nice walk on the trails here. They're very beautiful.'

Laszlo sat down beside Gretchen, crossing his long legs casually and patting Gretchen's thigh.

'I'm glad you took her to the forest,' he said to his wife proudly. 'It's gut for you to go now and then.'

Jenelyn desperately wanted to ask what he meant by that, but didn't want to be rude. Gretchen had told her that she often walked on those trails to get out of the house. It didn't make sense. Before Jenelyn could analyse it further though, Gretchen stood up and grinned.

'Well,' she exclaimed, 'it's almost time for abendbrot, which means dinner. I have the table set, so I need to make everything ready. Jenelyn, why don't you go sit at the table, and I'll join you?'

Laszlo looked over at Jenelyn. 'You go right ahead,' he told her. 'I'm going to go upstairs and change.'

Jenelyn nodded and followed Gretchen. She glanced at Gretchen as she walked by the kitchen to the dining room. Gretchen had opened the refrigerator and was taking out a baguette of bread and a package of large sausages. Jenelyn frowned in wonder, but settled into one of the small chairs in the dining room. Was that really all they were going to have for dinner? This prospect didn't seem too promising, and her stomach growled, voicing its frustration. Lunch felt like it had been hours ago, and she was hungry again for a full meal. She wondered if she was going to lose any weight here in Germany. Or, would she adapt to it the same as everyone who lived here? Obviously, people ate differently in every culture, and though they all shared the same basic human needs, they seemed able to adapt to different eating habits without ever feeling starved. So, she assumed that even if she were to lose weight, her body would simply adjust itself to this new schedule.

She didn't have much time to sit and ponder over this before Gretchen joined her, setting down a wooden board with slices of the baguette and sausages. Beside the cutting board, she placed a large bowl of peas and green beans, accompanied by three small dishes of butter, mustard, and pickles to Jenelyn's astonishment.

'It's Bratwurst tonight,' Gretchen announced, not noticing the look of surprise on Jenelyn's face.

No sooner had Gretchen sat on her seat than she popped back up again. 'Oh, I forgot the drinks!'

She quickly went back to the kitchen, while Laszlo came into the dining room. In Jenelyn's eyes, he was still dressed nicely, just a little more casual in brown corduroys and a blue, button-down shirt. He lifted the table chair slightly off the floor as he pulled it back and plopped heavily down on it.

With a contented sigh, he leant back comfortably in his chair, 'It's gut to relax. I'm always staring at a computer or drawing boards, so my eyes are constantly tired.'

Jenelyn gave him a sympathetic smile and then glanced longingly at the wooden cutting board full of food. She was famished, but she knew it was rude to start eating before everyone was seated. To her relief, Gretchen returned quickly, and set down a glass of carbonated water in front of her. Jenelyn looked at her in surprise.

'I forgot that I had more carbonated water,' Gretchen explained apologetically. 'I thought I had run out. This should work for you at lunch and dinner.'

Jenelyn thanked her. She had never had carbonated water, but being a soda addict, anything carbonated sounded appealing. She took a tentative sip and though it wasn't sweet, she found it tolerable, and it certainly helped to temporarily fool her stomach.

'Thank you Gretchen,' she said gratefully, 'This is perfect.'

Gretchen beamed happily, and Jenelyn turned her full attention back to Laszlo, interrupting his first sip of the large foamy beer Gretchen had set down for him.

'Gretchen told me you're an engineer at a company called Heller Funke Europa,' she said politely.

'Ja,' Laszlo answered, pausing over his pint, 'I've been there for over thirty years now. It's a good company to work for.'

He finally was able to resume his first sip of the beer and beamed at it gratefully. 'Danke, Gretchen,' he said warmly, flicks of foam lining his lips. 'I needed this very much.'

Gretchen grinned at Jenelyn and rolled her eyes playfully. 'Laszlo always needs his bier when he gets home.' She chuckled, 'I don't know what he would do without it.'

Jenelyn raised her eyebrows. She couldn't remember her father ever drinking after work, and though she wasn't against drinking alcohol at home, she simply wasn't accustomed to it.

Her surprised expression caused Laszlo to quickly add, 'But only one pint per night. I don't drink more than that.'

Gretchen had started serving herself, placing slices of sausage on her plate and covering them with butter. Jenelyn watched carefully, and wondered where the pickles came in. Laszlo wasn't touching the pickles either, but had simply started on the bread and sausages. She decided to do the same, though she wasn't brave enough to try the mustard. Its strong, spicy aroma seared her nose hairs even from where she was sitting. She thought the sausages looked delicious though and eagerly took a bite.

'Are you sure you don't want mustard, Jenelyn?' Gretchen asked. 'It goes with Bratwurst very gut. I also want to go to the store and you can show me what you usually drink at home.'

'Oh, I don't need mustard,' Jenelyn assured her, 'The sausages are wonderful on their own. But it would be nice to go to the store. I usually drink juice or soda.'

Gretchen nodded, taking a mental note. Jenelyn appreciated that she wanted her to feel at home. She turned back to Laszlo, who was happily smothering his bread with butter.

'What does your company do?' Jenelyn asked, curious to know more about what an engineer actually did.

Laszlo finished buttering his bread and took a bite before eagerly explaining. 'We manufacture and sell electric motors for underwater and drainage purposes. I design the motors, you see, and then we have people who build them, test them, and then sell them. We're an international company and growing every day.'

'I can see why that would be quite tedious work,' she replied. She wouldn't know where to start with something like that, 'It must take a smart person to figure out those designs.'

This made Gretchen turn to him quickly. 'That reminds me, do you have any positions open right now?' she asked hopefully. 'When Jenelyn and I went to the Ausländerbehörde to get her work and residence permits; she couldn't get a work permit because she didn't have a letter from an employer stating that they would hire her. She was, however, able to obtain her residence permit.'

Laszlo frowned thoughtfully. He put some Bratwurst slices into his bread and ate it leisurely, his thick brows drawn down in deep consideration. Jenelyn bit her lip anxiously, imagining herself penniless when the Spirits did finally contact her. It was her responsibility to be ready for them, and if she were unable to continue her Journey, it would be a humiliating failure to admit to Gretchen and Laslzo, and she would be trapped. After a few heart-racing moments, Laszlo finally answered, unaware of the mental turmoil Jenelyn was experiencing beside him.

'Many of the people we hire have certain skills,' he explained, looking at Jenelyn curiously. 'What work experience do you have?'

Jenelyn swallowed nervously, knowing her answer wasn't very promising. 'Not very much,' she said grimly. 'I was a part-time cashier for about a year when I was sixteen, but that's it.'

‘Hm,’ Laszlo grunted, and then said, ‘I want to help you, Jenelyn, but I have to be honest. I’m not sure if my field service manager would have a position you would be qualified for.’

Jenelyn looked down at her plate forlornly. She was starting to see why her mother had danced on the streets for money.

‘I understand,’ she said, feeling deflated. ‘I’ll have to find another way to earn money.’

Laszlo and Gretchen looked at her sympathetically, but then Gretchen turned to Laszlo, her eyes exuberant with an idea.

‘Laszlo,’ she exclaimed. ‘What about the salespeople? I remember you telling me once that you don’t require them to have any work experience.’

Laszlo brightened immediately, and Jenelyn felt a small wave of hope. He looked a lot happier and stared at her curiously.

‘Do you think you would be good at sales, Jenelyn?’ he asked, his voice eager.

Jenelyn thought for a moment. She wasn’t a strong salesperson, but she was willing to try. This might be her only chance!

‘Yeah,’ she blurted, trying to look confident.

‘Well then,’ Laszlo stated triumphantly, ‘I’ll talk to my manager tomorrow and get you an application. After your interview, if he likes you, I’ll have him write up a letter stating he’s willing to hire you.’

Jenelyn frowned. 'Will he mind that I don't have a work permit?' she asked.

Laszlo shook his head. 'Not if I explain the situation to him first. He's a very understanding man, and he likes me, so I might be able to persuade him.'

Jenelyn took a deep breath and bit into her bread, her hope degrading quickly to anxiety. What was she thinking? She had never sold anything in her life! She was starting to think her desperation was overtaking practicality, and thought perhaps it would be good to learn more.

'So, what do salespeople do?' she asked timidly, almost dreading his answer.

'They're on the phone mostly with potential customers,' he replied. 'Once in a while, we might have someone who needs to do a speech at another company, but that's very rare. Most of the time, everything can be done over the phone.'

Jenelyn stared at Laszlo, shocked. Her heart had frozen, and her face must have been white, because he instantly looked concerned.

'Are you alright?' he asked, reaching over the table to hold her hand.

Jenelyn nodded, struggling to find her voice through the thick wave of despair. 'I can't do it.' She gasped, 'Laszlo, I don't speak German.'

Laszlo and Gretchen's faces fell, realising she was right. 'Of course,' Gretchen said, throwing up her hands. 'How could we forget? Well, what do you think Laszlo?'

Laszlo shrugged and shook his head. 'She must learn German first of all,' he said matter-of-factly. 'But she simply couldn't learn it well enough to be a salesperson. I will talk to my supervisor and see if he can create a position for her as a favour to me. We're good friends, and he may have an idea.'

'I hope so,' Gretchen muttered, buttering her bread.

Jenelyn had lost her appetite, but she knew she wouldn't have a good meal until the next day at lunchtime. She simply couldn't wait that long, so she picked up her bread and took a small bite, frustrated that she didn't know any German yet. She had picked up a few words here and there already from Gretchen, but that was a far cry from what she would need to know. She couldn't say 'yes, 'no and 'hello' to people all day. They ate in contemplative silence, and after all the bread, sausages, and vegetables had been eaten, Jenelyn noticed that the pickles still hadn't been touched.

'Do you like pickles?' asked Gretchen, finally offering the bowl to her, 'We normally have them after dinner.'

Jenelyn shrugged. 'Honestly I'm not sure,' she said, picking one up and smelling it, 'I've only had them in burgers, never on their own like this.'

She nibbled a piece and was surprised by the burst of tangy sweetness that exploded in her mouth. 'It's good,' she said, and continued to nibble on the pickle, contemplating the task of learning German.

The next morning, Jenelyn woke earlier and went downstairs after her shower. This time, she wasn't surprised to see Gretchen already in the kitchen, though she was setting rolls on the island this time instead of standing over the stove. Gretchen looked up as she entered, her soft, golden-brown hair tied neatly back and dressed smartly in a yellow blouse and brown slacks. Jenelyn stifled a yawn and greeted her.

'Good morning, Gretchen,' she said, giving a yearning glance towards the rolls and jam sitting on the island.

'Guten Morgen, Jenelyn,' Gretchen chirped happily. 'Was wollen sie für frühstückt heute morgen?'

Jenelyn gave her a blank stare and shook her head. 'What?' she asked, still drowsy from sleep.

Gretchen chuckled and plopped an egg into a boiling pot. 'I've decided to start your German lessons today,' she clarified, 'There's no time to waste, and immersion learning is supposed to be very effective.'

Jenelyn leaned against the counter and shrugged, doubting her abilities to speak a new language. As much as she wanted to learn German, it was daunting to feel like she had to learn it immediately.

'Well, I'm willing to give it a try,' she admitted, 'You'll have to repeat yourself a lot more though. Like, what did you say to me?'

'I asked what you want for breakfast.' Gretchen explained. 'I'm assuming you want what you had yesterday?'

Jenelyn nodded and grabbed a slice of toast.

This is going to be an interesting day, she decided.

She hoped that she wouldn't frustrate Gretchen, although she seemed to have a lot of patience.

'Can we go to the store today?' Jenelyn asked, abruptly remembering what Gretchen had said yesterday about shopping.

'Ja,' Gretchen replied and eagerly added, 'I can teach you new words while we're there.'

Jenelyn admired Gretchen's tenacity and decided that this was probably the best way for her to learn and to comply.

'That sounds great,' she agreed, surrendering her doubts. 'Hopefully I can pick it up fairly quickly.'

Gretchen assured her she would and they sat down to breakfast, leaving for the store soon afterward. Jenelyn couldn't get over how tidy Wittlich was as they drove through the provincial town. Nicely dressed people casually walked past endearing shops clean of graffiti, and children ran freely. Jenelyn absorbed the carefree attitude like a sponge and found herself sinking further into the leather of the seat. She was fully relaxed outside of her home for the first time. Gretchen parked next to another car outside a large building, and Jenelyn got out and stretched in the gentle sunshine.

'Is May always like this?' she asked Gretchen. 'Does it ever get really hot?'

Although the soft warmth of this sun felt like a comforting friend, she still didn't prefer it compared to the hot intensity of the California sun that tried to emulate an oven.

Gretchen smiled. 'Nein, May is a nice time of year,' she said, not aware that Jenelyn wanted it to be hotter. 'It's cool but still hot enough to melt the snow.'

As they grabbed a trolley in front of the store, Gretchen said, 'This is a grocery store called Aldi. They have some other supplies as well, like toys and office supplies. Kommen sie, let's do our shopping.'

They walked into the store and lines of merchandise met them. Jenelyn immediately felt a sense of familiarity. It was similar to the small local grocery store near her house in Los Angeles, with narrow aisles of overcrowded shelves, a few cashier stands, and a miscellaneous array of everything imaginable along with food items. The only difference being that everything was in German. She pointed out a bag of crisps and turned to Gretchen.

'Could I have those?' she asked politely, 'I'm used to eating them as a snack in my room.'

Gretchen's eyes widened in shock, and she shook her head. 'Absolutely not,' she gasped. 'Späne are not a snack. If you ever get hungry, let me know and I will get you some fruit. My goodness, how have you stayed so thin with your appetite?'

Jenelyn was disappointed but not surprised at Gretchen's attitude. Her own mother had never allowed her to snack on crisps either, but she had wondered what Gretchen would think about it.

'I have a high metabolism,' Jenelyn explained. 'It's a good thing too because I love food.'

She scanned the aisle, looking for anything else that seemed familiar. Finally, she spotted a pack of soda and nearly fainted with relief. She knew she had a mild addiction.

'That's what I normally drink at home,' she informed Gretchen, who was looking at the pack of soda sceptically.

'Soda isn't very healthy,' Gretchen warned grimly, but she grabbed the pack anyway. 'I'll make you a deal. If you drink carbonated water every other night, you can drink soda the rest of the time. That way, you're not getting too much.'

Jenelyn gave her a tolerant grin. Gretchen was definitely a mother hen.

'Alright, it's a deal,' she said, her eyes twinkling mischievously. She had no doubt that she would be able to sneak a few into her room later on. Jenelyn glanced at the long list in Gretchen's hand as they meandered through the store. Her eyes widened in surprise.

'Wow, you're getting a lot of meat,' she exclaimed. 'Is it for all the lunches?'

Gretchen nodded. 'It's time for us to stock up,' she replied as she looked down at the variety of meat to choose from.

Jenelyn's eyes widened with amazement as she scanned the selection, from thick-cut bacon to roast beef wrapped tightly in string. She had never seen such a wide range of meats before, and certainly hadn't seen bacon so thick. American bacon was thin and streaked heavily with fat. These bacon cuts almost looked like ham! Gretchen picked up a package of strip loin steak, and decided to pursue educating Jenelyn.

'A lot of food is pronounced very similar as in America,' she explained. 'Like this for example. This is called steak in German just as in English, though you would say 'das' before using it in a sentence. Fruit is a little different however.'

Gretchen moved on to the vast produce section, repeating the word for each fruit, and completely oblivious to how overwhelmed Jenelyn was becoming. Thankfully there was a saviour from the monotonous lesson in the form of a woman they were walking past. She glanced over at them while selecting a head of broccoli and did a double-take.

'Frau Wenesievers?' she asked, disbelief lacing her polite tone.

Gretchen looked over quickly, putting on a polite smile, though her eyes were wary. 'Hallo Frau Becker,' she responded cordially. 'Es ist lange her.'

She then motioned toward Jenelyn and switched to English, much to Jenelyn's relief. 'This is a family friend, Jenelyn, visiting us from California in the U.S.'

Frau Becker flashed Jenelyn a quick smile, merely glancing at her, and then turned back to Gretchen. Jenelyn couldn't mistake the look of deep curiosity written all over the mild woman's face.

'It *has* been a long time,' she responded pointedly, politely using English so as not to exclude Jenelyn from the conversation. 'I haven't seen you in town for months.'

Gretchen chuckled. 'Our paths must have crossed,' she said dryly. 'I hope you have a nice day.'

Frau Becker could tell she had been dismissed. A brief wave of disappointment crossed her face but was almost immediately smoothed over by a patronising smile.

'I will,' she said shortly. 'Well, I must be going. It's nice seeing you again.'

She wandered off, Gretchen watching her carefully for a few moments. Jenelyn couldn't keep quiet any longer.

'What was that about?' she asked, amazed at Gretchen's obvious disinterest in the woman.

'What?' Gretchen asked, feigning innocence.

'That woman,' Jenelyn persisted, 'she seemed awfully disappointed not to talk to you more, as if she was missing out on some gossip or something.'

Gretchen shrugged as if getting rid of an annoying fly on her shoulder. 'Frau Becker is a very nosy woman,' she explained, 'I avoid her if I can.'

Her tone meant the conversation had ended. Jenelyn wondered why Gretchen wasn't more social. She was such a friendly, warm person that it didn't feel right that she wouldn't extend that kindness to everyone around her.

Perhaps it was only with this particular person, Jenelyn thought.

Either way, she was grateful to Frau Becker for giving her a respite from Gretchen's teaching. Unfortunately, it had been far too brief because Gretchen immediately started again and continued for the rest of the shop.

Later that evening, Jenelyn felt like she had finally accomplished her basics. It had taken hours of her and Gretchen sitting in the living room repeating each other, but she was sure that she had gotten most of it. When Laszlo entered the house, Jenelyn surprised him.

'Willkommenes heim, Laszlo,' she said in greeting, 'How was your day?'

Laszlo beamed at her and looked over at Gretchen happily.

'Well,' he cried jovially, 'I see Jenelyn has learned some German today. That's good news.'

Jenelyn and Gretchen looked at him expectantly. 'Did your supervisor find a position for Jenelyn?' Gretchen asked hopefully.

Laszlo nodded, a beaming grin widening across his face. 'Ja, he did,' he said, sitting down across from Jenelyn, 'You have an interview tomorrow at two o'clock. He has been thinking about having a personal assistant for a long time, and he thinks that it would be the perfect job for you. He speaks little English, but I thought both of you could help each other out. He wants to learn more, and I told him that you were still learning German. He's obviously doing this as a favour to me, but it does give him some help.'

Jenelyn felt scared and excited all at the same time. She rubbed her hands against her jean-clad thighs, subconsciously gripping the material in anxiety and happiness.

'Tomorrow? Oh my goodness. How am I going to be ready? Oh, thank you Laszlo!'

Laszlo laughed and waved her off. 'Don't worry about anything,' he assured her, 'I will help you. Gretchen, you can drop Jenelyn off. I have a feeling the interview will take over an hour. Now, we can discuss details over dinner.'

He rose from the sofa and Gretchen hurried to the kitchen. Jenelyn followed her slowly, her mind racing. She was about to get a job! At least, she hoped she was. She still had to pass the interview.

Chapter Nine

Jenelyn nervously straightened her blue blouse. She and Gretchen had gone shopping that morning in preparation for her interview. Jenelyn had been shocked to see all the departments in what Gretchen called 'hyper-stores.' They had all been in the same shopping centre and carried every available item one could think of. After a few hours of careful consideration, they had chosen an appropriate outfit Jenelyn had finally liked. White, pressed dress pants with black pumps completed Jenelyn's look, and although it was completely different from what she would normally wear, it was the best out of the limited selection she liked. She had wanted to purchase the clothes herself with the little money that she had brought with her, but Gretchen had refused, insisting that she had always wanted to go shopping with a teenage daughter but had never had the chance. Her eyes had become quite misty when she'd told her this, causing Jenelyn's curiosity to rise again. The depth of Gretchen's secret gnawed away at her like a pestering woodpecker each night, but she still didn't feel like she could approach the subject yet. It somehow felt too raw to bring up, even though Jenelyn had no clue what it was.

They were now heading towards Laszlo's office building. There was still an hour before the interview, but Gretchen wanted to be sure Jenelyn was on time.

'Well,' Gretchen warned her, 'I don't know what American interviews are like, but here in Germany they are extremely formal. It would be wise not to get too friendly.'

Jenelyn nodded her head quickly, her mind racing.

Please, please let me not mess this up, she pleaded silently.

'Interviews vary in America,' she explained to Gretchen, 'It depends on the company you're applying with. When I applied to be a cashier, the interview was extremely casual. I was wearing jeans and a T-shirt. But I've been told by my friends who have interviewed at business offices that it's more formal.'

Gretchen looked shocked. 'You were allowed to wear jeans and a T-shirt to an interview?' she asked, horrified.

Jenelyn nodded and Gretchen shrugged, shaking her head in amazement. 'You could never do that here, not even if you were applying to work in a department store,' she explained.

It didn't take them long to reach Laszlo's building. It was a single storey, long building made of red brick, with multiple windows, and Jenelyn felt as if it were staring her down in challenge. Four flagpoles stood in a straight line to the left of the entrance, and a small car park was situated on the side of the building. This surprised Jenelyn. Judging by the size of the building, she would have assumed that they would need a larger one. She mentioned this to Gretchen, who shrugged matter-of-factly.

'Many people choose not to drive to work,' Gretchen explained. 'Petrol is so expensive now, and we have buses and such to use. And people here try hard not to make a carbon footprint.'

Jenelyn frowned at the word petrol. Of course, she knew what it meant, but she would have to remember to say it instead of gas. For all she knew, maybe the word gas meant something else entirely. They were forty-five minutes early, so they sat down in a large waiting room. Jenelyn tried taking deep breaths, tapping the leather binder holding her Lebenslauf, pondering momentarily over the unfamiliar word for a CV that Laszlo had taught her while helping her type it up the night before. Unfortunately, it seemed pathetically empty, and she hoped the supervisor wouldn't be too disappointed. She was so nervous she was almost shaking. Gretchen noticed and patted her arm.

'Don't worry, Liebling,' Gretchen reassured her, 'you'll be alright. Laszlo told me only this morning that Edwin is a very nice man.'

Jenelyn swallowed and tried to distract herself from the frightening thoughts of the interview.

'Liebling?' she asked, not understanding.

'Literally, it means favourite, but it is used like darling,' Gretchen explained, looking a little worried. 'I hope you and Edwin can understand one another well enough.'

Jenelyn raised her eyebrows hopefully and shrugged. 'Well, I can say hello, goodbye, and now some small phrases, thanks to you,' she replied. 'Hopefully, he can say more in English. It's everything in between that makes me worried.'

After a few minutes, they both noticed a tall, blonde receptionist walking back to the front counter. The receptionist saw them and smiled.

'Wie kann ich sie helfen?' she asked politely.

Gretchen patted Jenelyn's knee and turned to her. 'She just wants to know if we need help,' Gretchen explained. 'I'll go and tell her.'

Gretchen walked purposefully over to the receptionist and began explaining everything rapidly in German. Jenelyn bit her lip and stared out the large window onto the snow-patched lawn. She could feel her heart beating nervously and wondered why she was so panicked. Other than not knowing the language, what on earth could this man do to her to make her feel so uneasy? Nothing. She needed to calm down and act professionally. Jenelyn folded her sweaty hands together on her lap, wringing her fingers together.

So much has happened in a week, she thought. *Maybe that's my problem. Everything seems to be happening so fast.*

She couldn't be too hard on herself. A week ago, she had been comfortably at home in America. Now, she was trying to get a job in a foreign country, away from her parents and all that was familiar, and under immense pressure to learn a new language. Of course, she was panicking. It was a small miracle that she wasn't hyperventilating at this point.

'Well, everything is settled,' Gretchen said, sitting back down next to Jenelyn, who sat frozen and pale. 'Are you alright?'

Jenelyn nodded woodenly, and Gretchen pursed her lips. 'Jenelyn,' she said curtly, 'you look like a frightened animal. Edwin is a nice man, and he understands your position. The worst that can happen is that you're not hired.'

Jenelyn finally looked over into Gretchen's friendly, light-brown eyes. What Gretchen said was true. So what if she didn't get this job? She could always find another way to make money.

'You're right,' she agreed, forcing the tornado whirling in her stomach to stop, 'I need to calm down. I'm trying to put on my professional face, but I don't think it's working.'

Gretchen shook her head and cupped Jenelyn's chin in her hand. 'You look beautiful,' she told Jenelyn firmly. 'Simply smile and don't stare the man down, and remember, do not shake hands with him. That is not a custom here and he may be taken aback. I'm sure he's run into it before, but probably not very often.'

Jenelyn swallowed heavily. It was so instinctual for her to shake hands with someone. She wasn't sure what else she should do.

'Oh, Gretchen, I'm scared,' she blurted, her heart pounding. 'What if I accidentally insult him or something?'

Gretchen shook her head. 'You won't,' she chuckled calmly, 'Laszlo told Edwin that you're American. In fact, Edwin is probably expecting you to do some things that are unfamiliar to him.'

Jenelyn nodded, concentrating on breathing through her tightening chest. She had only been to one interview in her entire life, and it was nothing compared to this. This seemed prestigious and intelligent. Her little drugstore had been exactly the opposite. She simply didn't have the confidence in herself to face this place. Time flew all too quickly for Jenelyn, as soon the receptionist called them over.

'Edwin ist bereit für sie,' she called, her voice light and sweet.

Jenelyn looked over at Gretchen questioningly. Gretchen stood up and smoothed down Jenelyn's blouse.

'She says that Edwin is ready for you,' she explained. 'I'll walk over there with you, but then you're on your own, Liebling.'

They walked to the receptionist's desk, and Gretchen asked where Edwin's office was. The receptionist told her and Gretchen turned to Jenelyn steadily.

'Go down that hall and turn right at the end. His office is three doors down on the left. I have faith in you, Jenelyn.'

Jenelyn gave Gretchen a tight hug for good luck. The receptionist smiled warmly at her, making Jenelyn feel a little more at ease. She took a deep breath and watched Gretchen leave. She knew that Gretchen would come back for her in an hour, but watching Gretchen walk through that door felt like when her parents had abandoned her on her first day of nursery. This was officially the first time she had been alone in Germany, and she was terrified. She felt her feet begin walking down the hall, but she could have sworn she wasn't moving them. Instead, she felt like she was floating outside her body.

I'm truly scared out of my mind, she thought, suddenly having an uncontrollable urge to giggle.

She reached the office door. It loomed in front of her as she tried taking small, deep breaths before she raised a shaky hand and tapped lightly on the wood. A deep voice answered from inside.

'Kommen sie herein.'

Jenelyn shrugged, assuming the voice meant what she thought. She opened the door slowly and peeked inside. It was a tidy, spacious office with a black and glass desk sitting in the middle of the room, and two potted plants standing behind it to the right. Two black chairs were placed in front of the desk, and behind it sat a wide man in his late fifties, with short, greying hair and a large bald spot. His round face smiled at her in welcome, causing thick wrinkles to bunch up on his forehead. His friendly blue eyes twinkled at her, and she quickly felt more comfortable.

He looks like Santa Claus without a beard, she thought happily. *He's no one to be scared of.*

'Hallo, my name is Edwin,' Edwin's voice was deep. 'Bitte setzen sie sich hin.'

When Jenelyn looked at him in confusion, he pointed to one of the chairs and motioned with his hand for her to sit.

'Oh!' Jenelyn quickly sat down, 'You do know a little English.'

Edwin nodded and held up his fingers, with a small space between his index finger and thumb.

'A little,' he replied, his thickly accented words broken and uncertain. 'It will be hard talk with you, but between us, we make work.'

Jenelyn grinned, already feeling relaxed now that Edwin appeared to be friendly. She had pictured him as curt and cold, like other businessmen she had heard of. Instead, he was almost like an old grandfather.

'Well, you know more English than I do German,' she said, then frowned when he looked at her uncertainly.

Jenelyn shifted in her chair and shrugged, not knowing what else to do. A few awkward seconds passed and then Edwin grabbed some paperwork.

'This is application,' he finally said, sounding the larger word out carefully. 'Take home, have Laszlo help fill out.'

Jenelyn picked up the papers and stared at them in horror. They were all in German, of course. Oh, that was going to be fun. She understood why Edwin wanted her to take it home instead of trying to fill it out then. She nodded in understanding and put the application in her leather binder. She wondered how she was ever supposed to be a personal assistant if she couldn't even read the paperwork given to her! She took out her Lebenslauf and handed it to him. Laszlo had written it in German, so she knew Edwin would at least be able to see her credentials.

'Danke,' Edwin said and then continued. 'I must ask of health and crime record.'

Jenelyn didn't have any difficulty understanding him, but he hadn't been able to understand her so far. She breathed deeply and answered as best she could.

'Good health,' she said shortly, hoping that if she kept her answers small, he could understand them, 'No crime record.'

Edwin nodded, seeming to understand. He smiled at her and gave a short laugh. 'Es ist gut,' he chuckled to himself, and then transitioned back into English.

Jenelyn thought it would be too rude to ask what he had said since she was sure he didn't mean it to be something for her to respond to.

'Benefits,' he said, pulling out another form from his desk. 'We have benefits here. Health, unemployment, and retirement.'

Jenelyn nodded slowly, not wanting to seem impatient. But Edwin was talking at a highly measured pace like he had to think out one word at a time. Jenelyn wished she could say something, anything, in German to help him out. She learned that employers paid for their employees' lunches, and would compensate them for the cost of getting to work. She was flabbergasted. She had thought American unions were good, but they were nothing like this! Her father would have a stroke if he knew.

'Is there a probation period?' she asked finally, watching Edwin's face scrunch in thought.

'Ja,' he replied, 'Drei zu sechs monaten.'

Jenelyn shook her head sadly, and Edwin held up three fingers and then six. Then he pointed at the months on the calendar on his desk. Jenelyn's eyes widened.

'Oh, you mean three to six months,' she confirmed, and Edwin nodded patiently.

'After that,' he stammered, 'I cannot fire you. Would have to convince union.'

Jenelyn knew that was similar to how it was in America and was eager to learn more about Germany's work system. Edwin gestured and pointed to pictured documents and signs to help her learn that sometimes workers could get housing subsidies and child subsidies to help raise them. She also couldn't believe the amount of vacation time that the law required every employee to have. She was required to have eighteen paid vacation days annually, but Edwin motioned that it could be as much as thirty days. She'd also get six weeks of paid sick leave, and then after six weeks, her health insurance would pay seventy percent of her salary. After nearly an hour of Edwin explaining all this to her, Jenelyn was so impressed that she hoped he would hire her more than ever.

'So, job would be simple. Paperwork, filing, some computer, und help in general.'

Hm, thought Jenelyn, listening politely, *so it's a receptionist position.*

Edwin studied her for awhile, and then he broke into a wide grin.

'Want job?' he asked.

Jenelyn nodded and laughed. 'I think we can teach each other a lot,' she said, hoping her point got across to him. It seemed to because he laughed.

'I teach you more German,' he chuckled, shaking his head. 'You need bad.'

‘I know,’ Jenelyn answered, being able to take a deep breath for the first time.

It was over. She had been hired. Unexpectedly, Edwin snapped his fingers.

‘Almost forgot,’ he said, picking up a form, ‘Must take drug test. And will run background check on you.’

Jenelyn nodded and took the form from him. ‘Where do I go?’ she asked.

Edwin only stared at her and shook his head. ‘Laszlo,’ he said, pointing toward the door dismissively. Jenelyn looked back at him in confusion and then understood. He needed Laszlo to explain it all to her. Of course, Laszlo would understand what needed to be done.

‘I’ll ask Laszlo,’ she confirmed, and Edwin nodded affirmatively.

‘Auf wiedersehen,’ Jenelyn told him, happy that she could at least say goodbye in German. Edwin’s eyes widened in surprise and he laughed.

‘Auf wiedersehen!’ he replied, and Jenelyn left to go meet Gretchen in the waiting room.

First Month

Chapter Ten

'Jenelyn, können sie mir meinen kaffee bringen?' a deep, male voice called.

Jenelyn looked up quickly from the filing cabinet. After a month of working for Edwin at Heller Funke Europa, she had finally grasped some German, mainly due to necessity.

'Ja!' she called back and quickly walked to the small kitchen down the hall.

She enjoyed her job immensely. There was always something new to learn, and she loved keeping busy with the multitude of tedious tasks that awaited her every morning. Her days went faster that way, and time didn't feel so stagnant.

She and Edwin had worked hard together to communicate, but it was becoming easier. Every morning, he always asked her to get his coffee, as he did now. It had been one of the first sentences she had learned, though she knew she would have difficulty saying it herself. It was easier to understand German than it was to speak it. She had learned a few words and sentences so that Edwin could understand her, and it was nice to have Anelie, the blonde receptionist, help her out. Anelie didn't know

English at all, but she had been able to tell Jenelyn what Edwin had asked her to do by miming out the word. It kept Edwin from doing it himself, which was helpful since he was a busy man and Jenelyn tried to inconvenience him as little as possible.

I may not know how long I'm here for, she thought dryly, *but I'll do the best I can while I'm here.*

She poured the fresh cup of coffee carefully, mixing in the exact amount of sugar and cream Edwin preferred. It hadn't taken her long to learn how finicky Edwin was about his coffee. She walked back to his office and set the mug down on the glass desk.

'Danke,' he said gratefully, sipped it, and then asked. 'How is filing?'

One of the rules Edwin and Jenelyn had decided for one another was to try and speak the other's language as much as possible, allowing them both to learn simultaneously. To her dismay, Edwin was having a much easier time of it than she was. Of course, they always corrected each other, but Jenelyn noticed that she was losing the game.

'Gut,' Jenelyn answered, hoping her accent was right. 'Es ist leicht.'

She looked at Edwin expectantly, waiting for him to laugh and shake his head and tell her that her accent had been wrong, or she pronounced the word so it meant something else. Instead, he beamed at her.

'Nice!' he said, 'Have been practising?'

Jenelyn nodded, ruefully thinking about the hours she'd spent burying herself in German language books every night before bed. She wanted to learn this language so badly, and knew it was the only way to secure her job. It hadn't gone unnoticed by her that Edwin's patience had been tested many times during the past month. She was sure that Laszlo was getting an earful for how much he owed him.

'Good,' he said, 'I hoping you was. Now, could you take papers, and initial for me?'

Jenelyn frowned. What would her initial do for him? She didn't know the German to answer, so she was forced to be the first to break the rule again.

'My initial?' she asked, 'Don't you mean, you want me to sign your initial?'

Edwin looked at her patiently, but his lips pursed with annoyance and strained lines of tension tightened his cheeks. She knew she was starting to wear him down.

'Ja,' he said shortly, 'Here.'

He handed her a large stack of papers, at least twenty centimetres thick. Jenelyn knew it would take her the rest of the morning to do it. She thanked Edwin and went back to her tiny, wooden desk that sat in the room right next to his so she could hear him call. Despite its tiny size, it was comfortable and perfectly suited her needs. She had quickly personalised it by getting a desk calendar and a small vase of fake flowers, knowing she would accidentally forget to water real ones. Their colourful presence added some cheer to the room, and she found they helped lift her spirits when the day was becoming difficult. Giving a daisy a quick flick of her finger in greeting, she picked up a black pen and began on the first page.

At four-thirty sharp, Laszlo came to Jenelyn's desk. Since it was more convenient, Jenelyn worked Laszlo's hours and took the bus with him to work. They were long hours, often including overtime, but she didn't mind. It helped her earn more money, and it wasn't as if she had anything else to occupy her time. Though she did miss the time she spent with Gretchen.

'How was your day?' Laszlo asked her, smiling broadly.

Jenelyn grinned and piled her papers neatly. She wanted to appear as efficient and tidy as possible, despite her language handicap.

'It went well,' she replied, following Laszlo out the door.

The evening was fresh and pleasant. The days varied from the low to mid-20s Celsius. It was cooler than Los Angeles, but Jenelyn had eventually adapted. Fortunately, the days were longer, and it helped her immensely to have some daylight left after work. She didn't know how she was going to cope in the winter. She settled into Laszlo's car, eagerly looking forward to going home for dinner. Despite the large lunch she'd had with Laszlo, she was famished. Meals were still a problem for Jenelyn, and she knew she would starve if it wasn't for the vending machine at work.

'Gut,' Laszlo replied. 'Are you and Edwin getting along together?'

'I think so,' she said hesitantly, 'but sometimes, I get the feeling I'm driving him crazy. There are so many times when he has to correct me.'

Laszlo chuckled. 'That doesn't surprise me after how much Edwin has vented to me,' he said, 'Though you've been a model worker, your language barrier has cost me quite a few pacifying pints over the last month. Fortunately, the pints seem to be all that's needed to appease him.'

He looked over at Jenelyn's downcast worried face and shook his head.

'But I think he's impressed with your work. You always have it done on time for him,' he assured her.

Jenelyn gave him a small grateful grin. She knew that was true. She may not be able to communicate with her boss, but she could do her work.

Then again, she thought ruefully, *a monkey could do my job*.

Soon, the car pulled into the driveway of their house and Jenelyn felt a cosy contentment wash over her. She loved the feeling of coming home to this house. It was nice being able to get out of the car without having to worry about being mugged. The sentry trees always seemed to stand guard by her bedroom window, and she could listen to the quiet sounds of nature in the evening. Most of all, she loved hearing Gretchen's voice when she and Laszlo walked through the door. It made her feel less homesick for her mother, especially since Gretchen never failed to be over-enthusiastic upon seeing Jenelyn again.

'Hallo!' Gretchen cried, hugging Jenelyn tightly as she walked through the door. 'I do miss you. I know you have only been working for one month, but I honestly don't know what I've always done without you.'

Laszlo laughed and set down his briefcase. 'Gretchen,' he chastised gently, 'you must get used to being on your own again.'

He gave his wife a pointed stare, and Gretchen stiffened. Jenelyn watched the two of them and waited expectantly. She always hoped that one of them would slip and say something that would inform her of why they acted like this. Unfortunately, they never did.

'True,' Gretchen agreed, her eyes smiling again. 'Well, abendbrot is on the table ready for you.'

She sniffed and hustled toward the kitchen. Jenelyn began to follow her while Laszlo went upstairs to change. She noticed that he walked heavily, obviously feeling bad about reminding Gretchen that she wasn't always going to be around. Frowning in confusion, she decided to spend a little time watching television while waiting for Laszlo. She never spent time in the living room since watching television had been impossible due to the language barrier, but she wanted to test her German skills now that she had studied for so long. As she sat down on the sofa and picked up the remote to turn the television on, the three framed photographs on the entertainment centre caught her eyes. She hadn't thought about them since she had glanced at them on her first day. Laszlo had quickly distracted her before she could look at them, and then Gretchen had always kept her busy since then. Never had she really had the opportunity to look them over. They were the only photographs she had seen in the entire house. She listened carefully for Gretchen and was pleased to hear that she was busy in the kitchen. She knew she had a few moments before either Laszlo or Gretchen called for her and quickly stepped over to the frames.

The photographs were of Laszlo, Gretchen, and a young girl that Jenelyn had never seen before. They were all smiling happily. Laszlo and Gretchen were much younger, and she judged the pictures had to have been taken at least twenty years earlier. The young girl was very pretty, with golden-brown hair and laughing blue eyes. Her hair hung down to narrow shoulders, and Jenelyn guessed her age to be around ten years old. She couldn't mistake the familiar arch of the brows and jutting chin. This girl was no doubt Laszlo and Gretchen's daughter. The conclusion made Jenelyn take an involuntary step back.

Daughter? she thought wildly.

She puzzled over why they wouldn't tell her. That little girl would be around thirty now and possibly married. Laszlo and Gretchen could even have grandchildren! Instead, they had never mentioned anything about her, nor were there any other family photos. Aside from death or being disowned, it didn't make any sense. And even then, why would it be a secret that her parents would want to hide?

She heard feet on the stairs and knew Laszlo was coming down for dinner. She didn't want him to see her staring at pictures that they obviously didn't want her to notice. She scrambled through the small living room door and into the kitchen. Gretchen looked at her suspiciously.

'What took you so long?' Gretchen asked, her tone curious but not upset. 'Usually, you're the first one at the table.'

Jenelyn's heart was racing as fast as her thoughts. She looked at Gretchen's kind, friendly face and couldn't understand why she wouldn't have told her about her daughter. Gretchen seemed so loving and maternal. Surely, she would have been proud of that beautiful girl in the picture. Jenelyn suddenly remembered she hadn't answered yet.

'Oh, I was looking out the window,' she lied, hoping she sounded truthful. 'There was a pretty bird in one of the trees.'

She had decided not to mention what she had seen. She didn't know why they were keeping this a secret, but they had their reasons. They could easily be angry with her for prying. Laszlo entered the kitchen and patted his stomach.

'What are we standing around here for?' he asked. 'Let's eat!'

They sat down in the dining room and helped themselves. Jenelyn ate slowly, her puzzled thoughts hindering her appetite.

How can I not ask them about this? she thought desperately. *I have to know.*

And yet, they could quickly get upset. Gretchen noticed Jenelyn's barely touched plate and frowned in concern.

'Are you feeling alright, Jenelyn?' she asked.

Jenelyn stared into Gretchen's face and saw the similar-shaped blue eyes of the daughter staring back at her. She knew she would never feel comfortable around either Laszlo or Gretchen again until she knew their story.

'Um,' she began softly, not really sure how to admit this. 'Not really.'

Laszlo and Gretchen both froze and looked at one another, making Jenelyn even more nervous.

Gretchen put down her bread and pursed her lips thoughtfully. She looked down at the table and then back up at Jenelyn.

'I have a feeling I know what is wrong,' she said, her voice raspy with emotion. 'What really took you so long to come into the kitchen, Jenelyn?'

This was it. Whatever dark, deep secret Gretchen and Laszlo were hiding was about to come out. Jenelyn took a deep breath and plunged.

'I saw the pictures on your entertainment centre.' She spoke quickly. 'I was so curious to see them! You don't have any other pictures in the house.'

Laszlo cursed under his breath in German, and Gretchen looked down sadly. They both didn't answer for a long time, and Jenelyn bit her lip nervously. Her stomach churned, and her heart pounded. In truth, she really didn't know Gretchen and Laszlo that well. They seemed nice, but there was obviously something very strange about them.

After a few moments, Laszlo turned to her.

'I was hoping,' he almost whispered, 'that you wouldn't look at those pictures. But I suppose it was inevitable if you're staying here.'

Jenelyn nodded in agreement, summoning her courage. She looked over at Gretchen, who was wiping her eyes with her napkin.

'I knew we should have put them away before she got here, but I hate them being away so much. I guess we need to tell you the truth, Jenelyn.'

Jenelyn stiffened, waiting for the story.

'The little girl was our daughter,' Gretchen explained, her voice catching slightly. 'She died a long time ago.'

Jenelyn waited to hear more, but Gretchen had stopped. This was information that Jenelyn had already figured out. True, she hadn't known the girl was dead, but it didn't surprise her. Parents like Gretchen and Laszlo would have had tons of pictures of the girl growing up around the house.

'I figured that much,' Jenelyn answered, trying to be sympathetic even though she was screaming to know the story. 'Would you mind sharing with me what happened?'

Laszlo shook his head firmly. 'It's too gruesome to tell you,' he barked. 'Be glad that now you know we had a daughter, and she died. That's the end of the story.'

He pushed back his chair abruptly and left the room. Gretchen and Jenelyn sat frozen at his outburst.

'I'm sorry for prying,' Jenelyn whispered after a few moments, a little shaken at Laszlo's reaction.

Gretchen shook her head apologetically and picked up Laszlo's plate. 'It's not your fault for being human, Jenelyn,' she said. 'He knows that. But Laszlo takes her death very hard.'

Jenelyn's appetite had disappeared entirely by this point. She stood up and helped Gretchen take everything back to the kitchen. Dinner was obviously finished.

'I can understand,' she replied gently, 'To lose a child is one of the worst things in the world. But, what did happen to her?'

Gretchen turned to her sharply, her face almost as stern as Laszlo's. 'Jenelyn,' she said. 'It would be best if you forgot about it. We don't like to discuss it.'

Her voice gave no room for argument. Jenelyn knew the conversation was over.

On her way to bed that night, Jenelyn noticed the daughter's picture missing from the entertainment centre. Laszlo and Gretchen must have moved it to prevent the chance that another conversation about her would happen again. Obviously, the pain of her memory was too hard for them to bear, and Jenelyn had accidentally opened an old wound. Apparently, Laszlo and Gretchen were deciding to pretend as if it had never happened.

As Jenelyn lay on her bed, looking up at the honey-oak beams, she listened to the trees swaying in the soft breeze through her window. Both Gretchen and Laszlo had sounded so serious about not discussing the death of their daughter. Jenelyn's natural curiosity was dying to know, but she respected both of them. She would hate to anger them more than anything in the world. They had made the beginning of this Journey so much easier for her, and she knew she could never repay them for taking her in like a long-lost...*daughter*, she thought, with a shiver rolling up her spine.

Everything they had said made sense to her about them being lonely for a long time: the maternal looks Gretchen had given her, the odd underlying tones when they would speak of a specific room or event. She hated to think of them dealing with a loss that big for so long. Tears welled up in Jenelyn's eyes. No wonder they had welcomed her with open arms. Based on the appearance of the pictures, she assumed the twenty years of living without their daughter had to have been torture. And to have lost her at such a young age was almost too hard to bear. Jenelyn shifted on her bed to look at the picture of her parents, imagining how they would react if they ever lost her. They would be devastated, to say the least, and she solemnly swore she would respect Laszlo and Gretchen's wishes to never mention their daughter again. It was the least she could do in return for them taking care of her. And, one day, when they were ready, perhaps they would tell her the story. She drifted off with one question thrown out into the night where the daughter's spirit might hear it.

What happened to you, dear one?

Second Month

Chapter Eleven

Jenelyn stretched in the warm sunshine, enjoying the goosebumps that prickled along her cold skin. It was a Saturday in early July, and she stood on the front lawn waiting for Laszlo and Gretchen. A whole month had passed since she had spoken with Gretchen and Laszlo about their deceased daughter. The next day had started awkwardly with Laszlo, but the more Jenelyn didn't speak about it, the more he became his old self again. Jenelyn was determined to keep her promise and never mention their daughter again. She prayed to the Spirits nightly to help her find out what happened. So far, they hadn't answered, but Jenelyn was patient. She knew without a doubt that one day she would learn their daughter's story.

Today, however, was not going to be the day. Laszlo had finally remembered his old promise to her two months before that he would take her back to Kaiserslautern. Since the city was only an hour away, they were going to make a day of it.

'You know,' she mentioned casually to Gretchen and Laszlo as they bustled into the car, 'today is the perfect day to do something fun.'

Gretchen looked at her in amusement. 'Why?' she asked, clicking her seatbelt while Laszlo started the engine.

'Today is the fourth of July!' Jenelyn proclaimed.

Laszlo and Gretchen stared at her curiously. They obviously didn't have any idea what she was talking about. With Laszlo and Gretchen both being born in Germany, Jenelyn figured they wouldn't know what it meant and was happy to explain.

'In America, we celebrate the day we became independent from England.'

'Oh!' cried Laszlo and Gretchen in unison, finally seeming to understand.

Laszlo merged onto the autobahn and looked at Jenelyn again. 'What do you normally do?' he asked.

Jenelyn described all the festivities: the fireworks, the apple pies, the rodeos, everything that made the Fourth of July an American tradition. Gretchen was intrigued mainly by the rodeos. They didn't have them in Germany, and she found the concept fascinating.

'Imagine,' she said in amazement, 'riding a bull! My goodness, what those western cowboys won't do.'

'Yeah, it's pretty incredible,' Jenelyn agreed, though she had only seen rodeos on television. She wondered if she would ever get the chance to see one in real life. She knew that it was mostly a western United States event, and that she could be in Europe for a long time.

Or forever, she thought, *depending on what the Spirits want to do with me.*

Before she knew it, they had reached the city limits of Kaiserslautern, and Jenelyn jiggled her leg in excitement. She had grown accustomed to the quiet town of Wittlich and its quaint houses. Kaiserslautern's city pulse was already reaching them with the streams of traffic pouring into the city centre and the tall buildings enveloping the sky. Exhilaration washed over her. This was her first trip where she wasn't tired or hungry.

'So,' Jenelyn said, leaning forward between the front seats, 'What are we seeing first?'

Gretchen shrugged her shoulders.

'Wherever you like, Liebling,' she said, 'It's your day, remember.'

Jenelyn appreciated the gesture but knew she could never take the whole day for herself. If Laszlo and Gretchen wanted to see something, she would make sure they would be able to.

'Well,' she admitted, aiming her question towards Laszlo, 'why don't you run through the sights for me?'

Laszlo thought for a moment while parking the car on a side street in the city.

'Hm,' he murmured, and then brightened. 'Ah, ja! The Betzenberg Deerpark. We must see it, and this would be the best time, at the beginning of the day.'

They all agreed and set off. Jenelyn couldn't have been happier with how gorgeous the day was. The temperature was only in the mid-20s, much cooler than the 40-degree temperatures in Los Angeles now. Still, she had adapted to the cooler temperatures in Germany to appreciate the sun's warmth instead of expecting it. It didn't take them long to catch a bus to take them across town to the deer park. Jenelyn was amazed at how large it was. Pine trees and grassy meadows covered an expanse acreage of land, and people were enjoying themselves walking on the trails, eating under the trees, or simply sitting in the shade and watching the red-coated deer graze. As they entered the park, Laszlo immediately began his dialogue.

'This park covers 62 acres of land,' he explained, patiently taking the time to give information about the sight and be Jenelyn's personal tour guide, 'and the deer are famous because they are the descendants of the deer that were here in our former times. We also have some in our hunting grounds, but this is a sanctuary for them.'

Jenelyn stared at a large buck that had wandered away from the trees. He lifted his proud, antlered head and called loudly.

'He's looking for a doe,' Gretchen gushed. 'How niedlich.'

Jenelyn was astonished and thought cute was hardly the word to describe such a majestic creature. She had never seen a deer like this before. They were a far cry from the white-tailed deer at home. The buck's coat was a deep blood-red, and his elk-like antlers were wide, long, and sharp, with several points. The buck stood for a moment longer and then lazily walked back into the pine trees. Laszlo, Gretchen, and Jenelyn continued slowly into the park, keeping their eyes open for more deer. They weren't hard to find. There were hundreds of them grazing around, and Jenelyn noticed one couple tossing apples towards a doe who was happily accepting them. Nearby, another young family was talking while a deer grazed unfazed behind them.

'They're not running away from people,' Jenelyn said to Laszlo.

'Of course,' he said matter-of-factly. 'The Betzenberg Deerpark is extremely popular. They see hundreds of people every day, and since they're protected here, they're never hunted.'

They walked for a long time, enjoying the cool breeze, warm sunshine, and beautiful landscape. It was thick with woods, and Jenelyn was reminded of the forest trails back in Wittlich. Since she had started working two months before, she hadn't had a chance to wander them again. She would have to ask Gretchen to take her. Jenelyn felt at peace in Kaiserslautern, loving the serenity of the deer park so close to a bustling city. There was something about this place that called to her. She could feel it in her bones that this city was important, and she needed to pay attention.

Are the Spirits contacting me? she thought. *Is this what it feels like?*

She was certainly feeling something racing through her, but it was so faint she couldn't pinpoint exactly what it was. Soon, they began to get tired, and Laszlo glanced ruefully at his stomach.

'I'm afraid I'm getting hungry,' he said apologetically. 'Who else could eat?'

Jenelyn shot her hand in the air eagerly, all thoughts of the Spirits vanishing at the mention of food. They had arrived in Kaiserslautern on their usual, light breakfast, and at least three hours had passed since then. Gretchen thought for a moment and then snapped her fingers.

'The Hannenfass!' she cried happily. 'That's where we should eat.'

Laszlo beamed at her, and immediately started walking with an enthusiastic purpose.

'Gut idea,' he replied jovially. 'They have excellent food, and I could certainly use a bier. And, of course, Jenelyn can get what Kaiserslautern is famous for.'

His teasing tone made Jenelyn turn to him curiously, though knowing that she would probably be better off unaware.

'What is it?' she asked warily.

Laszlo gave her an impish grin as he wrapped his arm around her and squeezed her shoulder.

'Stuffed pig stomach,' he said, relishing the words. 'It's better than it sounds. You have to try it.'

Jenelyn's eyes widened. She couldn't eat that! Although she knew that part of this Journey was trying new things, and if she was going to live in Europe for an indefinite amount of time, she would have to get used to eating strange foods.

'Alright,' she said grudgingly, 'But if I get sick, it's your fault!'

Laszlo agreed to take full responsibility, and soon they were outside the famous Hannenfass restaurant, which appeared to be a small pub.

'I can't wait to have one of their Deutsche Dunkels Biers,' Laszlo beamed and then explained to Jenelyn. 'They're famous for their drinking parties and traditional music, even if it can be a bit cheesy.'

Before Jenelyn could answer, they had walked inside, and she understood what Laszlo meant. Loud, traditional German music wheezed through the accordions played by the live band on a side stage. Women in traditional attire, arms laden with mugs of beer, danced gracefully between long, dark wooden tables and benches filled with customers drinking, eating, and chatting loudly with occasional shouts of 'Prost!' as they cheered. A heavy, ten-meter bar was situated near the front, its thick wood, aged with decades of spilt beer and damp cloths. Rich scents of yeast, hops, and grilled meat filled the air, causing Jenelyn's stomach to growl in anticipation.

They found space on one of the long benches, greeting people as they squeezed in beside them. Jenelyn was surprised at this casual camaraderie between strangers but found she enjoyed it. It felt much more hospitable and friendly than the stiff formality of a restaurant. They didn't have to wait long for a waitress to come and take their orders. Gretchen ordered first, then Laszlo. Finally, it was Jenelyn's turn.

'Hallo,' she greeted, happy that she was more comfortable now with her German basics. 'Ich würde den vollgestopften schweinmagen und ein wasser bitte mögen.'

The waitress jotted everything down and walked away. Jenelyn knew that her German probably sounded like Edwin's English, chopped and primitive, but at least she could order for herself now. The German language book had really been helping her.

'Are you sure you want the stuffed pig stomach?' Gretchen asked worriedly, 'I know Laszlo mentioned it, but you don't have to get it.'

'Oh, yes,' she said genuinely, 'It's good to try new foods, even if I don't like it. And if I don't, I can always give it to Laszlo.'

She smiled sweetly at him, and he turned red. She was well aware that he did not usually order stuffed pig stomach. She hoped she liked it. They enjoyed chatting and listening to the music, with Laszlo shocking her by joining in singing a ruckus chorus with everyone else sporadically, not caring at all that his booming voice was off-key. But then, so was everyone else's and Jenelyn loved that none of them seemed to care. The atmosphere was so warm and full of fun that inhibitions dropped and everyone adopted a communicative spirit.

A familiar American accent floated on the wave of voices and Jenelyn's ears immediately perked. She turned, eager to find the voice's source. So Kaiserslautern had tourists! She had gotten used to the local feel of Wittlich. Finally, she saw the woman sitting at another table with a group of Germans who were talking about her trip with her. Jenelyn felt sheepish about eavesdropping, but her ears were now so tuned to the woman she couldn't help hearing their conversation. Most of it was incomprehensible due to the loud music, but one particularly loud man's voice cut across clearly.

'Wherever you go, don't go to Wittlich!' he laughed, though his undertone made it clear he was serious.

The rest of the group chuckled as well, albeit slightly uneasily. The American asked why not, but between a sudden cry of 'Prost' and the band hitting a high note, Jenelyn only caught the last word of what the man was saying.

'...werewolf.'

Jenelyn's sharp concentration was interrupted as the waitress brought their orders. But her mind raced.

Perhaps that's why Wittlich doesn't get tourists. Locals are warning them away, she thought. *But do that many people really believe in werewolves*?

She thought this hard to believe and dismissed it as the ravings of a man having drunk too much. She hoped the American would find it as silly as she did, and visit Wittlich despite his warning.

After a permissive 'Guten Appetit,' the waitress left them to their meals. Jenelyn stared at the gross piece of meat in front of her. It was white, grilled brown on top, and looked like an oversized, gelatinous sausage. It was also huge and took up most of her plate. She grimaced and looked up at Gretchen.

'What is it stuffed with?' she asked timidly, poking at the bulbous mass with her fork.

'Normal beef,' she assured her. 'It's only meat, Jenelyn, no matter what it looks like.'

Jenelyn gathered her courage and forced herself to take a bite while Laszlo watched her curiously.

'Well?' he prodded and Jenelyn nodded with satisfaction after swallowing. The aromatic beef spiced with onions overtook the slimy texture of the sausage.

'It's different, but not terrible,' she assured him. 'It definitely tastes better than it looks!'

Laszlo laughed in relief.

'I think the next place we should see is the Kaiserbrunnen,' Gretchen advised, taking a bite of her sausage and sauerkraut. 'Laszlo, we haven't been there since 1987 when it first opened.'

He gave her a small, understanding smile and nodded. 'I think it's a fine idea,' he said softly. 'Are you sure you'll be alright?'

Gretchen nodded and Jenelyn stared at them, wondering what Laszlo's concern was. 'What's so special about the Kaiserbrunnen?' she asked.

Laszlo scowled at her and shook his head, his face heavy and strained. 'The last time we went was with our daughter,' he explained curtly, 'I only wanted to make sure Gretchen could handle it.'

His voice was thick and gruff, and Jenelyn knew she was on thin ice. She stayed silent until they had left the pub. Gretchen seemed uneasy but at last, turned to Jenelyn.

'I think you'll really like it,' she told her, continuing their earlier topic. 'It's where art combines history with humour, and it's famous for its architecture.'

Jenelyn gave Gretchen a polite nod, but she kept staring at Laszlo. His face was tight and drawn, and she could tell he was distraught. She couldn't stand knowing she was the cause of his distress and walked over to him, touching his arm gently.

'Laszlo,' she murmured. 'I'm sorry. I didn't mean to upset you.'

Laszlo exhaled a deep, shaky sigh and turned to her, his face softening a little.

'I'm sorry too, schätzchen,' he pleaded gently. 'I shouldn't get so upset.'

Jenelyn understood, however, that whenever he and Gretchen exchanged odd looks or said something peculiar, she wasn't to ask. Now she understood it would always have something to do with their daughter. She knew she couldn't keep making it harder for poor Laszlo even if she felt she still had to know what happened.

'I promise,' she said, smiling at him.

Laszlo grinned and they took the bus to the Kaiserbrunnen. The first piece of amazing architecture Jenelyn saw was the large fountain right outside the main building. It was simply the strangest fountain she had ever seen. It was made of dark grey stone, and the main statue was of a king sitting on the top with a sword in one hand and a ball in the other. He was sitting on what appeared to be an upside-down rook, with sculpted doves flying around the middle. Two carved elephants stood on each side of the rook, and stairs led up to the king in between them. Horses and other creatures pranced around the circle, spurting water out of their mouths. Jenelyn couldn't make any sense of it, but she knew it was masterfully done. Gretchen walked up to her, proud to show Jenelyn the impressive sights of her country.

'It's called the Emperior Fountain,' she explained, 'and is one reason why this place is so famous. Isn't it unglaublich?'

Jenelyn nodded, agreeing it was incredible.

'Wow,' she stammered, 'I don't know what to say to that.'

Laszlo laughed and shook his head in bemusement. 'I know how you feel,' he said. 'It is rather strange. Wait until you see what else they have.'

They turned to look at the main building and Jenelyn gasped. Out of everything she had seen in Germany so far, this building had to be the most comical looking. Everything was overexaggerated, the windows, the doors, and simply the architecture itself. It looked like a cartoon artist's and architect's drunken brainstorm, albeit with a touch of genius. As they stepped inside, odd, off-beat historical art filled the rooms. Jenelyn knew that she would probably never see another art gallery so unique again. The cacophony of colours in the paintings combined with detailed, creepy-faced statues made Jenelyn want to laugh hysterically at seeing something so bizarre flirt with being mentally disturbing. They explored every room for over two hours, and finally walked back outside into the bright afternoon sunshine.

'That was awesome!' Jenelyn exclaimed, her brain overwhelmed with the task of processing everything. 'I don't know what we could do that would beat that.'

'Well,' Laszlo laughed. 'There's still St. Martin's Square and the Kaiserslautern Zoo. That's always a fun place to go, and the Square is the gateway to historic Kaiserslautern. It's wunderbar.'

'I'm ready when you are,' she said, amiably taking Laszlo's arm.

'Then let's go,' he said and grabbed Gretchen's hand with his free arm.

Arm in arm, the trio marched down the street, ready to see whatever the city would show them. The streets were crowded with everyone enjoying the sunny weekend, and after a while it was too difficult to continue walking next to each other. They fell to a single file, having to weave their way around the swarm of people. Jenelyn tried to look at everything as they quickly walked past small stores. She found herself subconsciously slowing down, admiring the intricate jewellery in one store and beautiful glazed pottery in another. Before she knew it, Laszlo and Gretchen must have not noticed her slowing pace, and she had been swallowed up by the crowds.

Jenelyn looked around frantically. She didn't like being alone in a strange, foreign city. People knocked into her as they walked by, laughter was carried in the wind, and nobody was speaking German slow enough for her to understand a word. She quickly ran on, searching desperately for the sight of Laszlo's curly hair and Gretchen's sweet face, which would be strained with worry by now. But there were too many people. She tried to swim through the thick crowds that were pushing her back like an ocean tide, and before she knew it, the crowd had squeezed her off the main street and into a deserted alleyway. Jenelyn stopped for a moment, breathing heavily as her heart thumped against her chest.

She looked down the alley and noticed that it connected to another street that was around the corner. Forcing her fear down, she tried to think logically. Laszlo and Gretchen most likely walked quite far before noticing that she wasn't with them. They would have walked around that corner by now. If she kept going down this alley, she might possibly see them. Having a plan calmed her panic down, and she set off resolutely. However, she didn't get far before a male voice called out to her.

'Halt und spricht mit uns, zucker!' it cried, sounding unnervingly close.

Jenelyn's heart froze. She had been cat-called too often in her life not to recognise a punk. She turned around irritably, preparing to snap back at him, but her stomach dropped sickeningly. This punk was not alone. He had four other buddies with him. She felt icy terror rise up in her throat, choking her retort. They were walking with steady confidence towards her, their lean, athletic bodies stalking her. Their eyes groped her body unashamedly. Jenelyn knew she had two choices. Run, and pray to the Spirits that she made it, or confront them. She decided to try both. She took a few slow steps back toward the bright, crowded street.

'Hallo,' she replied nervously, trying to remember her basic German. 'Netten tag, huh?'

The punks all sneered and chuckled. They weren't fooled by her nonchalance. Jenelyn sensed this and prepared herself for a fight. They had walked faster than she had, and she was surrounded.

'So ein netter arsch. Zu nett verschwenden zu, gehen. Recht, Jungen?' one of them said, circling a little closer to her, staring at her backside.

Jenelyn couldn't understand their German when they spoke it so fast. At least in Los Angeles, she was able to fight back with her words. Her breath became faster as one of the guys, with short dark cropped hair, reached out and grabbed a fistful of her t-shirt. The dark blonde one also stepped forward, eager lust shining in his eyes and his white teeth flashing with a rakish grin as he pulled her shirt off her shoulder. Jenelyn's eyes frantically scanned the other two, seeing that they weren't far behind joining their friends. She screamed as fear took over her completely.

'Get away!' she snarled, knowing in her heart that it wasn't going to do any good. 'Stop it!'

They all laughed without humour. Their voices were hollow, consumed with only one goal. The dark-haired one laughed the loudest and stuck his nose in her face. He was obviously the leader. Jenelyn was too frightened to take notice of any details.

'Ach, ist sie ein Amerikaner. Sogar netter,' he panted with lust, his hot breath brushing her cheek.

All Jenelyn understood was the word, 'American'. Her face turned red with anger. Nicole had always told her she had a temper, and Jenelyn felt one rising now.

'Touch me again, and I'll neuter you,' she threatened, her voice low and deadly serious.

Unfortunately, her threat was lost on them. They recognised her accent as American but didn't understand English. She couldn't frighten them. They moved in closer in determination, pushing her a little more into the shadows. By this time the dark-haired guy and the blonde had almost ripped her shirt entirely off. As the other two moved in to help finish her, Jenelyn screamed even louder. Suddenly, one of the punks looked up down the alley towards the street behind them in fright.

'Es ist sie!' he warned and ran off.

The others looked in the same direction and followed him with horrified fear on their faces.

'Es ist sie! Wir wollen nächst nicht sein!' the leader shouted, and they were gone.

Jenelyn tried to cover herself with her hands, the cool breeze feeling alien as it crept inside her torn shirt. Her heart raced in her ears as she searched for what had scared them off. Maybe the police had come? But as she stared at the end of the alley, she saw Gretchen and Laszlo's slim frames. She was safe again. She ran to them, tears burning the backs of her eyes, and fell into Gretchen's tight embrace.

'Hush, schätzchen,' Gretchen murmured comfortingly. 'They're gone. We were so worried!'

Laszlo was staring after the punks, his eyes hard and his face set in stone. Jenelyn wondered what the hoodlums had said.

'What were they saying when they ran away?' she asked, still trembling and bewildered. 'I was surprised they ran.'

Laszlo flashed a warning look at Gretchen and she nodded infinitesimally. 'Nothing for you to be concerned with,' Gretchen replied sharply. 'They were only stupid boys.'

Jenelyn nodded as her body began to shake from her slowing adrenaline. The terrifying experience was starting to sink in, and the burning tears that threatened to fall finally cascaded down her cheeks.

'Kommen sie,' Gretchen coaxed. 'You need to sit down and relax.'

They walked back to the main street and quickly found a cafe where Laszlo ordered her a soda. Jenelyn groaned gratefully as she sipped the sugary drink and felt her tense muscles begin to relax.

'We'll get you a new shirt as well,' Gretchen said grimly as she lifted the torn sleeve from her shoulder. 'We can throw this away.'

'I was lucky they didn't tear more of it off,' Jenelyn mumbled shakily. 'I was so afraid they were going to do more. Thank you for coming when you did.'

Laszlo smiled tightly, his eyes still hard at the mention of the punks. Jenelyn wondered briefly if he would have gone after them had she and Gretchen not been there.

'Of course, Liebling,' he assured her. 'I only wish we had found you sooner.'

Gretchen agreed and hugged Jenelyn gently. Her soda was soon finished, and they went to find a clothing store. It didn't take long to find her a new shirt, and Jenelyn felt better once she was fully clothed again.

'Would you like to go home?' Gretchen asked, worry still lining her eyes. 'I think it might be best so you can relax.'

Jenelyn frowned. There was still so much for them to see, and she wanted to forget about that terrifying experience.

'No Gretchen,' she said, taking a deep breath and collecting herself, 'we had a fun day planned and I'm not going to let those creeps ruin it for us. I'll be fine.'

She forced a brave smile, reassuring both Laszlo and Gretchen that she would be able to enjoy the day. Gretchen wrapped her arms around Jenelyn's shoulders in comfort as they set off. Jenelyn hoped she could forget the terror of the experience in time, but she wasn't going to ignore the punks' words.

She snuggled into the backseat that evening as Laszlo drove home. The Kaiserslautern Zoo had been magnificent and the first large zoo she had visited. She had always wanted to see the San Diego Zoo, but her parents never had the money, so she had only seen small circuses and carnivals when she was young. St. Martin's Square had been beautiful. It was an actual square with historic buildings and churches surrounding it. Jenelyn had loved how the new buildings greeted the old like lifelong friends. It was like history meeting the present and what the two cities would look like if they had existed in the same time.

Maybe they are, she thought sleepily.

She was hungry, tired, and full of curiosity. Even after all the sightseeing, she hadn't forgotten the exact words the German punks had said. She wanted to remember the fun time that the three of them had, and nothing else, but her residual fear from the punks' attack overshadowed it. She could still feel the dark-haired punk's tight grip on her arm, and hear the tear of her shirt under the blonde's vicious hands. Jenelyn's stomach coiled as she thought about how powerless she had been, and what could have been the end result had Laszlo and Gretchen not arrived. A knot formed in her throat when she pictured herself lying on the street, bleeding, half-naked, and disposed of if they hadn't come. Yet despite these haunting memories, fear didn't outweigh her curiosity. She was desperately curious about why Laszlo and Gretchen wouldn't translate them for her. A traitorous part of her subconscious whispered in her ear.

You must find out, it urged, *because it means everything.*

The car sped onto the autobahn, and after several fitful starts, Jenelyn eventually fell fast asleep to the soothing murmurs of Gretchen and Laszlo in hushed conversation.

That night, Jenelyn spent an hour searching inside her German language books. She was determined to find out what the punks had said before she forgot. It was a relief to be back in her room, listening to the warm, gentle breeze outside sway her sentry trees. The soft, yellow glow from her nightstand lamp lit the small pages of her language book.

'Es ist sie,' she muttered, flipping the pages, 'I feel like I know what that means.'

Finally she found it. 'It's them,' she read, whispering aloud, then kept going, trying to find the other words.

'Wir wollen nächst nicht sein,' she said to herself again, searching for the leader's words. Again, she finally found the translation. 'We don't want to be next,' she read and sat back, puzzled.

'It's them. We don't want to be next?' she repeated, completely confused. What on earth did that mean? How could those words apply to Laszlo and Gretchen?

Jenelyn put down her book and stared outside, thinking hard. Perhaps Laszlo and Gretchen had a reputation for catching punks and sending them to the police, which was logical. But Jenelyn remembered the pure fear on the punks' faces as they stared at Laszlo and

Gretchen. That was more fear than being sent to the police. That punk had looked at them like they were predators. Jenelyn shook her head and laughed. She was being ridiculous. It had been too frightening of an experience for her to think rationally. Her feeling that the Spirits were near in the deer park had left and she couldn't even be sure that they had been there at all. She lay in her bed and closed her eyes, trying to picture the green fields of the Betzenberg Deerpark rather than the sneering faces of the gang.

August

Third Month

Chapter Twelve

Birds sang outside the sunny windows and the hum of the fridge filled the quiet kitchen. Jenelyn wrapped her hands around her warm mug of milk taking it all in and embracing the peaceful morning. Cosy contentment poured over her as she wiggled her toes inside the soft fuzzy slippers that hugged her feet. She thought of her usual Saturday mornings in Wittlich, exploring the surrounding parks and local shops, wondering if this time they might go to the bakery. They hadn't mentioned any plans, so for the first time, Jenelyn didn't know what to expect but she hoped it was somewhere as peaceful as this kitchen. She liked the local bakery, because not only was it a quiet place, but the warmth of the baked goods always comforted her.

To her surprise, she was awake before Gretchen, but it wasn't long before Gretchen entered the kitchen, snapping Jenelyn out of her daydreaming. She was dressed casually in jeans and a loose-fitting blouse, similar to when they would go for a walk. This piqued Jenelyn's interest since perhaps it meant they were going somewhere for the day.

'Guten morgen, Gretchen,' Jenelyn greeted.

Gretchen's mouth lifted in a blissful smile. 'I love Saturday,' she replied happily. 'It's nice having the company. I get too lonely during the week.' She poured some milk into a glass. 'Laszlo and I had a wunderbar idea about what to do today.'

Jenelyn took a bite of her apple. She had made her breakfast already but was still a little hungry. It had taken her two solid months of getting comfortable enough in Gretchen's kitchen to start making her own breakfast.

'Really?' she asked, raising her eyebrows.

Gretchen shrugged and began preparing her own breakfast, taking out butter and jam from the refrigerator and toasting her bread.

'We didn't think of it until this morning,' she explained matter-of-factly. 'But then, it didn't register completely what month it was until Laszlo remembered something one of his co-workers said. Then he remembered that of course, it's August, and what happens every year in August?'

Gretchen rattled on until she noticed that Jenelyn was completely lost.

'I'm sorry, Jenelyn!' she chuckled, 'I forgot that you wouldn't know. We want to take you to the Tübingen Summer Festival. It always comes in early August.'

Jenelyn smiled. A festival! That sounded like fun to her. She had never been to a fair or festival before and told Gretchen so.

'You must be joking!' she cried. 'But didn't they have festivals in Los Angeles?'

Jenelyn nodded, shrugging with mild embarrassment at Gretchen's shock. She didn't like admitting how much she hadn't seen or done.

'Yeah, they did,' Jenelyn replied sheepishly, 'but they're expensive. My parents couldn't afford it.'

She was uncomfortably aware of how many times she said that her parents couldn't afford things. Surely, Laszlo and Gretchen must have heard her say it at least two dozen times since she had come to them. She hoped they didn't judge her parents too harshly for it, but they never seemed to give it a second thought.

'Well, that's too bad,' Gretchen replied. 'Only a very few of our festivals cost. Most are free and are only for people to enjoy themselves. Tübingen's festival is one of them.'

Jenelyn's eyes widened. She was sure that every county fair, state fair, or little town festival in the States cost to get into. The only free event was a street market fair, but usually, it was too tiny to count as much. The fact that this festival didn't cost anything made her grateful. She always felt guilty when Laszlo and Gretchen spent money on her and made sure never to ask for anything when they were out unless she absolutely needed it. She even kept a record of how much they spent on her and set aside a little money every time she was paid to make sure she could pay them back one day. Even though she earned her own money now and felt more than responsible for herself, they still preferred to care for her and made her save every cent she earned into the separate savings account that Gretchen had opened on her behalf.

'It sounds like a lot of fun,' Jenelyn answered, finishing her milk, 'When do we go?'

'The minute my faul husband gets out of bed,' Gretchen's voice was laced with mild irritation, 'Which shouldn't be too much longer. You know how he likes to sleep in on weekends.'

Jenelyn could sympathise with Laszlo since she shared his work hours. But she was eighteen, not fifty-five. Poor Laszlo usually didn't get up until around eight-thirty on weekends, enjoying the two mornings he could luxuriate in unashamed laziness. Gretchen was finishing her breakfast when Laszlo, eyes drooping with fatigue, sauntered sleepily into the kitchen. Jenelyn always worried about him overworking himself, but she knew that no one could make Laszlo slow down. He loved to work and would probably never retire.

'Guten morgen,' Gretchen said dryly, handing Laszlo a cup of coffee. 'This should wake you up. I just told Jenelyn that we're taking her to Tübingen's Summer Festival today.'

Laszlo took a deep gulp of his coffee. 'That's besser,' he sighed, 'I'll need it today especially. One thing about the festival is that it's a lot of walking. I hope you have good walking shoes.'

He pointed to Jenelyn's fuzzy slippers and she nodded. She knew she could wear the tennis shoes she had worn when she first came to Germany.

'I do,' she assured him. 'I could walk a hundred miles in the shoes I have.'

'Gut,' Laszlo replied with a grin, 'You may have to. What time does the festival start, Gretchen?'

Gretchen looked at her watch and her eyes widened. 'Oh mein!' she cried in dismay, 'We had better leave immediately. The festival opens at nine and closes at five this afternoon. And we still have a three-hour drive to get there!'

Jenelyn frowned.'What time is it?' she asked Gretchen, 'I hope we won't be too late to not make the drive worth it.'

Gretchen shook her head but motioned for Jenelyn and Laszlo to hurry out of the kitchen.

'It's nearly eight-thirty,' she said quickly. 'The schlafmütze, here, has made us late.'

She looked accusingly at Laszlo, who gave her a disgruntled look as he grabbed the car keys and Jenelyn rushed to grab her shoes. In minutes, they were walking out of the house.

'I'm tired,' Laszlo said shortly, 'I work very hard.'

Gretchen rolled her eyes and settled herself into the car. 'Don't complain to me,' she snapped, 'You insist on working hard.'

Laszlo couldn't respond to that, so he stayed silent. Jenelyn jumped on the opportunity.

'What did you call him, Gretchen?' she asked, almost laughing at Laszlo's indignant face.

Gretchen grinned smugly. 'I don't know what you call it in English,' she admitted, 'but it means someone who is tired and has a hard time getting up.'

Jenelyn pondered over this for a moment. She could think of many words to explain that.

'Is it said as a joke?' she asked.

Gretchen nodded, and Jenelyn suddenly had an idea.

'I think you might be calling him a sleepyhead,' she chuckled. 'That's what we call people who are lazy getting out of bed.'

Gretchen snapped her fingers excitedly and nodded, her eyes gleaming. 'That's exactly what it is!' she said laughing, then sobered and turned back to Laszlo apologetically. 'Oh, Laszlo, you never got breakfast. I rushed us out too fast.'

Laszlo shrugged and pulled the car out into the autobahn. 'Don't worry,' he said shortly, 'I'll eat at the festival.'

Gretchen grinned playfully at Jenelyn, who smiled in return. She knew that Laszlo wasn't actually upset, but he was sensitive about being teased. His innate male pride and slight chauvinism made him very indignant. But he would be over it soon, and all would be back to normal. Jenelyn settled into her seat, fiddling with her thumbs as she eagerly waited for her first festival.

The traffic got more congested as they reached the city of Tübingen, which informed Jenelyn that the festival would be crowded. She could already see streams of people rippling down the cobble-stoned streets as they drove off the autobahn. She pressed her face excitedly against the car window. This little city was different from all the others she had seen. It was a rustic ancient town nestled on the back of a mountain that towered between two valleys.

'That's the Spitzberg Mountain,' Laszlo told her, gesturing towards the rolling, green ridge, 'and the two valleys it divides are the Neckar and Ammer valleys.'

Although it didn't have the height and splendour of California's Sierra Nevada mountain range, Jenelyn thought it had a gentle dignity with its lush green face lined with ragged peaks and rock crevices. California's mountains seemed young and wild, whereas this mountain had an aged ruggedness that was almost timeless.

After another half hour of Laszlo fighting traffic, they were able to park on a side street near the border of what Laszlo called 'the Old Town.' It was still in the city, but quite a walk to the main centre. As they got out of the car, Laszlo abruptly stopped and looked at his car, then ran his hand over his face.

'I can't believe it,' he muttered angrily to himself.

'What is it?' Gretchen asked.

'This is Tübingen,' he grumbled, slapping his hand on the car's bonnet in frustration. 'How could I forget? There's a Green Zone here, which means that every vehicle must have an environmental badge on it. I forgot to get one before we left.'

Jenelyn was confused, and her leg started jiggling nervously. If they needed to park again then they would lose more time at the festival. But she didn't want Laszlo to feel any worse than he did. Although she would prefer to see the city, the thought of upsetting Laszlo further softened the blow of disappointment.

'It's alright, Laszlo,' she assured him. 'We can come another day. I hate to cut our time even more.'

Gretchen nodded in agreement, but Laszlo shook his head stubbornly, refusing to allow his forgetfulness to ruin their day.

'Nein,' he ordered. 'You and Gretchen go on ahead. I'll go get an environmental badge and meet up with you later. Let's meet at the fountain in the middle of the marketplace at two o'clock. I can't imagine it taking longer than that.'

Jenelyn was about to protest about them staying together, but Gretchen spoke before she could.

'In ordung, Laszlo,' she agreed, understanding that he was trying to save the day for them, 'Hurry back, and be careful.'

Laszlo grunted grimly and gave Gretchen a quick kiss. 'Have fun,' he told Jenelyn with a tight smile. He hopped back into the car and drove off.

'I feel so sorry for him,' Jenelyn said as they walked toward the city. 'He shouldn't have to miss the fun. We could always come back.'

'What's most important to him is that you have a good time,' she explained, 'and Laszlo hates wasting trips. You and I can see a lot of the sights right now, and he knows it. It would be a waste of petrol to come back another day when you could be completely satisfied with the amount of time we have now.'

Jenelyn reluctantly agreed.

As they walked closer to the centre of Tübingen, Jenelyn's thoughts of Laszlo started dissipating. She couldn't believe her eyes. Looming before her were genuine, historical Renaissance buildings! Her heart caught in her throat and a gleeful laugh almost escaped her. The buildings were clustered together like close friends, and their pointed, rusty-red roofs shone in the sun. The dark timber-latticed slats around the stained glass windows and heavy oak doors told the story of their sixteenth-century past. Jenelyn knew this was her favourite city so far. Gretchen smiled down at her exuberant face and laughed.

'I suppose you like it?' she asked teasingly.

Jenelyn nodded mutely, not quite knowing what to say. She had never seen a town so wonderfully historic and quaint. Finally, she turned to Gretchen, her face beaming.

'It's absolutely amazing!' she exclaimed, her dark brown eyes shining.

Gretchen laughed and they turned a corner into the main section of the festival. Bright red, yellow, and black flags wove gaily above the windows. Vendors in booths sold their wares to the pedestrians walking by, calling in German. Jenelyn felt like a sponge, soaking in all the colourful sights, the sounds of people laughing and chatting, and the smells of different foods filling the marketplace. A large stone fountain stood in the centre with people sitting around it, relaxing, chatting and eating in the warm August sunshine. The breeze wafted the savoury scents of meats and yeasty loaves of bread, and once in a while Jenelyn even caught a whiff of something sweet. Her stomach growled, but she knew it was too soon to ask Gretchen to eat. She wanted to see everything first. Every building originated from the medieval ages, complete with narrow, cobbled stone streets overlooked for centuries.

'Oh, it's perfect,' she gushed in admiration. 'I've never seen a town look like this.'

'It is lovely, and there's a lot to see,' Gretchen said, then continued thoughtfully. 'It's eleven-thirty now, and we have to meet Laszlo here at two o'clock. So, we have two and a half hours to explore. We can eat and shop in the marketplace. But, if you would like to see more of the city, there are many historical buildings, such as the Hohentübingen Castle und museum, and the Old University Assembly Hall. Tübingen has nearly eighty-five thousand residents, but twenty-two thousand of those are students at their university.'

Jenelyn thought for a moment. The castle was intriguing since she hadn't seen one yet. She told as much to Gretchen, who instantly agreed. They set off happily toward the castle, which fortunately was less than a kilometre from the centre of the town. It was a steady climb the whole way since the castle sat atop part of the Spitzberg Mountain, which overlooked the town.

As they ascended, Jenelyn admired the beautiful 17th century stone gateway that greeted them at the castle's entrance. The thick stone was intricately carved above the archway with two archers flanking an ornate crest. The cobbled stone at their feet made her feel as if she were truly walking back in time. Jenelyn could only gape in awe at the domineering castle as they walked through the tunnelled archway. It certainly wasn't the elegant fairytale version of a castle but seemed to be more of a battle fortress, with four wings and a round tower. High stone walls formed a square with a large courtyard in the centre, its red roof gleaming in the sun.

They had climbed high, and the views were vast, overlooking the Neckar and Ammer valleys which Tübingen sat between. She could also see the entire town of Tübingen, with the red roofs clustered together amidst the maze of streets that connected the town like the strands of spider's web. Overlooking all of it stood the Hohentübingen Castle, centred in the heart of the town.

She had to admit that though it was impressive, it wasn't her interpretation of a castle. Gretchen seemed to read her mind.

'I know it might not be what you imagined,' she said, 'but it makes up for beauty with history. This building was built mainly in the Renaissance period, but it stands on the site of the older castle built in the 11th century.'

By this time, they had entered the courtyard, where many people were milling about. Cream walls towered around them, with multiple doors spaced along each wall. Jenelyn recognised the familiar, timber-latticed Renaissance architecture on the windows that gazed down at them from the top of the walls.

'It's certainly different,' she acknowledged. 'Where do all the doors lead to?'

'That is the most interesting part of this castle,' Gretchen explained eagerly, 'They are part of the museum called Alte Kulturen, which has 4,600 exhibits from seven archaeological and cultural collections from the university. Do you want to go?'

Jenelyn nodded enthusiastically. They headed towards one of the doors, where they had to pay a small fee to enter. Gretchen paid for her without hesitation, though Jenelyn wanted to argue.

'My treat,' Gretchen said shortly, not allowing any room for argument.

Jenelyn bit her tongue, and thanked her. For now, she would be polite, but one day she was going to pay them back and start paying for herself.

'It's a very large museum,' Gretchen mused as they read the brochure the employee had handed them. 'It's hard to know where to start. They also have the Bohnenberger Observatory and apparently the oldest giant wine barrel. Which exhibit are you most interested in, or perhaps we could start by seeing these?'

Jenelyn was overwhelmed at the variety of exhibits and shrugged helplessly. They needed to decide soon as people had to squeeze by them since they were standing in the entrance.

'I say let's visit the observatory and wine barrel,' she suggested. 'Perhaps we can see exhibits on the way to them.'

With the plan made, they began their slow meander through the rooms, admiring the ancient relics, from the oldest figurative art of mankind, known as 'Ice Age art', to Egyptian artefacts, such as the offering chamber of Seschemnefer III. Both she and Gretchen were mesmerised by everything, and it was almost with regret that they started to leave the exhibits to see the observatory and wine barrel. But as they began walking through the exit, a staff member called out to the room at large.

'Our new mythical creatures exhibit is opening today,' he announced, 'for anyone interested, come get a complimentary tour, bitte.'

Jenelyn looked eagerly at Gretchen, whose face was impassive.

'That sounds like fun, Gretchen,' she said. 'It may be a bit corny, but could be more interesting than a giant wine barrel.'

Gretchen seemed reluctant at first but gave Jenelyn a short nod. Jenelyn wasn't sure why Gretchen was so disinterested, but figured she might think mythical creatures were a bit childish. Although Jenelyn didn't hold a strong interest for mythological creatures, it seemed intriguing that there was a museum exhibit on them. She wanted to see what kind of artefacts people had thought they had discovered. They followed the staff member into the dimly lit room lined with multiple glass cases filled with various objects, from shining crystals to fossilised bones. Jenelyn smirked at most of them, figuring they were props placed there to disillusion people into imagining all kinds of fantasies about them. Gretchen seemed as sceptical as she was, but they enjoyed laughing at a few pieces together, softly so no one overheard and thought they were being rude.

'I have to go to the bathroom,' Gretchen said after looking at an artefact that could be nothing more than a sculpture of a unicorn's horn, 'I'll go find them. There is only so much of this I can take.'

She chuckled and winked at Jenelyn before walking away to source out the bathroom. Jenelyn pressed on, understanding Gretchen's scepticism but still enjoying the novelty of such an exhibit. Although she didn't believe in any of it, it was still fascinating to see what kinds of creatures had been imagined in age-old times. Her brows furrowed in confusion as she stopped at a glass casing holding a remarkably lifelike claw. It was at least 25 centimetres long and looked like it came from a large dog. It even had dark tufts of fur around the top of it. If it was fake, it was incredibly well done.

'Ah, you have come across the werewolf claw,' the staff member said, suddenly coming up beside her. 'It is said to have been taken from the last werewolf killed in Germany.'

'You mean the one in Wittlich?' she said, curious to know if the staff member also knew of the legend Gretchen had told her.

'You know it?' he asked, surprised. 'As an American tourist, I'm surprised you've heard of it. Wittlich is a small town.'

'I'm staying there,' she explained, 'but I don't know much about werewolves, just the legend.'

The staff member glanced around the room, assumingly to make sure other guests didn't need assistance, before continuing.

'Werewolves are monstrous creatures,' he said, his voice firmer than Jenelyn thought necessary for a person describing a fictional creature. But perhaps he was only doing his job as a tour guide. 'They hunt similar to a wolf, but are ten times bigger. It's said that they can jump over eight metres high and bound across five metres in one leap. Predators normally stalk their prey once they see it, following its every movement until it can attack. A true killer will track the prey, patiently following its scent and markings until they find it. Unlike normal predators, the werewolf doesn't stalk its prey. It's dead the moment the werewolf decides to kill it. They don't waste time hunting, they only track to kill. Except for the odd times when the prey is unlucky enough to come across them and get in their way.'

As grisly as this all sounded, Jenelyn knew it was fantasy and argued with her stomach to stop jumping around.

'It certainly sounds awful,' she said, keeping her tone light compared to the staff member's warning one. 'It makes you happy we don't have them anymore!'

She was teasing, but her chuckle died in her throat at the staff member's grave face. He flashed a tight grin, appreciating the jest, but it didn't reach his eyes.

'I would think this too,' he said. 'Except that there have been multiple sightings of the beasts in Wittlich. And more importantly, fairly recent sightings, not just ancient ones. If you're staying in Wittlich, I would be careful.'

He looked behind Jenelyn as Gretchen came walking up, smiling. His eyes widened slightly as she stood next to Jenelyn, and the colour drained from his face.

'Is this who you're staying with?' he asked, and Jenelyn nodded.

'Ja, she's staying with me,' Gretchen said, slightly quizzical at why he would be asking.

'Haben sie einen guten tag,' he said quickly, wishing them a nice day, and walked away.

Jenelyn and Gretchen watched him in bewilderment.

'Well that was odd,' Gretchen said. 'What were you discussing with him?'

Jenelyn shrugged and pointed to the werewolf claw.

'He was just telling me about werewolves and how there have been sightings in Wittlich.'

Gretchen's breath tightened, and her nostrils flared. Jenelyn's brows raised in surprise, then her eyes narrowed quizzically.

'Are you alright?' she asked, and Gretchen nodded immediately.

'Ja, of course.' She smiled, though her face was still tight. 'Let's continue on from here.'

They strolled back towards the museum, which inhabited the north and east wings of the castle, as well as the pentagon tower. As they wandered out of the west wing, Jenelyn noticed a tunnel behind one of the fountains.

'Where does that go?' she asked, intrigued.

Gretchen shook her head but followed Jenelyn, also curious to see where it led. She read her map that was part of the brochure and figured it out.

'Oh, it's a schänzle or little entrenchment,' she stated. 'And as we walk through this tunnel and to the next doorway, we should be able to see the western castle moats through what they call the rabbit hole.'

Sure enough, as they passed the entrenchment, they could look down upon the moats. Jenelyn loved exploring the castle this way and was delighted when she saw a doorway to their left.

'Gretchen,' she called, 'let's see where this goes.'

Gretchen happily followed, and they soon discovered that it led to a hiking path. Jenelyn was eager to keep walking and see where it took them, but Gretchen stopped her.

'Warten, Jenelyn,' she warned, reading her brochure, 'that path leads over the Spitzberg to the Wurmlingen Chapel, and takes over an hour to hike. We won't have time before we have to meet Laszlo.'

Jenelyn stopped, disappointed, but agreed that time was marching on, and poor Laszlo wouldn't want to wait for them for too long.

'True, we'd better start heading back to the marketplace,' she agreed, 'but it would be fun to hike that one day.'

'We could go to the north side of the castle,' Gretchen reassured her, continuing to read. 'There's a path called the Captain's Path on that side that leads to the lower city. We can make our way back from there.'

Jenelyn agreed, but she would much rather see something new than retrace their steps. It didn't take them long to reach the north side and start their way back down to the city. The descent was much quicker and easier than when they trudged the steep gradient to the castle, so it wasn't long before they had almost reached the marketplace. Right before entering the busy square, a heavy-set, middle-aged woman with light blonde hair and quizzical brown eyes interrupted them.

'Gretchen?' the woman asked curiously. 'Ist das sie?'

Gretchen stopped and stared at the woman in surprise, and then a look of recognition and excitement crossed her face.

'Adele!' she cried happily, giving the woman a warm hug. 'Es ist so nett, sie wieder zu sehen.'

Adele's mouth dropped and the corners of her mouth lifted as she nodded in agreement, her eyes still surprised.

'Ja,' she said and then looked over at Jenelyn, who was waiting patiently to be introduced to what was obviously an old friend. 'Wer ist mit ihnen?'

Gretchen suddenly remembered Jenelyn and motioned her to come forward.

'This is Jenelyn,' she said, slipping back into English. 'She's a daughter of an old friend of mine who is coming to stay with us from America.'

Adele seemed pleased, but her eyes were quizzical as she gave Jenelyn a welcoming smile.

'Hallo,' she said pleasantly. 'How do you like Germany?'

Her accent was extremely thick, but Jenelyn had listened to German long enough to be able to understand her easily. After working with Edwin, she was sure she could understand anyone.

'I like it very much,' she replied. 'Tübingen is magnificent. I think it's going to be one of my favourite places.'

Adele nodded politely and then turned back to Gretchen, a hint of sadness in her eyes and tone.

'It must be nice to have company again after all these years,' she said softly.

Gretchen nodded briskly. 'Ja,' she said, her voice clipped, 'Jenelyn has been very good for me.'

Adele moved closer to Gretchen and switched back to German. She spoke lowly in her ear, almost inaudibly, but slowly enough that Jenelyn could understand.

'I'm glad to see that you're out doing things again, Gretchen,' she said, 'I'm sure you feel the same.'

Gretchen nodded, looked over at Jenelyn in concern, and tried to position herself so that her back was to her.

'I do, ja,' Gretchen answered dismissively, 'but Jenelyn and I must be going. It was nice seeing you again, Adele.'

Adele smiled and waved goodbye. Jenelyn turned to Gretchen as they walked away towards the castle.

'What was that about?' she asked.

Gretchen shook her head sharply. 'Adele is a very nosy woman,' she said, 'don't bother listening to her.'

Jenelyn couldn't help thinking that Gretchen had said the same about Frau Becker when they had gone grocery shopping. She was obviously trying to stifle Jenelyn's curiosity by acting as if these women were nothing more than unimportant busybodies. But these women treated Gretchen as old friends, not nosy busybodies looking for the latest gossip. There had been genuine concern in Adele's voice, not to mention the staff member's reaction towards Gretchen at the mythical creature exhibit. He had seemed almost afraid of her. Something wasn't right, and she was determined to find out what.

September

Fourth Month

Chapter Thirteen

Jenelyn stared at the computer screen with blurry eyes. Edwin was trying to teach her the new data entry system Heller Funke Europa had recently received, but she was having difficulty paying attention. She was feeling near tears and was emotionally exhausted.

'Jetzt klicken dort, und dieser schirm erscheint,' Edwin was telling her patiently, standing beside her, his finger pointing at the screen in explanation.

She looked up at him with a tremulous sigh. After four months of working with Edwin, she was finally becoming almost fluent in German. She loved working with him and living with Gretchen and Laszlo, but she was becoming terribly homesick. Perhaps it was because of the seasonal change from the warmth of summer to chilly autumn, but the novelty of being in a new country was beginning to fade as she settled into the mundane daily routine of work and home. She was starting to miss her old life, such as watching movies while throwing popcorn at Nicole every time she talked through a scene, and cuddling up to her mom at night to hear how her day had gone, or listening to her dad play his guitar in the evening. Germany was proving to be a wonderful place to live, and she certainly didn't miss her neighbourhood, but working a full-time job for the first time was becoming tedious and didn't help ease her homesickness. Edwin looked down at her and noticed her disheartened expression.

'Are you alright?' he asked, switching back to English. While Jenelyn became better at German, Edwin was excelling in English.

'I guess so,' she murmured, shrugging her shoulders despondently.

Edwin cocked a sceptical eyebrow and pulled up a chair next to her, settling into it comfortably.

'I highly doubt that,' he stated. 'You've seemed very sad lately. Is there anything I can do?'

'I'm homesick, I suppose,' she admitted. 'I miss my parents and my best friend Nicole.'

'Ah, ja,' Edwin said under his breath. 'Heimwehkrank is so depressing. Well, you have almost been in Germany for half a year. It's understandable.'

This didn't make Jenelyn feel any better. She hadn't thought of her four months in Germany being half a year.

'Ja, it has,' she said, unaware of her easy use of the German word for yes. 'It feels so much longer.'

She watched Edwin sit back, studying her thoughtfully. She wondered how he was interpreting her behaviour. Over time, he had seemed to warm to her. Each day she'd walk in with a cheery attitude, and his stern demeanour would lift. He'd even complimented her work ethic and patience. Jenelyn didn't want to feel like she was letting him down by having a day where she just felt like she wanted to wrap up in her blanket and cry about missing home.

'But you do like it here, ja?' he asked with pure concern laced in his voice.

'Oh ja,' Jenelyn assured him, 'I appreciate everything that has been done for me. I love working here, and being with Gretchen and Laszlo is fantastic. It's only that I've never been away from my parents before. It's starting to catch up to me.'

She didn't add that working full-time was also putting a strain on her. The last thing she wanted was to sound like an inept employee.

Edwin nodded slowly, deep in thought. Jenelyn was sure he didn't know why she was really in Germany, and not once had he asked.

'Well, I have enjoyed your company very much,' he said kindly. 'You're a very good, honest worker, and we Germans appreciate that. But you'll go back home one day and see your parents. How long are you planning on staying in Germany?'

It had always surprised Jenelyn that Edwin had never asked about why she was in Germany, even in the interview. She supposed it was simply a matter of time, but telling him the truth might make him sorry he hired her since she wasn't guaranteed to stay.

'It's anyone's guess,' she mumbled, shrugging and staring back at her screen, her eyes distant. 'No one knows, much less me.'

Before he could reply to this mystifying response, Jenelyn lifted her chin bravely, shrugged her hair off her shoulder, and gave him a cheeky grin, her tobacco brown eyes shining with sanguinity once more.

'So, before I take any more of your time, Edwin, go ahead and show me the rest of this system,' she waved off the subject.

After all, her life was none of his concern as long as it didn't affect her work, and he couldn't help her anyway. She could see that her mysterious reply to her length of time in Germany confused him, but being a professional, he didn't interrogate into her personal life any further.

'Abendessens bereit!' Gretchen announced, setting down the cutting board of cheese and bread with a flourish.

Jenelyn stared at the display of golden Gouda cheese and the large, toasted baguette of Dutch crust bread. She usually loved Gouda and bread for dinner and was getting used to eating so much cheese. But this evening, she barely had an appetite.

'Jenelyn, what's wrong?' Laszlo asked, setting down his cheese and placing his hand on her own.

'Nothing,' she smiled at him, 'It was a long day. I'm a little tired.'

Gretchen cocked a suspicious eyebrow. 'I doubt that,' she said, shaking her head, 'In all the months we've known you, I have yet to see you tired. Now, what is wrong, schätzchen?'

Jenelyn frowned, tired of having to explain herself to everyone. She scraped her chair back angrily and stood, staring at Gretchen's shocked face.

'I'm tired, alright?' she snapped. 'Is that not allowed?'

She stormed out of the dining room and up to her room, her heart pounding in horror at how she'd acted. It would have never occurred to her in a million years that she would yell at Laszlo or Gretchen. But she felt like an emotional wreck. Tears streamed down her cheeks uncontrollably as she collapsed on her bed, watching the sentry trees outside her window sway in the light breeze. Choking sobs attacked her chest, and it was all she could do not to burst out in hysterics. She wanted to be home, cuddled next to her parents watching TV, or cooking with her mom as they listened to their favourite music. She wanted to know what her future was and if she'd ever see her parents again. Most of all, she wanted stability. A few minutes passed, and then a light knock rapped on her door.

'Go away,' Jenelyn choked, her voice stifled from her face being buried in her pillow. 'Please, leave me alone.'

The door opened slowly, revealing Gretchen's worried face and a small tray of cheese and bread.

'You left the table so quickly you didn't eat,' Gretchen said in a low, soft tone.

She set the tray down on the nightstand and sat on Jenelyn's bed, waiting for a response. When Jenelyn didn't bother to look at her, Gretchen gave a throaty *hmm* and continued thoughtfully.

'I haven't been a mother in a long time,' she said, 'but I do remember when to comfort and when to let things be. Jenelyn, you need comfort. What's wrong?'

Jenelyn sniffed and then gave in. After all, she wasn't sure why she wasn't confiding in Gretchen and Laszlo about her problems.

'I'm homesick,' she confessed, feeling slightly embarrassed at her dramatic outburst.

Gretchen's eyes widened.

'Is that all?' she asked. 'Meine güte, from the way you were acting, I assumed it was something we had done.'

Jenelyn understood since she had completely overreacted at the dinner table, but she couldn't help it. Her emotions were balancing on a knife's edge at this point.

'Well, if I'm going to be honest,' she continued, her voice catching a hiccupping sob, 'it's more than that. Gretchen, why do I have to be here?'

Her chocolate eyes looked at Gretchen's face, searching for some kind of answer from the older woman. Being a young woman, a primitive instinct born from a necessary need for guidance and comfort persuaded her to ask the only other maternal figure in her life. It was so natural that Jenelyn was hardly aware of it.

'Schätzchen, you know why you have to be here,' she replied, unsure of what Jenelyn wanted from her. 'The Journey is part of your family's culture, it's your -'

'Exactly what I mean!' Jenelyn interrupted. 'Why do I have to follow this culture? Why couldn't I have been normal? I could have stayed with my parents and lived a stable life.'

Gretchen looked down and rubbed her hand over the plush white comforter on the bed, thinking carefully. She had never followed a bohemian culture and really didn't know everything there was to know about it. What Jenelyn was asking needed to be answered by her mother, not her. Jenelyn was only eighteen years old. She still needed a lot of guidance.

'Ja, you could have lived a normal life,' Gretchen agreed. 'But, would you have enjoyed it?'

Jenelyn opened her mouth to protest. But Gretchen saw the look on her face and continued quickly before she could.

'Think about it,' she persisted. 'Had your parents not believed in this way of life, then you would still be in Los Angeles, in the neighbourhood that you hated. Ja, you love your parents, but that is not enough to make a life. Nun, I'm a Christian woman and don't believe in the Spirits that you believe in. But I do believe that there is a higher power that controls our fates. And if you were born into a bohemian culture, then there is a reason. We don't know why, but we have faith in both our beliefs that they will make the right choice, recht?'

Jenelyn reluctantly agreed with her. She did have faith in her Spirits to guide her, but she still wished she didn't have to do it alone.

'I know what you're saying, Gretchen,' she conceded, her voice calm again. 'I know there must be some reason why I'm doing this. But it's hard that I have to be without my family and friends. I mean, no, I wouldn't have wanted to stay in L.A., but couldn't there have been another way for me to make my own life without having to go on a Journey where I'm alone?'

An escaped tear rolled down Jenelyn's cheek, and she brushed it away impatiently. She couldn't believe how much she was crying.

'Alone?' Gretchen asked. 'What do you mean, alone? You have Laszlo and I, ja?'

Jenelyn couldn't help but smile at Gretchen's put-out expression. She gave her a hug, immediately feeling guilty for insulting her.

'I'm sorry, Gretchen,' she apologised. 'You're right; I'm not completely alone. But, when I leave Germany and both of you, I will be. Every step I take on this Journey will be me doing it on my own. And it's frightening to think that I could be doing it forever. What if the Spirits never find my true home?'

Gretchen shook her head resolutely. 'That will not happen,' she stated, her tone steadfast and confident. 'Every person finds their true home eventually. We can't help it. We adapt to whatever life we have settled with and become happy. Some more than others, of course, but I have no doubt that you will. As for you being alone in the process, that is absurd.'

Jenelyn shook her head in exasperation. 'Gretchen, how is that absurd? You know that the whole point of my Journey is for me to be alone.'

Gretchen shrugged matter-of-factly. 'People who are alone choose to be,' she explained. 'There are too many people in this world for someone to always find themselves alone unless they wish it. You may *travel* alone, but there will always be someone waiting at your destination. You simply have to find them.'

'That's a nice idea Gretchen,' Jenelyn mumbled, 'but how am I supposed to always find them?'

Gretchen grinned with patience practised after years of logical thinking.

'You'll learn to watch and listen.'

Jenelyn cocked an eyebrow at such a theoretically simple idea. If only she could believe that it was true. Despite her scepticism, she knew Gretchen was helping her as best she could, and she had given good advice. Jenelyn only had to learn how to follow it.

'Danke, Gretchen,' she whispered gratefully, 'I'll try to remember that.'

Gretchen gave Jenelyn a tight hug and rubbed a tear off her cheek. 'Sleep tight, liebling, and don't worry. One day, I'm sure you'll be happy with the life that your Spirits have given you.'

She left the room, leaving Jenelyn lying on her bed, wishing that Gretchen was right. She looked out her window in pensive thought. She was born into her parent's world and had a Journey to fulfil. She sincerely hoped that she had the courage to do it. She remembered what her mother had told her before she left.

'*My blood runs through you, and you have the same freedom of spirit that I have. You have the strength and courage to do this. I know you will succeed in finding your true home.*'

Jenelyn felt a warm comfort fill her. She wasn't the only one who had to have faith in her ability to do this.

Her parents also believed wholeheartedly that she was capable, along with Gretchen and Laszlo. She needed to believe in herself with the same confidence. Maybe then she would find her courage. She had to stop being afraid of what she was meant to do and embrace it instead, learning how to navigate and master every challenge life would throw at her.

She turned over and looked at the picture of her parents she had brought with her, framed in old mahogany wood with a faded gold trim. It was placed lovingly on her nightstand, where she could look at it every night before going to sleep. Seeing their faces always comforted her and gave her courage, as they did now. She lifted her finger and traced her mother's face with the tip, her heart aching with longing, but her soul at peace once more.

'Okay, Mama,' she whispered. 'I'm on my way. No more tears, no more worries.'

October

Fifth Month

Chapter Fourteen

Laszlo chuckled; his large frame settled on the cream brocaded sofa. They were sitting in the large, bright living room, enjoying their tea and discussing Halloween. Jenelyn yearned for the American custom, though it wasn't accompanied by the same aching homesickness she had experienced the month before. She had felt a lot better after that day and had not forgotten the wise advice Gretchen had given her. However, this was her first holiday away from her parents. She remembered the decorations her mother would put up; the orange pumpkins in the windows, small enough to fit in her palm. The Dracula costume her father would wear, and the fairy costume she wore year after year until she grew too big for it. She and Nicole would go trick-or-treating until their plastic pumpkins were full and their small round bellies churned with sugar. But if she focused too much on those memories, she'd start running to the nearest airport. She needed the distraction of a different custom. So, she had decided to ask Gretchen what they did for Halloween.

'I can't believe you've only been celebrating Halloween for ten years!' cried Jenelyn.

'Surely you knew our customs would be different here,' Laszlo replied. 'What's so surprising?'

Jenelyn shook her head and grinned. 'I guess I assumed Halloween was everywhere since it's a pagan holiday,' she explained, still feeling a bit bewildered.

'Well, we didn't know anything about it,' Gretchen said in amusement, taking a small sip of tea, 'but we did have something close to it before it was brought over. What did you do for Halloween?'

Jenelyn paused, nostalgically reminiscing back to all of her childhood Halloweens. They hadn't been easy for her parents, since they lived amongst so many gangs that considered trick-or-treating open season for mugging and mischief. Her parents had always tried to take her to houses that didn't smell of weed, or have suspicious men or women lurking about outside, sniffing with puffy eyes or a gun in their pocket. She'd seen news reports of muggings increasing at the season, but her parents quickly learnt where not to go, and told her the same. Still, she could remember clutching her candy bag as a stranger tried to take it away from her, but that had been when Nicole and her were older and allowed to go on their own.

'My parents and I would go to the malls or friends' houses to trick-or-treat,' she explained, not wanting to admit how dangerous her neighbourhood was. 'Then we would come home and carve our pumpkin.'

Jenelyn remembered briefly the last time she and her parents had set a pumpkin outside their apartment door. Gang members had destroyed everyone's pumpkins as a prank, and it had been the last year her parents had had a pumpkin. That had been five years ago. She decided to tactfully omit this occasion from her explanation.

'It sounds fun,' Gretchen told her. 'Though here we do not say 'trick or treat.' We say 'süß oder saur,' which means 'sweet or sour.' I admit Laszlo and I had a hard time accepting the new tradition. After losing our daughter, it was hard not to feel like we were mocking the dead.'

Jenelyn nodded in consideration. Laszlo stayed quiet and took a sip of his tea while Gretchen watched him.

'We're becoming used to it now,' she continued, taking a sip of tea, her expression pensive. 'But it did take us a little time.'

Jenelyn didn't want the conversation to become depressing or awkward, so she gently steered Gretchen to another track.

'You said that you had had another custom similar to Halloween?' she asked. 'What was it?'

But before Gretchen could answer, Laszlo spoke up, his voice eager.

'It was called Walpurgis,' he explained. 'But it didn't take place in October. The only holiday we had in October was for the Protestant church, which did take place on the thirty-first. But it was to celebrate and remember Martin Luther, who started the Reformation. Some Protestant Germans are still quite upset that Halloween has overshadowed that day. But aside from that, Walpurgis was celebrated on the first of May.'

'In May!' Jenelyn's eyes widened. 'What a difference! Did it have anything to do with the dead?'

Laszlo shook his head. 'Not really,' he continued, unperturbed by Jenelyn's interruption. 'It was created to honour the witches on Brocken Peak, which is located in the Harz Mountains. The witches were believed to have been there in the eighteenth century. The tale was that the witches would come alive on the first of May and haunt the villages. So, it started that children would dress up as witches and pretend to haunt everyone, but we didn't have trick-or-treating.'

Jenelyn was fascinated by this different and novel tradition for Halloween. She pictured the kids in bedsheets and pointy hats and thought the tradition not too different from the present day Halloween.

'It sounds like fun,' she said. 'Do people still celebrate it at all?'

Laszlo frowned and shook his head. 'I'm not sure,' he replied, 'Gretchen and I haven't celebrated it in twenty years. Ever since…'

He stopped and looked at Gretchen, who squeezed his hand. 'It's been a long time.' Gretchen spoke for him, and Jenelyn knew precisely what they meant.

'Well,' she chirped, determined to keep the conversation positive, 'I think we should have a small Halloween this year. It could be fun!'

Gretchen and Laszlo brightened, the shadows on their faces lifting away. 'What a wunderbar idea, Jenelyn!' Gretchen cried. 'We can go down to the market and buy a pumpkin.'

'I'll show you how to bake the pumpkin seeds!' Jenelyn offered. 'They're delicious, and my mom always made them.'

Laszlo's face beamed, and his eyes sparkled. Jenelyn liked seeing that light in his eyes that she'd helped to put there. It meant he could focus temporarily on something other than his deceased daughter.

Jenelyn breathed in the crisp October air as she, Gretchen, and Laszlo stood outside the market, picking out their pumpkin from huge cardboard bins. Today was Halloween, and Jenelyn wished she could call her parents. Halloween hadn't been terribly important in their family, but it was still a holiday when they did something. She wondered what her parents were doing. Gretchen and Laszlo's voices faded into the distance as she pictured her mother bending over the oven, a hot sheet of freshly baked pumpkin seeds in her hand. Jenelyn could almost smell the savoury scent of them. A painful squeeze in her chest made her hide her fallen face into the carton of pumpkins. Laszlo put his arm over her thin shoulders, squeezing gently.

'Which pumpkin do you like, schätzchen?' he asked, his eyes full of understanding.

Jenelyn smiled, not fooled by his question. He knew how she was feeling today. She looked back at the pile of pumpkins in front of her and saw a plump, round one that was the perfect shade of Halloween orange.

'This one is perfect,' she answered, picking it up and turning it around. 'Doesn't it have a great face?'

Gretchen laughed and shook her head. 'We wouldn't know,' she said, chuckling. 'Laszlo and I haven't celebrated that many Halloweens. We're not experts like you are.'

'I'm not an expert like my parents,' Jenelyn said quickly, feeling humbled that she would be considered an expert in anything, 'but I do know what makes a good jack-o-lantern. And this pumpkin is great! You see, you set it down and if it sits up nicely with the front-facing up, that means it has a good face. Of course, it all depends on what you want to carve.'

Gretchen listened intently, but Laszlo was digging through the other pumpkins. 'Don't you always carve a wicked face or something?' Gretchen asked, confused.

'Oh no,' Jenelyn said, shaking her head. 'Some people carve cats or goblin faces. My friend once carved a whole village!'

Jenelyn remembered how Nicole had always been proud of that Halloween memory. When she and Jenelyn were sixteen, Nicole had decided to carve a very intricate village in her pumpkin. Nicole had always been craftier than Jenelyn, but that year she had really outdone herself. Jenelyn's heart squeezed painfully at the thought of her best friend. Who knew when, or if, she would ever see her again?

'That sounds like a lot more fun than simply carving the same old face every year!' Gretchen remarked.

Laszlo finally lifted a giant pumpkin that was tall and skinny.

'That's the perfect pumpkin to carve a tall face on!' Jenelyn gasped, taking it from Laszlo and setting it on its bottom, 'You could carve Frankenstein or even a howling werewolf on this one!'

Dead silence. The world suddenly seemed to be in a vacuum, all noise extinguished from the echo of her words. Her smile faded as she looked up. Laszlo's face had gone completely ashen. Gretchen looked remarkably uncomfortable and anxious, and Jenelyn shrugged nervously.

'Or not?' she asked meekly.

Laszlo brushed past her toward the car without saying a word. Jenelyn stood frozen beside the pumpkin bin, unsure of what she'd said and how to act. Gretchen immediately rushed to her and patted her shoulder.

'Let's pay for these and go home,' she mumbled.

'I'm sorry if I said something wrong,' Jenelyn said apologetically as they walked to the cashier. 'I didn't mean to upset you.'

'It's nothing,' Gretchen said shortly. 'Forget about it. We can take these pumpkins home and begin carving immediately.'

Forget about what? Jenelyn's mind whirled.

As they walked to the car, Jenelyn saw that Laszlo was still pasty white, and she knew that this was something she would never forget. For some inexplicable reason, she had shaken both of them badly.

Everyone was silent on the drive home. The tense, gloomy atmosphere in the car was contrary to the cheerful laughter when they had left for the store. It made Jenelyn feel guilty for upsetting them. She loved Laszlo and Gretchen and couldn't imagine what she had done. They acted as if she had mentioned their daughter again. She desperately thought back to what she had said. Could it be something about Frankenstein? She shook her head at that ridiculous thought. Surely not the howling werewolf bit?

Then she remembered. Werewolf. That must have been it. She had forgotten Wittlich's old legend. The word werewolf was taboo here in Wittlich, and she had said it without a second thought! That must have been what bothered Laszlo. But what a reaction! Surely he couldn't be that sensitive to the legend? She leaned forward and spoke softly.

'I'm sorry, Laszlo and Gretchen. I didn't mean to speak about a werewolf. I forgot about the legend.'

Gretchen looked back at her in surprise, but Laszlo answered, his voice hoarse and deep.

'Danke, Jenelyn,' he said, 'Please try to remember.'

Jenelyn swore she would and spent the rest of the drive home in contemplative silence.

To Jenelyn's profound relief, Gretchen and Laszlo cheered up as they were carving their pumpkins, refreshing the atmosphere back to being festive. She was cautious not to mention anything about werewolves or their past. They simply stuck to mundane conversations about how to bake the seeds and how Jenelyn's parents had decorated the house for Halloween.

'We would hang paper ghosts from the ceiling,' Jenelyn was saying as she dug her large spoon into the slippery, orange guts of the pumpkin. 'All of our decorations were normally homemade since we didn't have much money. But it was nicer that way since it seemed more special.'

Gretchen nodded in agreement. She was busy digging out her own guts and didn't seem to particularly like how slimy the process was.

'You all sound very creative,' she said, sounding impressed before grunting as her spoon got caught in the pumpkin's flesh, 'I could never make half the things you did.'

Jenelyn laughed and shook her head. 'Oh, it was mainly my mom,' she admitted. 'I don't have an ounce of crafty skill in me. My dad is better than me, but my mother is amazing.'

Tears threatened to fill her eyes as Jenelyn thought about her mother. But Laszlo quickly interrupted her nostalgic thoughts.

'Don't worry, you have other talents, Jenelyn,' he told her. 'You just have yet to discover them.'

An appreciative warmth filled Jenelyn at this, and she was about to reply when a sudden, piercing howl split the air. Gretchen and Laszlo's faces both turned white, and Jenelyn's heart jumped.

'What was that?' she whispered in alarm.

'Laszlo,' Gretchen spoke urgently to him. 'Lock the windows and doors.'

Laszlo quickly left the kitchen to do as she said. Jenelyn's heart pounded, and she grabbed the carving knife, almost dropping it since her palms were sweaty with nerves. She wasn't sure what she would do with it, but it made her feel better knowing she could use it if necessary. The howling became louder and closer.

Gretchen gripped Jenelyn's shoulder so tightly she was sure it was bruised.

'Hide in our bedroom closet,' she ordered, whispering frantically. 'It mustn't find you!'

Jenelyn looked at Gretchen as if she was daft. It was hard to think over the screeching, blood-curdling sound coming from outside. It was a demonic noise that made Jenelyn certain that a portal from Hell had opened and unleashed its fiery demons, but she wasn't about to hide.

'I will not,' she told Gretchen firmly, the howling cacophony making her voice faint. 'I will stay here with you and Laszlo.'

Gretchen gave her a long stare, her brown eyes stark with fear, and then nodded when she saw that Jenelyn wasn't going to budge.

'Alright.' She relented, her lips tightly drawn into a thin line. 'Come with me.'

As they walked into the living room where Laszlo was, they could hear the howling much clearer. Laszlo was crouched beside the front door, a large rifle in his hand. His face looked ten years older, and it had returned to pasty white.

'Gretchen, get her out of here!' he commanded as he saw Jenelyn approaching him.

'I'm staying right here, Laszlo,' Jenelyn said stubbornly. She was more afraid of being trapped away where she didn't know what was happening than of the demon outside. 'Whatever that howling is, it's not going to scare me into your bedroom!'

Laszlo was about to argue, but then a loud scratching rasped at the door. Icy cold tendrils of fear walked up Jenelyn's spine. The howling was frightening enough, but the scratching nearly made her as panicky as Gretchen and Laszlo. Her heart was pounding so hard she could hear every beat in her ears. The scratching intensified, peeling away tiny slivers of wood with every stroke. Jenelyn hardly remembered to breathe as she waited for the door to succumb to the claws raking it at any second. Laszlo cocked his rifle, and Gretchen whimpered a little. The scratching became louder as the howling grew fiercer.

'Laszlo,' Gretchen whispered, 'who do you think could have blown the candle out?'

Laszlo shook his head. 'I could have sworn that after twenty years, no one would do it again,' he said grimly. 'I was wrong.'

Twenty years? There was something that needed connecting here, but she couldn't concentrate on it through the howling. Suddenly, there was howling all around the house, at the front, sides, and back. The howls became almost comically shrill, and Jenelyn started becoming a little suspicious.

'Gretchen, Laszlo,' she began, but Laszlo had jumped up as scratching and pounding sounded on the front windows. She could feel Gretchen's terror as the woman clung to her, her fingers digging into the flesh of her arm.

'Gretchen, I think this may be a-' she started, only to be interrupted again.

Laszlo turned around from the windows, his face white as snow and old. His eyes were white-walled and terrified.

'I saw it!' he rasped in horror. 'Through the window! We must get out of here!'

Jenelyn was about to ask how and why, but there wasn't time. Again, she had a strong feeling that something was wrong, but she couldn't get a word in. Laszlo and Gretchen each had one of her arms and were dragging her up the stairs.

'Is it the same, Laszlo?' Gretchen's voice shook.

'Ja,' he answered quickly, breathlessly climbing the stairs two at a time.

Jenelyn tried again, becoming frustrated at being handled like a rag doll.

'Laszlo, Gretchen,' she said sharply, trying to break through their cloud of fear. 'I really think we need to look into this more carefully. Let me open the front door and see what's going on.'

That statement made Gretchen cry out in horror, and Laszlo gripped her arm tighter. 'Nein, Jenelyn,' he rasped out harshly. 'You will be killed!'

Jenelyn wasn't so sure. The scratching had faded, and the howling was becoming strained. Whatever it was, it was getting tired. She wrenched her arm free of Laszlo's hand and raced down the stairs before they could catch her. She swung open the front door, and a grey, hairy body slammed into hers. She almost screamed but then felt the body shaking with laughter. She pulled the head up and stared into a gruesome werewolf mask, the face that

Laszlo had seen through the window. She snarled with irritation and stood up, dragging the person with her. Laszlo and Gretchen were creeping slowly down the stairs, their every limb trembling with fright.

'As I tried to say,' Jenelyn stated, pulling off the kid's Halloween mask. 'I think this could be a prank.'

Laszlo sank onto the stairs and buried his head in his hands. Gretchen became furious and screamed at the laughing prankster, every threatening word enunciated with a cold fury.

'Wie sie herausfordern! Sie erschreckten uns aus unseren witzen! Wir sollten die polizei rufen!'

The kid only laughed harder at this stream of German, but it was nervous laughter. Jenelyn peeked outside and noticed that his companions had already disappeared.

'I agree, kid,' Jenelyn told him in disgust. 'We should call the police for scaring us out of our wits.'

By now, the boy was starting to sober up and pleaded with them to let him go. Laszlo took the boy from Jenelyn and dragged him to the phone by the neck. Gretchen was still shaking, her face white. Her panicked emotions seemed to boil to the surface and she erupted, bursting into tears, hugging Jenelyn tightly. Jenelyn didn't know what to say or do. It had been obvious that Laszlo and Gretchen had honestly thought the werewolf from the legend had been outside of their house. It was one thing to believe in a legend, but another to actually believe it could come to life. Jenelyn was starting to wonder if Laszlo and Gretchen were quite sane.

‘Happy Halloween,’ she mumbled over Gretchen’s heaving sobs.

November

Sixth Month

Chapter Fifteen

Jenelyn folded her comforter carefully on the bed, her mind racing. Four weeks ago, Laszlo and Gretchen had frightened her at Halloween when she had realised that they genuinely believed in the werewolf. Though they went about their lives as usual, Jenelyn's opinion of them had altered. Being from a spiritual, bohemian culture, superstition was not something she took lightly. However, she was also a product of her time, and it was hard for her to accept that such myths were actually true. She was superstitious enough not to blow out the candle, but not enough to believe in the consequence.

Jenelyn sat on her bed, deep in thought. She loved Gretchen and Laszlo dearly, like surrogate parents. But she yearned to talk with someone about this! She wished fervently that she could call Nicole and tell her about everything that had happened on Halloween. She could easily imagine Nicole's response as if her friend were sitting right beside her with her sparkling green eyes and bouncy red curls.

'They what?' her friend would shriek loudly. 'You've got to be kidding me, Jen! They actually thought it was a real werewolf? Wow, girl, and we thought L.A. was dangerous.'

Yes, Jenelyn could hear her friend's thoughts all too clearly. She smiled wistfully and then stood up. She was simply going to have to endure hoarding her anxious thoughts.

'Laszlo and I realised something last night,' Gretchen told Jenelyn when she came downstairs. 'We completely forgot about Erntedankfest!'

Jenelyn looked at Gretchen patiently. Thanks to Edwin, she was ninety percent fluent now in German, but often Gretchen would forget that Jenelyn was still learning.

'Translation, Gretchen?' Jenelyn asked.

'Oh, of course,' Gretchen laughed, slapping her forehead. 'Sorry. Erntedankfest is a holiday that's normally celebrated on the first Sunday of October. It's our Thanksgiving, basically.'

Jenelyn looked at her in surprise while she spread jam on her toast. They were standing in the kitchen, where Gretchen was busy laying out everything for breakfast.

'I didn't know Germany honoured Thanksgiving!' she exclaimed. 'I thought that was a true American holiday because of the Pilgrims.'

Gretchen nodded in agreement. 'It is,' she said dryly. 'But we have our own version of it. Over time, some traditions have been shared with us.'

At this point, Laszlo joined them, yawning. 'What are you two talking about?' he asked, stretching and then giving Gretchen a light kiss.

'Thanksgiving,' Jenelyn answered, a tingle of excitement trickling inside her. She thought of roasted turkey, the vibrant autumnal colours dressing the trees, the cinnamon smell of sweet potatoes, and bounced a little in anticipation.

'Oh, Erntedankfest,' Laszlo said, smiling. 'Ja, Gretchen and I forgot all about it since we haven't had company to share it with for a long time. We seem to be celebrating the holidays more on your schedule, Jenelyn, than ours.'

'But, we don't mind,' Gretchen hurriedly added, not wanting to make Jenelyn feel uncomfortable.

Gretchen walked into the small dining room and laid out the breakfast tray, Jenelyn reaching for another boiled egg. The four of them sat down comfortably, chatting as if they had known each other for years.

'Our Thanksgiving is a bit different than yours,' Laszlo explained. 'But, some parts of it have come over from America to us.'

'So, what do you do on Erntedankfest?' she asked.

'A typical celebration starts at church,' Laszlo explained. 'The best church to have the celebration is the Evangelisches Johannesstift church in Berlin. It's a Protestant and Evangelical church, and the celebration is an all-day affair. A typical day begins with a service at ten a.m. and then a Thanksgiving procession that concludes with presenting the traditional harvest crown called an Erntekrone. There's music, dancing, food, and an evening service that's followed by a lantern and torch parade called Laternenumzug for the kids. It even has fireworks! The ceremonies end around seven pm.'

Jenelyn liked the sound of such an event, though she knew Berlin was six hours away from Wittlich.

'So, where do you go to church for Erntedankfest?' she asked, knowing there must be a local parish nearby.

'We no longer attend,' Gretchen said shortly. 'We used to go, but many years ago. After…'

She stopped there and shook her head. Laszlo continued for her, his voice grave.

'It's been many years since we have gone to Berlin for Erntedankfest. There's a Protestant church here, but they don't do as much. But we decided long ago that we choose to worship God at home instead.'

His voice made it clear that he wouldn't say one more word about it. Jenelyn decided not to pry.

'So, it's not exactly like our Thanksgiving because it isn't always inviting family over for a large dinner,' Jenelyn stated. 'That's interesting.'

Gretchen's brows furrowed, the sadness in her eyes replaced by curiosity. 'You have a large dinner? We cook our truthahn, but only for ourselves. What sort of dinner do you eat?'

Jenelyn laughed. 'What don't we eat?' she teased. 'Everyone makes tons of food because we invite all our friends and family over. We have turkey, mashed potatoes, sweet potatoes, corn, bread, cranberry sauce, and many families have other traditional dishes that they make special. After that, we have a lot of pies to choose from. Apple, cherry, blackberry, pumpkin-'

'Ah yes!' Laszlo interrupted. 'You have pumpkin pie in America!'

Jenelyn, confused by his excited tone, nodded slowly. 'Yes, with whipped cream. It's my favourite.'

Gretchen's eyes were also wide with eagerness. 'I'd forgotten about your pumpkin pies,' she said, shaking her head in wonder. 'Sie Amerikaner!'

She laughed in bemusement, and Jenelyn smiled, entertained at their reactions to such a mundane dish. *Who would have thought that pumpkin pie could be so incredible*?

'I can make one for you this year,' Jenelyn offered.

Gretchen beamed, her eyes shining. 'I have a better idea,' she said, sitting up with excitement. 'Why don't we celebrate it anyway? We no longer attend church, so the only way we celebrated it was a dinner with only us at home. But this year, we can combine your tradition with our own. We'll invite our friends over and have a large dinner. What do you think, Laszlo?'

Laszlo's face lit up. 'I think that's wunderbar, Gretchen! I'll call them right now and tell them the day.'

'Wait, wait,' Jenelyn said, a little panicked at their sudden eagerness to her offer while also trying to catch up with the fact that they had friends. 'I need some time to prepare. Why don't we plan it for next weekend?'

Laszlo nodded and then hurried off to call their friends. Gretchen gave a gleeful laugh.

'Do you have a lot of family here?' Jenelyn asked as she cleared the table, wondering if her offer had been premature. She was also desperately curious to know about these so-called friends and wondered if family would suddenly appear out of the woodwork as well.

Gretchen helped her, her eyes dimming a little. 'Nein,' she answered softly. 'They are gone.'

Jenelyn didn't bother pushing for more information, and wondered how many friends they had to invite. In all the months staying with them, no one had visited, or mentioned the topic of friends in conversation. So she wondered what friends Laszlo was calling and why she hadn't heard of them before.

The following week, when she and Gretchen were grocery shopping, Jenelyn came across a problem she hadn't foreseen. Jenelyn searched for the yellow can of pumpkin pie mix she always got at home, and when she couldn't find it, she concluded that Germany wouldn't have any. How could she make pumpkin pie without the mix? She had never seen it done any other way. Gretchen noticed her concern as Jenelyn paced frantically up and down the baking aisle.

'There's no pumpkin pie mix!' she cried. 'I think I'm going to have to make it from scratch!'

Gretchen frowned and tapped her lips thoughtfully. 'How do you do that?' she asked.

'I don't know!' Jenelyn flung her arms up. 'I've never seen it done. I guess I have to start with a pumpkin. Are there any left?'

Gretchen looked sceptical, but they hurried outside the store to check. Luckily, it was only November, so there were still some pumpkins left over from Halloween. They weren't very pretty, and some were rotten, but Jenelyn was able to find one that looked good enough to use for cooking. It was a small pumpkin, so she hoped it would work. Jenelyn looked at Gretchen and grinned.

'Thank the Spirits for the Internet,' she said, relief saturating her voice. 'I can research how to make the mix from scratch. Now I have to find the pie crust!'

Fortunately, she was able to find a ready-made pie crust and decided that she could cheat in this one area. They hurriedly bought their groceries and rushed to begin cooking for that night's dinner.

Laszlo and Gretchen's friends had agreed to come, excited at the idea of a large dinner and seeing the American guest. That thought alone made Jenelyn's leg jig as she stood peeling vegetables. The idea of being the centre of attention with strangers, questioning her culture, and judging her German was nerve-wracking. However, trying not to ruin dessert was her main focus for now.

'Alright,' she stated, reading the recipe from the bright computer screen in Laszlo's office. 'I'm pretty sure we can do this, but it's going to take a little longer.'

'How much longer?' Gretchen asked.

'A while,' Jenelyn said grimly. 'Let's get started.'

The kitchen was a madhouse. Pots, pans, and groceries were scattered everywhere. Gretchen was stuffing the turkey, preparing it for its five-hour baking time, Laszlo was busy chopping the potatoes and reading how to make sweet potatoes from scratch. Jenelyn's jobs were the pie and the corn. The corn was easy, but the pumpkin pie was still daunting to her. She was reading her printed directions, focusing on deep breaths and keeping her shaking to a minimum. Fortunately, the recipe was straightforward. All they needed was a roasting pan and a food processor.

'Perfect! Do you need the oven soon for the turkey?' she asked Gretchen.

Gretchen shook her head, her wavy hair flying out of her clasps as she wrestled the stuffing into the hollow cavity of the turkey.

'Nein,' she said, grunting. 'This will take a bit more time. Then it can sit for a while since it's not defrosted all the way.'

After forty-five minutes, the pumpkin pie was ready, and the warm spicy scent of cinnamon, nutmeg, and cloves perfumed the air, reminding Jenelyn of sitting at the table with her parents, holding hands as they said a thankful prayer to the Spirits. Her stomach churned with homesickness, and her appetite vanished.

'I knew you could do it,' Gretchen said proudly, wrapping her arm around Jenelyn and giving her a squeeze. 'That smells wunderbar.'

'Danke, Gretchen,' Jenelyn replied. 'It was easier than I thought it would be.'

Laszlo was finished with his potatoes, so after tidying the kitchen, they decided to relax in the living room until the turkey was ready.

Four hours later, Jenelyn sat at the dining room table, lengthened with extension leaves for the guests, admiring her handiwork. All the food smelled fantastic, and her stomach growled appreciatively, despite her lack of appetite. She was grateful that she would have a Thanksgiving dinner this year, even though she yearned for her parents. This thought caused a knot in her throat, but she pushed it down firmly. She was not going to ruin this moment by pining. It was a day for celebration, fun, and meeting new people. She smoothed her shirt and quickly fluffed her hair, hoping to make a good impression as Laszlo and Gretchen's friends entered the dining room, delighted to see her.

They were an older couple, around their mid-sixties. The man was tall, with a large paunch of a belly. His snow-white hair was balding, and laugh wrinkles edged his mouth and eyes. Jenelyn knew she would like him. His wife was shorter, but not by much. She had dyed golden yellow hair and was dressed very fashionably, with large sparkly earrings, flashy pumps, and a trim suit. Her smile was warm and friendly as she greeted Jenelyn. With them was their granddaughter, Liesl, who was around Jenelyn's age. She was a stocky girl with a round, pretty face and long blonde hair.

Jenelyn glanced at Liesl. So far, Liesl was quiet, but Jenelyn was confident that she could draw her out of her shell. Jenelyn peered towards the door and raised her eyebrows when she noticed that no one else was coming. These were the only friends Laszlo and Gretchen had.

'Erdmann,' Gretchen said warmly. 'I'm so glad that you and Felicie brought Liesl with you. I haven't seen her in years!'

Erdmann squeezed Liesl's shoulder lovingly. 'Ja, we thought that it would be good for her. She needs more socialisation.'

Liesl's face flushed with embarrassment as Laszlo started serving the food. They were all talking in German, but Jenelyn found she could keep up easily.

'Opa,' Liesl grumbled. 'You make me sound like a dog! I get out and do things all the time.'

'Ja, Liesl, but with who?' Felicie chuckled, then turned to Gretchen. 'Honestly, the child is eighteen and barely has any friends. She needs someone other than our next-door neighbour.'

Gretchen looked over at Jenelyn, her eyebrows raised pointedly. Jenelyn knew that was her cue, and decided to join the conversation. She spoke in German, figuring that would comfort Liesl a little more.

'I need friends, too,' she said, giving Liesl a friendly smile. 'The only people I see are Laszlo, Gretchen, and my boss Edwin. But I don't have anyone my own age to hang out with.'

Liesl's eyes sparkled with curiosity. She leaned forward, her eyes and voice animated now that she knew Jenelyn spoke German.

'You are fluent in German?' she asked, 'How long have you been in Germany?'

'Six months,' Jenelyn said. 'And the only reason I can speak German so well is because of my boss.'

She briefly explained the private language game she and Edwin played at work, and Liesl pursed her lips, impressed.

'What part of America are you from?' Liesl asked. 'I've never been, but I've always wanted to go.'

Jenelyn swirled some mashed potato with her fork, pretending to eat. Her appetite still hadn't returned, even though the food looked delectable, and the added tension of meeting new people didn't help. Fortunately, no one seemed to notice.

'I'm from California,' she replied.

Erdmann leaned forward to talk to Jenelyn before Liesl could answer.

'Laszlo and Gretchen told me that you're on a Journey?' he asked. 'That sounds very interesting.'

Jenelyn's heart froze for a moment. She really didn't want to talk about her family's tradition in front of Liesl. She was desperate to find a friend, and she didn't want Liesl to think that it would be a waste of time to be friends with her if she was only going to leave. It didn't help that talking about her culture always made her feel like she was from a circus. Jenelyn continued, her eyes guarded.

'I suppose you could call travelling a journey,' she explained carefully. 'My parents decided it was time for me to see more of the world.'

Her tone implied that this topic was finished. Fortunately, Erdmann got the hint and refrained from asking further questions. Liesl seemed to miss it altogether, which Jenelyn was truly thankful for.

'So, what do you like to do with your spare time?' Liesl asked.

'I like to read and shop,' Jenelyn answered. 'But living here away from the city really made me realise how much I like hiking.'

'I like shopping, too!' Liesl cried, sounding as if this common interest was Fate stepping in, 'We should go some time.'

Jenelyn nodded enthusiastically. She had more than enough money saved in case she needed it to travel, and she could afford to splurge a little.

'Sure, that sounds great. Where's the best place to go?'

Liesl thought for a moment. 'Wittlich is pretty small,' she said, sounding almost apologetic, 'But I bet we can find something.'

Jenelyn liked Liesl's optimism. She knew that she would have a lot of fun with her and was about to ask her more questions when Liesl's grandparents interrupted, asking Jenelyn many questions about being American, living in California, and how she was enjoying Germany. The dinner went by quickly, and Jenelyn enjoyed speaking with more people. But she was really looking forward to having some time alone with a new friend.

December

Seventh Month

Chapter Sixteen

'Gretchen, we'll be fine,' Jenelyn insisted, grabbing the front door handle to leave quickly before Gretchen could fuss over her further. Liesl was standing next to Gretchen, and Jenelyn motioned slyly with her hand for her to join her.

'I simply want you two to be careful in Kaiserslautern,' Gretchen said while she fretted. 'I know you're smart and mature, but you don't know this country. I really would feel better if Laszlo or I came with you. We don't want a repeat of what happened last time in Kaiserslautern.'

Jenelyn shivered at the memory of the group of men and gave Liesl a quick glance. She hadn't told her friend about that incident and wondered if Liesl would ask about it, but Liesl didn't seem to have noticed and spoke before Jenelyn could answer.

'I'll take care of her, Gretchen,' she assured her, 'I've been to Kaiserslautern many times.'

This seemed to comfort Gretchen a little, but not enough to relax her pursed lips or worried eyes. Jenelyn hugged her and chuckled.

'Don't worry so much,' she said. 'We'll be back before you know it. It's only an hour's drive.'

This was the soonest she and Liesl could get together to go shopping, per their discussion last month at dinner, which was perfect since it was in time for Christmas. After looking around the small city of Wittlich, Liesl had decided that the best place to go Christmas shopping was in Kaiserslautern. But unlike Laszlo and Gretchen, who had shown Jenelyn the tourist sites, Liesl was going to show her the great department stores that the city offered. Jenelyn was so excited that she had been up and ready to leave an hour before Liesl arrived. She'd been waiting at the door when Liesl came, prepared to swoop them out before Gretchen could pull them aside to make sure they had everything to be safe, such as an emergency kit in the car, their mobile phones, and the most important of all, her warning to be careful. Unfortunately, Gretchen had been too fast for her.

Gretchen reluctantly agreed that Kaiserslautern wasn't too far and the girls waved goodbye to Gretchen as they got into Liesl's car and drove off. Jenelyn felt elated to finally go somewhere in Germany with someone her age on their own. It was a cold, snowy day, but she didn't care, having seen snow in the mountains near Los Angeles and not being impressed by the cold. She was eager to go shopping without Gretchen and Laszlo because she wanted to buy their Christmas presents. Liesl's round, pretty face was flushed with excitement.

'This is fantastic,' she exclaimed. 'I've never gone shopping with a girl my own age before!'

'You haven't? My friend back home, Nicole, and I used to go all the time.'

Liesl merged onto the autobahn before answering, keeping her eyes on the road. Jenelyn relaxed against the seat, happy to find that Liesl kept to the speed limits and checked her mirrors regularly.

'The only friend my age I ever go shopping with is Alfred, my next-door neighbour,' she confirmed. 'He and I have been friends for years.'

Jenelyn thought back to Felicie's comment about Liesl needing more friends at the Thanksgiving dinner. Her eyes twinkled at Liesl.

'Alfred, huh? Is he like a brother or something else?'

Liesl blushed, but her eyes sparkled with mischief. 'Something else,' she admitted. 'He and I have been secretly dating now for three years.'

Jenelyn gasped. 'Three years? How could you keep something like that from your parents for that long? And why on earth would you? Fifteen isn't too old to start dating.'

Liesl grunted. 'Not according to my parents. My grandparents are suspicious, but they don't say anything. They only want me to find more friends. Like you.'

Liesl flashed a friendly smile at her, and Jenelyn returned her own, even though she felt Liesl should defend her relationship with her parents. She didn't want to start her friendship on the wrong foot, though, so she decided to keep it to herself for now.

'So, are you two planning on getting married?' Jenelyn asked.

'Ja, right after he graduates college,' Liesl nodded happily. 'We've gotten so used to dating secretly that it's not hard anymore. We've always told everyone that we don't like each other that way and feel more like brother and sister. They believe it often enough.'

Jenelyn shook her head and watched the scenery as it passed by. It was beyond her comprehension to keep secrets like that from family. But she had been very close to her parents, whereas it didn't sound like Liesl was with hers. Jenelyn knew that if she had found a boyfriend, her parents would have nearly adopted him. Her mother would have had him over for dinner almost every night, and her father would have been thrilled to show him his vintage record collection. She was so busy envisioning this cosy scene for herself that Liesl's next question surprised her.

'What about you? Any boyfriends back home or anything?'

'No,' she said, chuckling. 'I was never interested. I only had Nicole, and she dated sometimes. But men have never interested me that much.'

Liesl turned to her in shock, her eyes round. 'Du machst witze, no one? But you're cute! I bet there are a lot of men who would want to go out with you.'

Jenelyn knew this was true. It had always been an awkward time for her when boys would flirt with her or ask her out. She had never known how to respond.

'There were, but I always turned them down,' she explained. 'There had been guys who were my friends, but they always ended up wanting more. It used to drive Nicole mad.'

'It would have driven me mad, too,' Liesl agreed. 'Especially if your parents didn't mind you dating. How ironic. I want to date, and my parents won't allow it. You don't care, but you have parents who wouldn't mind. Life isn't fair.'

Jenelyn stared at Liesl, hoping she hadn't made her mad. But Liesl was still smiling, her eyes gleaming with disbelief. Jenelyn had a feeling Liesl didn't mind too much because she had Alfred.

'I'll probably date someday,' Jenelyn mused, 'but it's not really a priority right now.'

Her priority was following the Spirits and finding her true home; having a relationship would cause unnecessary hassle. She smirked to herself at the thought of stuffing a boyfriend in her suitcase wherever she went. 'Hope you don't mind, honey,' she'd tell him sympathetically. Liesl glanced at her, but Jenelyn knew she couldn't tell her, or the girl would think her strange. As it was, Liesl didn't seem to understand.

'I can't imagine not wanting to find a man at eighteen,' Liesl persisted. 'That would be my main priority. I mean, don't you want to get married?'

Jenelyn shrugged. 'Maybe, but I haven't really given it much thought.'

'Well, I suppose there are people who want to focus on a career first,' she said thoughtfully. 'I guess you're one of those.'

Jenelyn agreed, figuring this was the best excuse she could give and hoping it would end the conversation. She made a mental note to remember to use it the next time the subject inevitably came up. Liesl was right. At her age, people would expect her to date.

The drive passed quickly, and they were soon in Kaiserslautern. Liesl drove into the city and parked a little farther away from the centre than Jenelyn was expecting.

'Parking in the centre can cost quite a bit, so we can walk the rest of the way,' she explained, wrapping her scarf tightly around her neck. 'You're going to love the department stores here. There's Karstadt, that's the largest one, and then Peek & Cloppenburg is also big. What are you looking for?'

Jenelyn thought for a moment about what Laszlo and Gretchen would like as she put on her own scarf and gloves. She knew they would be happy with anything she got them, but she wanted to make sure it was something they would enjoy.

'I'm not sure. What's in Karstadt?' she asked Liesl as they power-walked toward the vast shops.

She was sure getting her workout for the day! Though she had to admit it was the perfect way to stay warm in the biting wind.

'A little bit of everything,' Liesl replied. 'They have some good bargains for some nice quality stuff.'

Jenelyn liked the sound of that. She may have some extra money, but she didn't want to splurge it all in one trip.

'Let's try it,' she said, hoping it was one of the nearer stores to them. It was certainly a day to be indoors.

Kaiserslautern was larger than Jenelyn remembered it being five months ago. But she knew how foggy her memory could be after so long. Liesl expertly led the way, crossing streets and weaving through the crowds, completely comfortable. Jenelyn was a little nervous being in a strange, crowded city without Laszlo or Gretchen, but as Liesl guided them through the streets, her worry was soothed away, knowing that Liesl wouldn't get them lost.

'There it is,' Liesl said, pointing to a massive concrete building. Jenelyn's jaw dropped. She was used to large malls back home, but Los Angeles didn't have individual department stores like this. The building was four stories tall, with beautiful architecture. In the right-hand corner, there was the name 'Karstadt' in simple, white block letters, dwarfed by the colossal walls surrounding it. Jenelyn knew she would have probably missed the name of the store if it hadn't been for Liesl.

'It's enormous,' Jenelyn said in awe as they walked through the doors.

'Is it?' Liesl asked. 'Don't you have large stores in America?'

Jenelyn nodded, her eyes soaking in everything. If she had thought the building was impressive from the outside, she was positive of it now from the inside. She stopped Liesl when they walked inside so that she could simply stare. Two enormous, ornate chandeliers hung elegantly down from the high vaulted ceiling. The ceiling itself was a skylight encased in beautiful stainless glass. The rays of light streaming through it exploded against the walls in multiple refracted fragments of light that seemed like dancing fairies. Looking up, she could see all four floors, separated by multiple stairs and escalators. The wood and white-painted walls were well-designed, but simple. It was made all the more spectacular by the festive

Christmas decorations adorning every balcony and wall; from the gigantic evergreen Christmas wreath covered in shining balls, red poinsettias, and golden ribbon to the life-sized sleigh scene with Santa and his reindeer hanging from the ceiling, flying over everyone's heads. Jenelyn knew that she would never see another store so lovely.

'This is incredible,' she muttered in disbelief, 'So much better than any of our stores. I mean, we have large malls, but not individual stores that look like this. This one store is the size of one of our malls!'

'I always assumed that America built everything huge,' Liesl confessed.

Jenelyn shrugged and kept walking. 'I did, too.'

They started by browsing on the first floor, Jenelyn making sure she checked the price of everything. She could tell everything was high quality, but she had to admit that there were some outstanding deals. They shopped in silence for a while, simply pointing out things to each other. Jenelyn rifled through racks of soft cashmere jumpers, knitted scarves, and pressed trousers, but was overwhelmed with the choices. She simply had no idea what she was going to get Gretchen or Laszlo. Karstadt mainly had clothes, and she was wondering how much Gretchen would appreciate something to wear. She was pretty sure she knew her style and taste by now. In contrast, Liesl was avidly grabbing anything that appealed to her. It seemed that she enjoyed shopping much more than Jenelyn did.

'Look at this cardigan!' she cried, holding up a soft yellow knit-top. 'It's adorable! And it's on sale, so I'm going to get it.'

Jenelyn nodded in silent agreement, knowing a response from her would be unnecessary. Liesl was a happy personality - but bold. All of her initial shyness when Jenelyn first met her had melted away. It made Jenelyn quiet and willing to go along with whatever Liesl wanted, which suited her fine.

'I think I'm going to get Gretchen something to wear and find something electronic for Laszlo,' Jenelyn finally decided. 'I can't think of what else to get them.'

Liesl agreed, and they started looking at a table full of Christmas-themed jumpers. 'So, how long have your grandparents known Laszlo and Gretchen?' Jenelyn asked.

'Oh my, at least twenty-five years,' Liesl answered. 'Maybe longer. Opa was Laszlo's co-worker before he retired. They have always been good friends.'

Liesl's face shadowed briefly, and then it was gone as suddenly as it had appeared. But Jenelyn had seen it.

'What?' Jenelyn asked, her intuition coming alive like a hot wire.

Liesl shrugged, waving her hand dismissively. 'Oh nothing, just something I remembered.'

Jenelyn knew that Liesl wanted to end it there. But she was tired of being left in the dark. She might have to tiptoe around Laszlo and Gretchen regarding their deceased daughter, but she could be bolder with Liesl.

'Does your grandfather know something about their daughter?' she guessed, trying to sound nonchalant.

'How do you know about that?' Liesl paused, her whole body going stiff, 'Opa and Oma told me that Laszlo and Gretchen never talk about it.'

Jenelyn proceeded to explain what happened months ago when she had seen their daughter's picture in the living room.

'All they told me was that she died twenty years ago,' she finished unhappily, 'They never told me how. Do your grandparents know?'

Liesl bit her lip in hesitation. It was evident that she wasn't supposed to gossip about it, but Jenelyn pleaded with her eyes. Liesl glanced around them and noticed that they were pretty much alone in the corner of the store. She gave an acquiescent sigh and hung a shirt back on the rack.

'I guess it won't hurt to tell you,' she said, her tone cautious. 'I mean, you are living with them, and they like you. It's not that they wouldn't want to tell you; it's because it's too painful for them. Opa said that after the accident, Laszlo was never the same man again.'

Jenelyn leaned in closer, her voice barely a whisper.

'Accident?' she asked, trying to keep her voice mild, though her mind was racing. She had always assumed that the daughter had died of an illness.

'Ja,' Liesl replied quietly. 'Agnes was killed in a terrible accident. It's really something that we haven't spoken of in years.'

So, the daughter's name had been Agnes. Jenelyn felt a surge of pity for the child. Hearing her name gave her a personality, a life. It was as if having a name suddenly made her real. Jenelyn knew that finding out how Agnes died would help her on her Journey. How, she wasn't sure, but she knew.

'How did you find out about it?' she asked Liesl. 'I mean, you weren't even born until two years later.'

'When I was ten years old, Oma took me to visit Gretchen for the first time in twelve years,' Liesl explained. 'Apparently, after Agnes died, Gretchen and Laszlo isolated themselves in their house, Laszlo only leaving to go to work. They didn't talk to anyone. It was like they wanted to shut themselves away from the world. So, when we visited, Gretchen couldn't stop staring at me and hugging me. Of course, I asked Oma about it when we left, and she told me.'

'So, what was the accident?' she persisted with forced patience, trying not to sound too eager.

Liesl frowned and shook her head, her eyes puzzled. She answered slowly. 'That's the weird part of the story. You see, Gretchen and Laszlo's explanation of what happened doesn't make any sense. My parents and grandparents all think they lost their minds a little with grief. There have been some nasty rumours going around Wittlich because of it, too.'

'Liesl,' she insisted, her patience snapping. 'What happened?'

Liesl looked into Jenelyn's determined eyes. 'I assume that Gretchen told you about Wittlich's legend? About the werewolf and the shrine?'

Jenelyn nodded. She would never forget that strange hike in the woods near their home, or the ancient shrine with the maroon candle burning incessantly.

'Well,' Liesl went on haltingly. 'Did Gretchen tell you that the werewolf supposedly came back in 1988 and was seen by Air Force personnel?'

Jenelyn thought for a moment, thinking back to that long conversation. It sounded familiar, and she nodded. Liesl shrugged sheepishly.

'Well, Laszlo and Gretchen claim that when the werewolf returned, it killed their daughter,' she stated, her voice flat.

Jenelyn simply stared at her. She searched for signs of jest in Liesl's face, and found none. The years made sense, but the story didn't.

'What?' she asked, confident that she had heard her wrong. 'They actually believe that their daughter was killed by a werewolf?'

Liesl nodded almost apologetically as if she was sorry she didn't have a more logical story to tell.

'That's why there are a lot of people in Wittlich who think they're insane. It's why they locked themselves up for a long time. Some wanted them to get mental therapy. My grandparents were one of the few people who decided to forgive them. They figured that whatever did happen, there was no reason for Laszlo and Gretchen to be punished further. But it was a difficult time.'

Jenelyn was frantically trying to wrap her mind around this. It was too unbelievable. Her desperate thoughts raced back to Halloween, and suddenly, their panicked reactions made sense to her. She felt horrible for them and even madder at the pranksters who did it. Of course, now she knew why they did. Thinking of the pranksters also reminded her of the strange looks and obscure interactions Gretchen would have with people, and why she was greeted by women acting as if they hadn't seen her in years. Everything made more sense now.

'That's so awful,' she muttered as they drifted back through the racks of clothing. 'But, how did they think it happened?'

Liesl stared at her in surprise, as if she didn't think that Jenelyn should take this too seriously. Jenelyn couldn't blame her, but she was curious to know their side of the story.

'I'm not sure,' Liesl said carefully. 'My grandparents wouldn't tell me. They simply thought I should know what Laszlo and Gretchen were saying to be prepared for the rumours. I'm glad they did. I really like Laszlo and Gretchen, even if they are a little strange.'

She smiled at Jenelyn, her shoulders seeming to slump as if a weight had been lifted from her chest. Jenelyn sighed with disappointment. It looked like she was still going to be left in the dark for a while. She didn't know what to think. She couldn't seem to agree that Laszlo and Gretchen were insane. They seemed too normal for that. Yet, they thought a werewolf killed their daughter.

Her thoughts deepened, plunging her down into a maze of theoretical possibilities and choices, shopping utterly forgotten. There were only two possible solutions. One, a werewolf killed Agnes, and Laszlo and Gretchen were right, which sounded highly unlikely. Or two, Laszlo and Gretchen were insane, and Agnes died some other way. But, if that were true, then how did Agnes Weneseivers really die? Jenelyn shivered at the thought. She was faced with a real mystery, and she was living with the only people who knew the truth.

January

Eighth Month

Chapter Seventeen

Jenelyn shivered with cold, her hair rising on her arms. It was snowing outside, the tiny, delicate flakes floating softly to the ground. But the snow wasn't the only reason for her shivering. For the past month, ever since Liesl had confided in her about how Laszlo and Gretchen thought their daughter had died, Jenelyn had been nervous. It wasn't a normal nervousness either, and this concerned her more than anything else. It felt like a premonition, a foreboding of something coming, and it wasn't simply the New Year, which she usually loved with all of its promises and fresh opportunities.

She was lying in bed, staring out her window. It was time to get up, but she didn't want to leave her cosy, warm cocoon. She also needed to mentally prepare herself for talking with Laszlo and Gretchen, who didn't know that something was wrong. Jenelyn prided herself on her acting skills. After living with Laszlo and Gretchen for so long, she felt like family. She trusted them, loved them even. Knowing that they believed something so impossible made her wary.

Are they insane? she thought for the thousandth time.

Shaking off these unpleasant thoughts, Jenelyn forced herself to get up. The biting cold attacked her, and she quickly wrapped the heavy blanket around herself. Laszlo and Gretchen were used to the winter cold, so they didn't turn the heat on high. Jenelyn felt like she was standing in a freezer as she stood in the bathroom, brushing her teeth. She was wearing sweatpants and a jumper with long johns underneath and double-thick woollen socks, but they were little help to her. Last month the snow had started, and the bitter cold had arrived. It was almost painful dressing for the day, but she was finally ready to go downstairs.

Inhaling deeply, she forced a smile on her face. She would act naturally. They would never know she knew. And while she was with them, she would try and forget that they believed in werewolves.

'Guten morgen,' Jenelyn greeted airily as she walked into the kitchen. As usual, Gretchen was preparing breakfast, and Laszlo was reading the paper. It was a quiet Sunday morning, the snow outside blanketing all noise. She sat at the dining room table with Laszlo and studied him. He appeared like he always did, fatherly, loving, a kind man. Jenelyn's heart warmed. How could she possibly believe what she thought?

'Guten morgen, Jenelyn,' Laszlo replied, smiling at her above his paper. 'How do you like the snow this morning?'

Jenelyn grimaced, wrapping her arms around herself for warmth. 'It's not my favourite,' she admitted. 'Too cold.'

Gretchen walked up to them, a cup of tea in one hand and a platter in the other. She set the platter on the table, and Jenelyn helped herself to her light breakfast, grateful for the warm cup of tea that she had learned provided more comfort than she could have ever dreamed of. It not only kept her warm, but there was a delicious cosiness in drinking it as if it was wrapping her in a snug hug as she drank. She had almost forgotten how she had eaten back home and didn't miss it in the slightest. Though she had to snack way more here in Germany, she had adapted to the light meals and was actually beginning to prefer them.

'So, what are your plans today?' Gretchen asked Jenelyn as she sat down.

Jenelyn grinned at Gretchen's pointed consideration. Ever since she had met Liesl, Gretchen had understood about Jenelyn being an adult. She admitted that it was hard for her, but she knew Jenelyn needed to get out on her own. Jenelyn was more than grateful. As much as she adored Gretchen, it wasn't the same as being with someone her own age.

'Liesl and I were going to shop around Kaufland,' Jenelyn lied smoothly, naming one of the hyper-stores in Wittlich. She hoped that Gretchen couldn't see the truth in her eyes.

'You girls really do a lot of shopping,' Gretchen said. 'I hope you're still able to save enough money for your next trip.'

Jenelyn sobered at the thought. She was having so much fun with Liesl that she was starting to feel like a sister to her. She didn't like to think of the fact that she might be forced to leave her forever like she had been forced to with Nicole. Although they hadn't come, the Spirits could tell her any day that she needed to say goodbye to Germany and head elsewhere. Saying goodbye to friends was one part of her family's tradition that Jenelyn loathed. Fortunately, she could confidently say that she still had plenty of money because she and Liesl had not been shopping as much as she let Gretchen believe.

'I still have enough,' she assured Gretchen. 'Trust me, we mostly window shop anyway.'

Gretchen seemed appeased, and Laszlo grunted. 'I don't understand how you girls can spend so many hours stuck inside a shopping centre. We do have beautiful trails around here. You two should spend some more time outside.'

Jenelyn shrugged noncommittally and nodded in agreement. The fact was, she agreed with Laszlo wholeheartedly. She would be senseless if she were really shopping as much as they thought!

'It's so interesting here,' she explained, hoping she didn't sound as lame as she thought, 'Your stores are a lot nicer than the ones back home.'

'What time is Liesl coming to get you?' Gretchen asked.

'She'll be here in an hour. We wanted to get an early start.'

Gretchen frowned a little. 'I like that you have a friend, Jenelyn, but for the past month, I feel as if we've been growing apart. We used to spend so much time together. I really miss doing things with you.'

Jenelyn tried to ignore a stab of guilt. What she and Liesl were doing was important, and she knew that if they succeeded, Gretchen and Laszlo's life would be better.

'I miss that, too,' Jenelyn answered truthfully. As much as she loved being with Liesl, she did miss Gretchen's sweet presence.

Gretchen smiled at her and stroked Jenelyn's hair. Jenelyn's heart skipped a little. She was a little jumpier around Gretchen now. She didn't know exactly why, but she assumed it was because she didn't really know how Agnes died.

'Well, let's make plans for next weekend,' Gretchen said brightly. 'I'm sure Liesl can be without you for two days.'

Laszlo jumped as if he had been kicked under the table. He looked surprised but then looked over at Gretchen.

'Oh, ja,' he agreed quickly. 'That would be excellent. We can discuss what we want to do later this evening. That gives Gretchen and me some time to think.'

Jenelyn stifled a giggle at their obvious lack of subtlety. 'That would be great.' She said, chuckling and meaning it wholeheartedly.

Exactly one hour later, the doorbell rang. Jenelyn could never get over how prompt Liesl was. She wondered if the girl had any other life than hanging out with her or Alfred.

'Hallo, Jenelyn! Are you ready?' Liesl cried when Jenelyn opened the door. Her eyes were shining with excitement. Jenelyn hoped Gretchen and Laszlo wouldn't get suspicious.

'Ja, I'm ready,' she agreed quickly. 'Gretchen, Laszlo, I'm leaving now!'

Gretchen hurried into the living room, wringing her hands. ‘Be careful,’ she warned. ‘Snowy days make me nervous.’

Jenelyn assumed Gretchen was concerned about the road conditions for driving, but looking at Liesl’s face, she wondered if it was something else. Liesl seemed deeply concerned.

‘We’ll be fine, Gretchen,’ she assured her. ‘We’re not going far.’

Gretchen gave a tight smile, the worry never quite leaving her eyes. ‘That’s true. Have fun!’

Jenelyn and Liesl walked to the car, Jenelyn shivering the whole way. When they started driving, Jenelyn felt safe to ask her questions.

‘Why does Gretchen not like snowy days?’ she asked.

Liesl looked at her and rolled her eyes, her mouth set in a thin line.

‘Well, my grandparents told me that it’s because she’s nervous that the snow will blow out the candle. She doesn’t trust the protective plastic around it,’ she replied grimly.

To anyone else, that sentence wouldn’t have made much sense, but Jenelyn immediately understood.

‘Hm,’ she muttered. ‘I’m glad we’re doing this today then.’

Liesl nodded, and they drove in silence for a few minutes. For the past month, Jenelyn and Liesl had been researching Agnes’ death. They had gone to the local library, found her obituary, and read all the newspaper articles written in that year. Only one had mentioned a mysterious death in Wittlich, explaining that the cause of death was unknown. That had made Jenelyn even more nervous. A paranoid thought still haunted her. She wouldn't allow herself to believe it, but it was always there lurking underneath her practical thoughts. Would Gretchen and Laszlo have staged Agnes' death by blowing out the candle, then saying that the werewolf did it, when in fact, they had murdered her?

Jenelyn shuddered. It was a horrible thought, and she simply couldn't picture it. Laszlo seemed too disturbed by his daughter's death to have been the cause of it.

Or, Jenelyn thought cynically, *is that why he's so disturbed because he feels guilty? It is odd how he never wants to talk about it.*

This train of thought made Jenelyn feel sick to her stomach. The Gretchen and Laszlo she knew would never have done such a thing. Then again, she also didn't know them that well, especially since it had happened twenty years ago. People change.

'So, how do you know that this is the cemetery where she's buried?' Jenelyn asked Liesl, trying to interrupt her own dismal thoughts by focusing on their destination.

'Because Wittlich only has one cemetery,' Liesl explained matter-of-factly. 'And though the papers said that the cause of death was unknown, there was a body, which means there's a grave.'

Jenelyn's fingers clutched her seat until they were white and her leg jiggled nervously. She was going to have to calm down! The more she thought about Agnes' death, the more her heart pounded and her tightened fingers began to feel bruised. Her innate premonition weighed increasingly heavier the more they researched.

'How far is it?' Jenelyn croaked, trying to calm her nerves and heaving stomach by talking.

Liesl noticed her discomfort and looked at her in concern, but simply answered. 'Only a few more minutes.'

They were driving outside of the town, toward a rural area. The roads and landscape around them were covered in a light blanket of white. No one was out, not even the birds. Jenelyn stuffed her hands under her armpits, despite the warmth of the car, and shivered at how small and alone they were. Looking at the dense trees surrounding them, she could easily imagine a mythic beast, with large talons perfect for ripping flesh, charging out of the woods. She tried her hardest to thwart her imagination. She wasn't doing herself any favours by freaking herself out.

'I hope the grave will be easy to find,' she said, forcing the words through her dry throat. 'I don't want to be out in this for too long.'

'I agree,' Liesl replied, looking at the ominous dark clouds looming in the distance. 'It is cold.'

Jenelyn still couldn't believe that it had taken them this long to think of going to Agnes' grave. They had felt that they could learn more by reading past newspapers, which, of course, they did, but only a little. Seeing Agnes' grave seemed to be elementary, as if it should have been the first place they wanted to go. It would show them how often the grave was visited, confirm the date of death that the newspaper articles had stated, and possibly have an inscription that would give them some kind of clue as to what happened. It was a long shot, but was one of few resources to go on.

Finally, the tiny cemetery was ahead of them, a dismal collection of scattered stones overshadowed by rolling clouds that were dark and heavy with snow. The snow-covered ground looked crunchy and hard. The gravestones were shadows in the distance. Some looked like jagged teeth, and others too polished. Jenelyn strained her ears for any sounds of life, but not even a bird cawed, let alone any sign of people.

'We're here,' Liesl whispered, as if she, too, was a little spooked. 'Let's go.'

Jenelyn gathered up her courage and got out of the car. The two girls walked into the graveyard, their arms touching. The cemetery was dead silent, only their footsteps making soft crunching noises as they walked.

'Where should we begin?' Liesl asked Jenelyn, her breath frosting in the air.

'Anywhere, I guess,' Jenelyn shrugged. 'Let's go over there.'

They shuffled over to a collection of headstones like a pair of wrapped-up Siamese twins. It only took them a minute to see that Agnes Wenesievers's name was not there. They quickly walked around, trying to remain calm in such a cold, desolate setting. The cemetery had appeared to be tiny from the road, but upon walking in it, Jenelyn found that it was much larger than she had thought. Graves were scattered over a large expanse of land, with only a few rows clustered together, making the cemetery appear small. Jenelyn's heart pounded as she glanced at all the headstones. Some were new, while others had obviously been there for hundreds of years.

Normally, she would have liked to read them and think about the past peoples' lives, but today, her stomach was so queasy that it made her nauseous. Unexpectedly, the sky opened. Chunks of snow whirled madly around them, so thick that Jenelyn couldn't see the grave in front of her.

'How are we going to find our way back?' Jenelyn asked, struggling to see through the thick white, her heart hammering in her chest.

'Perhaps it's just a cloudburst. It may clear soon,' Liesl assured her, though her voice wavered.

'And if it doesn't?' Jenelyn replied through her scarf.

From behind them came loud, crunching footsteps. They were slow at first but then quickened rapidly. Jenelyn felt like her heart was as ice-cold as the flakes around her.

'Run!' she cried, her instincts screaming.

They dashed forward blindly, but after a few steps, they both tripped headlong over a grave and sprawled helplessly into the deep snow. Jenelyn screamed in horror, her fear completely dominating her. Even Liesl was starting to cry in terror. A large hand descended out of the white blanket around them, grasping each of their jackets firmly.

'Was sind sie mädchen, die hier machen?' a gruff voice snapped at them.

Neither girl was able to register the words through their thick fog of fear. Liesl screamed, and Jenelyn began hitting the hand, forcing it to drop them. After a few seconds, the spoken words finally cut through the fog, and they were able to focus on their source. The man standing before them was short but round. His bald head was uncovered, and Jenelyn wondered how cold he was. His unfriendly dark eyes narrowed, and his thin lips pursed with annoyance. Liesl was the first to respond shakily.

'We're looking for a certain headstone,' she gasped. 'Maybe you can help us.'

The man grunted and shrugged. 'Kann sein,' he replied shortly, his tone noncommittal. 'Who are you looking for?'

Jenelyn's heart was slowing down fast. She knew they had overreacted and felt foolish for it. The old man was obviously the caretaker.

'We're looking for Agnes Wenesievers,' Jenelyn answered finally, her voice back to normal.

'Now, why would you want to visit her grave?' he asked, scrutinising Jenelyn with a steely gaze. 'No one's visited her for years.'

This took Jenelyn aback. Why wouldn't Gretchen and Laszlo come to visit their daughter's grave? It didn't make any sense. Jenelyn's premonition that Agnes's death was connected with her Journey swelled like a wave in her chest.

'I'm staying with her parents,' Jenelyn explained, feeling uneasy talking about Agnes as if she was still alive.

'Are you?' the old man asked with dry humour. 'Now, that must be an interesting place to live.'

He spat a wad of tobacco, the pungent brown liquid melting instantly on the snow, and began leading them towards the back of the graveyard. Liesl and Jenelyn looked at each other in disgust. As he led them, Jenelyn heard him mumble to each headstone, a salutation to one, and a guttural chuckle to another. Others he simply placed a hand on, almost as if shaking hands with the person.

'Laszlo and Gretchen are two of the craziest people I know,' he continued gruffly, looking around the headstones. 'Ah, here she is.'

It didn't go unnoticed by Jenelyn that the caretaker had a habit of talking about the dead around him as if they were people staying at a hotel. She figured it must be because he was around them so much.

'Excuse me, sir,' Liesl said, after regaining her confidence. 'What is your name? I'm Liesl, and this is my friend, Jenelyn.'

The old man was still staring at the headstone, a look of deep pity etched on his face. At the question, he looked up in surprise, as if he had forgotten about them. His eyebrows fell heavily over his eyes, and the corners of his mouth drooped as he answered.

'Dierk,' he spat, and then muttered, 'Nosy females.'

Jenelyn barely heard him. She was staring at Agnes' grave. The headstone was plain and unadorned; a simple block of granite with a carved message that read:

Agnes Wenesievers

Born: April 11th, 1978

Died: May 3rd, 1988

The Lord giveth and the Lord taketh away

Underneath, roughly carved, and in messy writing as if the carver were inexperienced, were the words: *Too soon.* Jenelyn felt tears well in her eyes. It was apparent that whoever had carved that into the headstone had been deeply grieved.

Poor girl, she thought sadly, *she had just turned ten. What happened to you, little one?* Jenelyn stroked the headstone thoughtfully, her fingers outlining the words 'too soon.' Who had carved them? Liesl and Dierk were both silent, watching her. Jenelyn frowned and looked back over at Dierk.

'How long have you worked here?' she asked firmly, her courage returning at last.

Dierk seemed surprised and then instantly annoyed by the interrogation.

'Thirty years, more or less,' he said. 'Long enough to have known a lot of the people in here.'

Jenelyn wondered how that could affect someone's psyche. Dierk seemed like he preferred the dead to the living. Though his tone was curt with them, she noticed it softened when he mentioned the dead, or when he mumbled to a headstone in passing.

'So then, you would know the last time someone visited this grave,' she stated. 'When was it?'

Dierk sneered at her. 'And why would you want to know?' he huffed. 'You aren't family, are you?'

Jenelyn glared at him. She was getting tired of his attitude, and her anger renewed her courage.

'Dierk,' she snapped, trying to force her temper down. 'I have been living with Laszlo and Gretchen for eight months now. They are very good friends of mine, and I wanted to pay my respects to their deceased daughter. Now, you said that no one had visited her grave for a long time. I simply want to know when the last time was.'

Dierk stared at her for a moment as if trying to decide whether to bother with her, but then he rolled his eyes in resignation.

'Like I remember every time someone comes to visit a grave,' he said sarcastically, folding his arms.

Liesl narrowed her eyes at him. 'But you do remember *this* grave, don't you?' she asked. 'Everyone should know about this grave.'

Dierk and Liesl stared each other down for a while, but then Liesl won. Dierk sighed heavily.

'No one's visited Agnes for at least twenty years,' he said. 'Now, are you happy?'

'Not yet,' Jenelyn persisted, happy to have found someone who could give her more information, unpleasant as that person might be. 'What do you know about Laszlo and Gretchen?'

Dierk gave a choppy, coarse laugh. 'Those two?' he hissed. 'Crazy as cuckoos they are. Doesn't surprise me that they don't visit their daughter. They're probably afraid that the big, bad wolf is haunting her grave!'

He laughed hysterically, his face turning bright red. Jenelyn glared at him. She wasn't surprised that he thought Laszlo and Gretchen were crazy. Liesl had told her that the whole town thought they were.

'You know they aren't,' Liesl growled with repulsion, and a stubborn loyalty to Laszlo and Gretchen. 'In fact, my grandparents still visit them, and Jenelyn's been living with them! They aren't crazy.'

Dierk sobered, his eyes narrowing at Liesl's in challenge. A solemn calm came over him, and for once, a cold soberness replaced his nasty demeanour. The sudden change gave Jenelyn goosebumps.

'Not crazy, mädchen?' he asked, all humour gone, his voice firm. 'I'm sure you know the story. Those people believe that a werewolf killed their daughter! That's called crazy! Or maybe that's an alibi, and this one here should watch her back!'

He jerked his thumb toward Jenelyn. Jenelyn found it unnerving that Dierk had the same theory she had, but hearing it the way Dierk said it made Jenelyn remember her attack in Kaiserslautern in July. Those punks had been terrified of Laszlo and Gretchen, and their words suddenly rang all too clear. *We don't want to be next.'*

In a flash, she connected their fear and Dierk's warning words. Now she understood that it wasn't only fear of their mental health that had kept everyone in Wittlich away from Laszlo and Gretchen. An icy tendril of panic slithered down her back. To her amazement, Liesl didn't back down.

'Now look, Dierk,' she continued, her voice low, 'Laszlo and Gretchen have been living under that shadow for twenty years. Some people have let it go. We simply want to know the truth.'

At this, Dierk raised his eyebrows in confusion. 'The truth?' he asked, looking from Liesl to Jenelyn in surprise.

'Ja,' Jenelyn took over, pushing down her panic in a dogged pursuit to prove that her doubts about them were untrue. She was anxious for someone to tell her that her fears were unnecessary. 'However, I do believe they are mistaken. What have you heard about Agnes' death?'

Dierk stared at her, dumbfounded. Finally, he gave a deep snort and shrugged.

'Nothing different than what everyone else heard,' he said firmly. 'The Wenesievers came storming into the hospital carrying their dead daughter, screaming 'Werewolf! Werewolf!' Of course, everyone thought they had lost their minds. The doctors examined the body and found multiple abrasions and cuts, so something certainly attacked her, as was confirmed by the post mortem. She died from her injuries. Police investigated the Wenesievers, but couldn't find conclusive evidence that they had done anything. Like everyone else, they just assumed they'd gone crazy. The next day, they buried her here.'

Jenelyn looked back at the headstone. 'And they never came back here to visit?' she asked in disbelief.

'Nein,' he grunted. 'As I said, they're both nuts. Whatever happened to that little girl was a tragedy. Anyone would agree to that. She was a happy little thing.'

His gruff voice drifted off in thought, his eyes looking back at the headstone. Jenelyn felt a ray of hope.

'You knew her?' she asked.

'Ja, I knew her,' Dierk replied, settling against a headstone. 'I'd see her in the grocery store, around town. She was always out with Gretchen doing something. Laszlo and Gretchen seemed to adore her. Agnes was happy, bold, daring. Everyone loved her.'

Dierk stopped in obvious reminiscence. Liesl watched him. Jenelyn looked at her and wondered what she had heard about Agnes. Unexpectedly, Dierk went on, surprising them. She had thought that he was done.

'Wouldn't surprise me,' he muttered, then stopped again.

Jenelyn and Liesl shared a look.

'What?' Jenelyn whispered, almost afraid to break Dierk's patient mood by talking to him.

'Agnes and Gretchen used to walk in the woods all the time,'he mused, his thick finger rubbing his chin with subconscious thought. 'It wouldn't surprise me if Agnes had gone in there one day without Gretchen. There are many animals in those woods big enough to kill a tiny child of ten. Now, it's ridiculous to say it was the legendary werewolf, but it was something; there's no denying that.'

Jenelyn waited for more, but Dierk had finished. He stood up and glared at them, as if he was ashamed to have said so much.

'Spend some time with her,' he ordered gruffly, pointing at Agnes' headstone. 'She's been lonely for years.'

He shuffled off, leaving Liesl and Jenelyn standing in the snow, shivering with cold and adrenaline.

'Are you thinking what I'm thinking?' Jenelyn asked Liesl, her lips frozen.

Liesl nodded. 'I think so,' she whispered, and they both turned to Agnes' lonesome headstone.

February

Ninth Month

Chapter Eighteen

A cool breeze whistled through the dense snow-covered trees, rattling the pine needles that broke the muffled silence of the blanketed forest. Jenelyn shivered and looked over at Liesl. They were walking in the forest near Gretchen and Laszlo's house, both acutely aware of the heavy quiet. It was unnerving that there weren't any sounds of skittering animals, or birds crying in the trees. The forest felt as solemn and still as the cemetery they had visited a month ago. Between work and Gretchen wanting to do things, it had been challenging for the girls to get together.

Their footsteps crunched noisily on the icy snow, the sound keeping Jenelyn's wild imagination grounded and stopping her from panicking. She felt as if this was forbidden, even though she had walked this trail a dozen times with Gretchen. Without her, Jenelyn felt like she was trespassing. It had taken a lot of convincing on her part to keep Gretchen from coming with them. Jenelyn felt immensely guilty for consistently lying to her, and was becoming uncomfortable with how good she was getting at it. Lying was not in her nature, and she hoped it wouldn't be too much longer until she could stop. Gretchen hadn't seemed entirely convinced by her story of new shops they had found, but she had hesitantly agreed that they didn't sound like shops she would enjoy. Jenelyn had breathed a sigh of relief, since she and Liesl had wanted to go to the forest ever since they had visited Agnes's grave.

'Why is it so quiet?' Liesl whispered, making Jenelyn jump.

'I don't know,' she replied, not daring to speak too loud. 'Maybe it's because of the snow.'

They kept walking in silence, both girls trembling with nerves. Jenelyn didn't know what they would find at the shrine, but she had a good idea. She and Liesl had both had the same thought at the cemetery that day. Jenelyn knew Gretchen and Laszlo too well to believe that they would never visit their daughter at the cemetery. To Jenelyn and Liesl, this could only mean one thing: Agnes was not at the cemetery. She was somewhere else, and Jenelyn had a pretty good idea where that somewhere else might be.

'Is it much further?' Liesl asked, her voice a little above a whisper.

Jenelyn looked around at the tall evergreens towering over them, though they seemed vaguely unfamiliar now that their winter attire adorned them. She knew this trail reasonably well, but Liesl had never been here. She wished that she could have shown Liesl this forest in a much happier way.

'Not much farther,' she finally answered, hoping she was right. 'Probably another kilometre or so.'

Liesl nodded, and Jenelyn was grateful that Liesl was with her. To be honest, she was a lot more nervous than she appeared to be. Finding Gretchen and Laszlo's dead daughter's grave wasn't exactly fun. As inexplicable as it was, Jenelyn still had a strong feeling that if she found out how Agnes died, it would help her with her Journey, though she sometimes questioned if she was going insane.

For months, Jenelyn had waited for the Spirits to contact her. She knew that they would come when they were ready and that it could be years, but she also understood that she had to listen for them. Jenelyn was happy with her life in Germany, the wonderful couple she lived with, her boss, and especially her new friend, Liesl. She felt as if she was finally settling, and that scared her. The number one rule for her Journey was simple: Never settle until the Spirits leave, which was heart breaking. She knew eventually that she would find her true home. But *when*? The question haunted her. She loved everything about Wittlich: the seasons, the people, and the town. Although she had experienced many moments of homesickness, the small village had found a special place in her heart. How many places would she have to fall in love with, only to leave again? The prospect was daunting. The Spirits already predestined her life. They knew what her purpose was. She only had to trust them.

'Is that it?' Liesl whispered, jarring Jenelyn from her thoughts. The shrine stood only a few hundred yards away, the candle flickering brightly.

Jenelyn nodded slowly, her voice barely above a dry whisper, 'Ja.'

They kept walking, Liesl's eyes widening more and more as they got closer.

'My grandparents would talk about this place,' she murmured, 'but they never brought me here. I guess maybe they thought it would scare me.'

They had arrived at the large shrine now. Hundreds of flowers scattered at the base, now blanketed with snow around the headstone of Thomas Johannes Baptist Schwytzer. Jenelyn stared at it for a moment. Her skin prickled, and goosebumps rose on her arms as a light breeze whistled around them. There was something about this particular place that called to her. She knew that even if Gretchen and Laszlo were insane and a werewolf hadn't killed Agnes, there was something that felt almost magical here. Every instinct screamed at her to pay attention. She wondered why she hadn't gotten this strange feeling the first time she came here with Gretchen.

It wasn't time, a small voice inside her said, and she knew that deep in her heart, it was the truth.

Liesl was reading the headstone. 'Poor man,' she said sympathetically. 'What an awful life. So, where do you think it is?'

Jenelyn looked around. A week ago, she had noticed Gretchen leaving the house carrying a bouquet of flowers while Laszlo had run an errand. Finding it strange that Gretchen didn't invite her to go along, Jenelyn had followed her. She had only gotten as far as seeing Gretchen head towards the trail when the sound of a car made her scurry back to the house, fearing it was Laszlo coming home. An hour later, when Gretchen returned, the bouquet was gone. Jenelyn knew at that moment where Gretchen must have taken the flowers and why.

After telling Liesl, they had agreed that Gretchen and Laszlo must have moved Agnes's body from her grave and put it somewhere they considered more suitable. Jenelyn didn't have a doubt that they would have thought of this place.

‘When I was here before, Gretchen was only showing me the shrine,’ she explained, walking the perimeter of the circle. ‘Of course, I was so amazed by it that I didn’t look around very much. Gretchen wouldn’t have wanted the grave to be noticeable, but I’m sure it’s here somewhere.’

Liesl joined her, and they kept circling the surrounding area, walking further and further each time. The forest was still dead quiet, and Jenelyn kept checking down the trail to see if anyone was around. Although she was brave when she had to be at scary times, she still didn’t enjoy them. She didn’t even like watching suspense or horror movies.

Fantastic, she thought sarcastically, *looking for an unmarked grave. Just the sort of thing I love.*

She brushed and kicked aside snow, uncovering leaves and pine needles, and wondered if perhaps trying to find it in the deep snow wasn’t a good idea. Gretchen would have wanted to keep it hidden, so it was only going to be harder in this weather, but she couldn’t stop herself from stubbornly continuing to look. After a half-hour or so, Liesl called to her.

‘Jenelyn! I think I found it!’

Jenelyn charged across the shrine circle over to the other side, where Liesl was deep inside the forest, staring at a large boulder that sat beside the trail. Deep enough in the forest for no one to be aware of it, but not so deep that it couldn’t be found if someone knew where to look. Jenelyn was shaking as she stared at it.

‘Agnes,’ she breathed, reading the rough writing hand-carved into the boulder.

Our Dear Agnes

May your Spirit Shine Bright enough to Blind the Darkness

Tears filled Jenelyn's eyes as she read the meticulously carved words. She knew it must have taken Laszlo days to carve it. She had seen his handwriting at work too many times to not recognise his specific style. Liesl was also sniffling. Jenelyn sank to the ground, tracing the letters with her finger.

'I would give anything to know what happened to her,' she muttered. 'It's so sad.'

'Ja, it is,' Liesl agreed. 'Can you imagine dying at ten?'

Jenelyn shuddered and shook her head. The thought was so tragic that the tears overflowed down her cheeks. Suddenly, she heard a sharp, muffled breath gasp behind them, the sound magnified in the silence of the forest. Jenelyn leapt up, her heart racing, her body tense, and her hands instinctively curling into fists as she prepared for anything to happen. Her heart slowed and turned cold as she saw who it was.

Liesl jumped and gave a small whimper.

'What are you doing, mädchens?' Gretchen asked, her soft voice toneless but her eyes full of anger.

Jenelyn swallowed heavily. All the blood had drained from her face, leaving her as pale as the snow around her.

'Saying hello to Agnes,' she squeaked, her voice trembling. Liesl stayed quiet, obviously too frightened to speak.

'I see that,' Gretchen snapped, her hands clenched tight around the bouquet of flowers she held. 'But why?'

Jenelyn understood what Gretchen was really asking. How had they known to come here? 'We went to the cemetery last month to see her grave,' Jenelyn explained cautiously, not wanting to admit that she had followed her a week ago. 'But when Dierk, the caretaker, told us that you and Laszlo never visit, I knew something was wrong. So, it occurred to me that Agnes was somewhere else. This place made the most sense.'

Gretchen's brows rose in surprise. Her lips pursed as she walked to the boulder and delicately laid the flowers against it, her face etched in pain.

'Mein liebster, süße liebe,' she whispered to the boulder and then stood up, staring hard at Jenelyn.

My dear, sweet love, thought Jenelyn, repeating the words Gretchen had muttered, *poor woman*.

'So, you know then?' Gretchen asked harshly, her face white and her eyes glittering in anger. 'I can see that you've been told that Laszlo and I believe Agnes was killed by the werewolf. Who told you?'

Jenelyn didn't have to answer. Gretchen's eyes bore angrily at Liesl, who was looking down in shame.

'As I thought,' Gretchen continued tersely. 'So, Jenelyn, do you also believe we are insane?'

There was such deep hurt in Gretchen's eyes behind the anger that Jenelyn thought Gretchen would never look at her in the same mothering way as before. All of her misgivings and suspicious thoughts washed away at the sight of Gretchen's agony.

'Never, Gretchen!' she cried, running to her and hugging her. 'I know what everyone said, and some believe, but they're wrong! You and Laszlo are not crazy.'

Hearing the words said aloud, Jenelyn realised that in the far corners of her soul, she had always believed this, and she felt herself soften in Gretchen's warm arms, wanting to soak up the comfort she always offered. For the first time in weeks, her heart felt at peace. Gretchen relaxed a little, her eyes softening. She gave a wry grin and sat down beside the boulder. Liesl seemed undecided whether to run or stay. Gretchen noticed this and motioned for Liesl to sit next to her.

'I don't blame you, Liesl,' she said. 'It was bound to come out sooner or later. I'm actually surprised, Jenelyn, that you didn't say anything after Halloween.'

Jenelyn sat down across from them. She purposely had stayed quiet after Halloween, since she was still trying to wrap her mind around what they believed and had to convince herself they weren't crazy. She was glad that Gretchen didn't seem angry anymore, simply very sad and resigned.

'I won't tell you the story without Laszlo,' Gretchen stated. 'It wouldn't be fair. Laszlo has a big part in it, but I will explain why and when we moved the body.'

A shiver ran up Jenelyn's spine at the words. Spoken so matter-of-factly, and yet, it was a terrifying thing.

'It was the night after the funeral,' Gretchen began, her eyes far away. 'Laszlo and I could barely stomach the thought of our daughter being buried in the cemetery. Knowing how she died, it seemed wrong. I had no doubt that our daughter didn't want to rest peacefully among others. Laszlo and I discussed what we believed Agnes's spirit would want to do. We agreed that her spirit would want to help. Agnes was so full of life. I knew her spirit would be restless in that desolate cemetery. So, we moved her here the next night so that her spirit could keep away the darkness of the werewolf. I think of her as the guard here, a soldier to protect the shrine. It's what she would have wanted.'

A gentle smile lit Gretchen's face. Jenelyn looked at Liesl, who shrugged, knowing it sounded crazy. Jenelyn knew that the death of a child was the worst sort of tragedy a parent could live through. If Laszlo and Gretchen had gone a little mental, she wasn't going to judge them for it.

'I'm sure you're right,' she agreed kindly, making Gretchen smile wider. 'So, that's why Laszlo carved the inscription?'

Gretchen nodded, looking over at the boulder's words.

'Ja, he spent a full day carving it,' she explained, her voice soft with admiration for her husband. 'And two days after making sure it was deep enough to read. He doesn't visit very often. He says it's too painful. For some reason, he doesn't believe that I visit here often, either. Little does he know that I come faithfully every day.'

Jenelyn quickly remembered what Laszlo had said to Gretchen when she had first come here. After she and Jenelyn went to the forest. '*It's good for you to go now and then,*' he had said. Now Jenelyn understood completely.

'Why don't you tell him?' she asked.

Gretchen shrugged. 'I don't want him to feel guilty that he doesn't,' she replied. 'He's already haunted enough.'

Jenelyn nodded in understanding and looked over at Liesl, who still seemed amazingly uncomfortable. Jenelyn wondered why. Liesl almost looked scared. Finally, Gretchen noticed as well.

'Liesl, what is the matter?' she asked. 'Are you afraid of me?'

Gretchen's tone was teasing, but her eyes were genuinely concerned. Liesl abruptly burst into tears and hugged Gretchen fiercely.

'I'm sorry!' she erupted. 'My grandparents told me what you and Laszlo believe, and I thought you were crazy! I feel so guilty when I think about what you and Laszlo have gone through.'

Gretchen patted Liesl's back comfortingly, but her eyes were grave. 'It's alright, schätzchen,' she said stiffly. 'But you don't know the half of it. Come, let's go talk to Laszlo.'

The clock ticked loudly. Jenelyn, Liesl, Laszlo, and Gretchen sat in the bright living room. Jenelyn fingered the brocade fabric of the sofa anxiously and waited. Waited for the imminent explosion she knew was going to erupt from Laszlo at any second. Gretchen had just finished telling him that Jenelyn and Liesl had found Agnes's grave and that she had found them when she went to visit. Laszlo was frozen, his body taut and stiff. His face was white, and his eyes wild as he stared at Jenelyn.

'This is true?' he asked, his voice low and deflated.

Jenelyn nodded and looked at Gretchen. Laszlo followed her gaze.

'And you?' he asked his wife, his voice hoarse. 'You have been visiting her without telling me?'

His deep tone of betrayal made Jenelyn surprised that Gretchen didn't crack on the spot. But she stayed strong, her gaze and voice direct.

'Ja, Laszlo,' she stated firmly. 'I didn't want to hurt you.'

Laszlo gave a harsh laugh.

'Hurt me!' he growled, making Jenelyn sink meekly into the sofa. 'Do you honestly believe that I couldn't take it, Gretchen? Haven't I already survived the worst pain a man can feel other than being in Hell?'

Gretchen's face was impassive, but her eyes welled with tears. Laszlo's face was ferocious, and Jenelyn felt afraid of him for the first time.

'Liebling,' Gretchen murmured soothingly. 'I know you're strong, and I know what you have gone through. But I will never put you through any pain again if I can help it.'

They stared at each other for a moment, and then Laszlo wrapped Gretchen in his arms, giving her a bone-crunching hug.

'I know,' he muttered, his voice edged with pain. 'I wish I was strong enough to visit her too.'

Gretchen nodded sympathetically and then seemed to remember Jenelyn and Liesl waiting for them. She looked deep into Laszlo's tortured eyes.

'Laszlo,' she pleaded. 'I don't want to put you through pain, but there is one more thing I must ask of you. Bitte, tell Jenelyn and Liesl how Agnes died. They deserve to know.'

Laszlo closed his eyes and then took a deep breath, his voice shaking.

'I'll try, Gretchen, but you may have to help me.'

'They already know about the werewolf, Laszlo,' she said. 'But they need to know the whole story. Not just the story that the rest of the town has heard.'

This startled Laszlo enough that, for a brief moment, he seemed to forget his agony and his body relaxed infinitesimally.

'They know?' he asked with a deep sigh. 'Then it will be much easier than I imagined.'

He inhaled a shaky breath, and Jenelyn imagined that he was collecting and organising the horrendous memories he had attempted to bury years ago. She had felt impatient this whole time, but suddenly, she was almost frightened to hear the story. Unlike the ghost stories she had heard growing up, this one was real. It was easy to doubt when one person believed in a crazy story, but quite another when two people shared the same memory.

'It was twenty years ago when the werewolf came back,' Laszlo explained, his deep voice raspy with emotion. 'Gretchen, Agnes, and I were hiking in the woods like we normally did. Agnes loved the woods. We forbade her to stray too far since there are large animals in there, but we allowed her to venture a little. Gretchen and I tried to give her as much freedom as she needed. Agnes was an adventurer and was never scared of anything. We knew we couldn't rein in that kind of spirit without breaking it. Gretchen and I didn't know yet that the candle had been blown out. We didn't know that the werewolf had been seen at the Air Force base until we reached the shrine. I'll never forget the sight of that flameless candle as long as I live.'

Laszlo paused and shook his head, his eyes shut with horror. Gretchen shuddered, reliving their tragedy with him.

'At first,' he said bravely continuing, 'We were like everyone else. We knew the legend, but we didn't necessarily believe in it. Agnes had hiked ahead, enjoying herself. We were amazed that the candle had blown out and were in the middle of discussing how to light it again when we heard the scream. It was short but bloodcurdling. I would know that scream anywhere. It still haunts me. We ran frantically into the woods, Gretchen following behind me.'

They looked at each other then, their faces mirroring one another in shared anguish. Laszlo suddenly looked ancient as he continued to release the soul-destroying memory that haunted him.

'I found her,' he whispered, his voice cracking with despair. 'I found her with…it. No demon could ever scare me after that. It had just killed her. I knew she was dead the moment I clapped my eyes on her. The werewolf saw me and snarled viciously, raising itself on its hind legs. I was petrified and felt sick all at the same time. The monster was enormous, at least three metres tall, with red eyes and black fur. It came after me. I was so stunned that I don't believe I even thought of my own life. My only thought was to kill the monster that had murdered Agnes. I yelled at it and grabbed a stick, ready to meet it head-on.'

Jenelyn had been listening intently, but this made her eyes widen in surprise. He had grabbed a stick? What on earth had Laszlo thought he could do with a stick against a nine-foot werewolf? Laszlo looked over at Gretchen, obviously handing her the rest of the story. Apparently, his side of it was over.

'I also ran toward the scream, fearing for Agnes,' Gretchen explained softly. 'But Laszlo was ahead of me and yelled at me to turn back, that there was a werewolf. I don't even think I entirely registered what he said, but instinctively turned and went home for matches to light the candle. I've never run so fast or hard in my life, but by the time I got back to the shrine to light the candle, I knew Agnes was dead. I could feel it in my bones. It was as if when she died, a part of my heart went with her. I could hear the werewolf snarling and Laszlo cursing at it. Fortunately for me, I never saw it, so I don't have the terrifying image of it burned into my mind like Laszlo does. I lit the candle, and a few seconds later, it was quiet. I rushed to Laszlo and found him lying on the ground next to Agnes's body, convulsing with sobs. The werewolf had disappeared, back into the fiery pits of hell where it belonged.'

'Gretchen saved my life,' Laszlo choked, taking his wife's hand and kissing it. 'I would be dead if it wasn't for her. She lit the candle right as the werewolf lunged at me. Thank God the curse lifts after only a few seconds.'

The room was eerily still, no one quite sure how to respond. Jenelyn couldn't speak, her mind reeling from the images Laszlo and Gretchen had painted for her.

'And then you brought Agnes's body to the hospital,' Liesl finished for them, her voice awed. 'I can't believe either one of you haven't gone mad.'

It amazed Jenelyn as well. She couldn't imagine anyone living through something like that and surviving another twenty years sane. Laszlo and Gretchen shook their heads, both shrugging despondently.

'We couldn't do that to Agnes,' Gretchen confessed. 'It would be an insult to her memory.'

Jenelyn sighed and closed her eyes. Now she knew the whole story, but in her heart, she felt that somehow it wasn't over.

March

Tenth Month

Chapter Nineteen

'Gretchen?' Jenelyn asked at dinner. 'Could you take me to the sparkassen tomorrow after work?'

Gretchen's brows furrowed, and even Laszlo seemed a bit taken aback. Jenelyn had figured that they would. They would be curious to know why she was asking to go to the bank. Ever since she had arrived in Germany, Jenelyn had never asked to see her account. She simply had Gretchen deposit her checks when she deposited Laszlo's checks, but Jenelyn knew it was time to find out how much money she had.

'Of course, Jenelyn,' Gretchen replied. 'Why would you want to, though?'

Jenelyn shrugged and grabbed a piece of cheese.

'I think it's time I see what I have,' she answered. 'And since tomorrow is Thursday, they'll be open late enough for me to go.'

Jenelyn knew that though the bank usually closed at four-thirty, they were open an hour later on Thursdays. Since she worked until five o'clock every day, Thursdays were the only days she could go.

'That's true,' Laszlo agreed. 'I need you to make a deposit anyway, Gretchen.'

Jenelyn smiled warmly as she looked at Laszlo. Ever since he had told her the story of Agnes's death, they had become closer. Laszlo scowled and grunted less. He asked her to have tea and lunch with him more at work, and she found herself relaxing and not stressing about saying the wrong thing with him more. It was almost as if he was a true father to her, which terrified her. It would only be a matter of time before that would have to end.

Dinner finished quickly, and Jenelyn hiked up the stairs to bed. She felt withdrawn and strange. Her time was running out. She could feel it instinctively. Since Laszlo had told her and Liesl about the werewolf, she felt like the Spirits were coming. She didn't know the signs to look for when they actually arrived, but she could just feel that it wasn't long from now. She sat on her bed and stared at the framed picture of her parents sitting on her nightstand, taking comfort in her parents' smiling faces. She missed her mother's warm hugs, her father's loud laugh, and the closeness they shared as a family. Jenelyn lay down in bed and shivered. It was still snowing, even now in March! Since December, it had been snowing, but she knew that the snow wouldn't stop until late April, early May. She curled herself into a warm ball and drifted off to sleep.

'Jenelyn, bitte kommen sie in mein büro,' Edwin commanded, disrupting her work.

Jenelyn, frustrated, stared at her screen in dismay. She had so many files to sort out in the system! She hoped whatever Edwin wanted her for wouldn't take too long. Typically, when he called her into his office, it was to show her something new, which usually took up some time. Today, she was too busy for that. She walked into his office prepared to insist that he make it quick.

'Ja, Edwin?' she asked quickly in German. 'What is it?'

Edwin settled into his black leather chair and smiled.

'Jenelyn, you are one of my favourite employees,' he stated. 'I'm never disappointed in your work or attendance. In gratitude, I would like to offer you a raise.'

Her mouth gaped open, and all thoughts of the mountain of work she had to do evaporated. She sat slowly in the chair in front of Edwin's desk.

'A raise?' she asked, her voice sounding small.

Edwin laughed.

'Of course!' he said. 'It's only a small one, but you deserve it.'

'Danke,' Jenelyn murmured in disbelief.

'I'm giving you a fifty-cent raise,' Edwin continued. 'I'm putting the paperwork through today.'

Jenelyn felt frozen, not believing that her work was worthy of a raise. It was so simple. She abruptly realised that Edwin was waiting for her to respond!

'Oh, danke, Edwin!' she cried, shaking her employer's hand gratefully. 'You won't be sorry.'

Edwin chuckled at her, his eyes twinkling. 'Oh, I know.'

Jenelyn walked out of the office and back to her small desk. A raise! She wished for a moment that she could tell Edwin that every bone in her body told her she wouldn't be there for much longer. But she loved her boss and her job. Telling him would somehow make it more real, and she wasn't ready for that yet. She stared at her tiny desk and knew she wanted to live in denial a bit longer. She would miss all of it too much. Heller Funke Europa had been very good to her. Edwin had been superb, and her work was elementary. Now she also had work experience to carry with her for her next job, wherever that was. She shook her head and decided to be happy in the moment. Though time was running out, she was still here for now.

Jenelyn was curious to see the bank in Wittlich as she and Gretchen walked toward it later that day after she had gotten off from work. The building was bland, simply a grey concrete with red block letters in front saying *Sparkasse.*

'I can't wait to see how much I have!' Jenelyn squealed in excitement.

It was the first money she had ever saved, and she felt like she could walk on air. Gretchen draped her arm around Jenelyn's thin shoulders, her face bright.

'This is an exciting day,' she agreed. 'I hope it's enough to last you.'

Jenelyn nodded in agreement. She, too, was worried about that, especially now. Whatever she had in her account would probably be all she would have by the time she had to leave. There weren't any guarantees that she would be lucky enough to find a job in her new destination. They walked into the bank and went up to the teller. Gretchen spoke for her simply because she knew what she was doing.

'I assume you want a print-out statement?' the teller asked.

Jenelyn nodded. She wanted to be able to remember. Two seconds later, she was staring at a ridiculous sum in her hand.

'This can't be right!' she gasped.

Gretchen looked at it and nodded.

'But it is! That's fourteen thousand Euros you have,' she said matter-of-factly, not seeming at all surprised.

Jenelyn's head whirled, and she felt like she was going to faint. She had never thought of so much money in her life, much less owned it! She sank onto a nearby chair and looked at Gretchen in panic.

'How can this be?' she stammered. 'I mean, I'm only Edwin's secretary!'

Gretchen whipped out a calculator from her purse and punched in some numbers.

'It's right, Jenelyn,' she assured her, showing her the statement with every check deposit. 'See, in ten months, that adds up to quite a bit of money. Especially since you shop so rarely and don't pay any bills. In another couple of months, you'll have another three thousand.'

Jenelyn felt sick. She had no idea what she was going to do with so much money. Gretchen saw her panic and hugged her.

'Don't worry, Liebling,' she assured her. 'This is wunderbar. Now you don't have to worry about paying for your next destination, and in fact, you'll probably have some money left to live off of while you look for work! This is very relieving.'

Jenelyn nodded woodenly, knowing Gretchen was right. Jenelyn felt a weight on her chest ease, but it reappeared when she started to think about travelling with that much money. She could all too clearly remember the LA gangs and regular muggings. When she voiced this concern to Gretchen, she laughed.

'Don't worry about that,' she said. 'The funds can transfer to the new bank wherever you are. Simply pull out a few hundred for necessities, and then transfer the rest later.'

'Ja, but how do I transfer it later?' Jenelyn wondered, biting her lip and her leg jigging in panic at how little she knew of banking.

'We'll ask the teller and see,' Gretchen replied, ever practical, and leading her to the teller once more.

Fortunately, the teller was more than helpful. She explained how Jenelyn could simply sign up for online banking. This was a novelty for both Gretchen and Jenelyn, but she could see how convenient it would be. Especially in her situation since she never knew where she was going.

'Once you are signed up,' the teller said patiently, 'you can put in your new account details and transfer the money electronically.'

Thanking her profusely, Jenelyn and Gretchen walked back to their car. Jenelyn knew that Laszlo would help her sign up for her online account on the computer at home. Online banking certainly seemed like the solution to her problem, yet Jenelyn still felt the weight of the few hundred Euros she carried trailing along beside her.

'Just think, Jenelyn, you'll be nineteen in two months!' Liesl cried a couple of weeks later as they were hanging out in Jenelyn's room. 'This is so wunderbar! What do you want to do to celebrate?'

Jenelyn smiled at her friend. In a way, Liesl sounded exactly like Nicole had last year when her eighteenth birthday had been around the corner.

'Oh, Liesl, I don't know,' she said, leaning her head against the pillow on her bed. 'Birthdays aren't that big a deal to me.'

Liesl's eyes widened. 'Not a big deal?' she shrieked in disbelief. 'That's absurd! I mean, why not? Isn't it exciting that you're one year older?'

Jenelyn shrugged. She always felt older, especially now. Her feelings about having to leave soon were only getting stronger. It made her sad to think that she might not be around to celebrate her birthday with Liesl, just like she hadn't been able to celebrate Nicole's birthday.

Am I not supposed to be able to celebrate birthdays with friends anymore? She thought sadly.

'Ja, I guess it's nice to be older,' Jenelyn agreed, trying to humour her friend. 'But I don't know what to do.'

Liesl jumped on this.

'We can have a party!' she cried. 'With me, Gretchen, Laszlo, and my grandparents. That isn't too many people. Come on, it'll be fun!'

Jenelyn wanted so much to know that it would happen, but her heart warned her not to get too excited. Her birthday would be full of goodbyes, not fun. She wished that she knew whether her feelings were right or not, but she wasn't going to take any chances of getting her hopes up.

'We'll see,' she said, smiling at Liesl's excited face, but cried internally.

'We'll make you a Black Forest cake.' Liesl went on, her face beaming with her plans. 'It's the most common chocolate cake here, filled with fresh cream and cherries, and of course soaked in Kirschwasser, a cherry schnapps. You'll love it!'

Liesl laughed and jumped on the bed, unaware of Jenelyn's sad expression. Jenelyn gave a light chuckle and couldn't believe she had considered the girl shy when she first met her.

'Of course,' she agreed, laughing at Liesl's antics as her friend danced on the bed. 'Would I have a choice?'

'Nein.' Liesl laughed. 'We'll force it down your throat! I can't believe you've never had it.'

That gave Jenelyn an idea. She didn't know how to tell everyone that she felt like she would be leaving soon, but she did have a way to make sure she would be able to celebrate her birthday.

'Hey, Liesl, what if we celebrate my birthday a little early?' Jenelyn asked, not wanting to make the girl suspicious.

'Why?' Liesl immediately asked, confused. 'Who celebrates their birthdays early?'

Jenelyn knew she was walking on eggshells.

'Um, some people,' she said lamely. 'I'm just looking forward to it, I guess.'

Liesl's eyes narrowed suspiciously.

'Why? It's a fun dinner, but no need to celebrate it early. What's going on, Jenelyn?'

Jenelyn stared at Liesl's confused face and resigned herself. What difference did it make? She was going to have to tell her at some point.

'My family has a different kind of culture, Liesl,' she confessed softly. 'We believe that Spirits guide us to our true homes. I may have to leave soon.'

Liesl's face fell. 'What?' she asked. Her voice was flat.

'I'm on my Journey,' Jenelyn continued. 'My family's tradition is when you turn eighteen, you have to go on a Journey to find your true home. Well, this was my first destination. Gretchen and Laszlo happened to be friends of my mother's. But, I can feel that my time is coming to an end here, and I don't want to miss celebrating my birthday with you. I had to miss celebrating my friend Nicole's birthday last year because I moved here, and it was awful. I want to make sure I can still celebrate my birthday with friends before moving on.'

Liesl's face scrunched in anger. 'Why didn't you tell me?' she snapped, 'Did you think I wouldn't understand?'

Jenelyn shook her head quickly. The last thing she wanted was to make Liesl mad. She didn't want a repeat performance of what she went through with Nicole.

'Nein, Liesl!' she pleaded. 'I didn't want you to think that you would be wasting your time being friends with me. I wanted to enjoy the time we had together. Besides, I didn't know how long I was going to stay here. Now, I can feel that it's not much longer.'

Liesl stayed quiet for a moment, her upset face gradually relaxing as she avoided Jenelyn's pleading eyes. Then, finally, she looked at Jenelyn again.

'How long?' she asked matter-of-factly, as she fiddled with the throw pillow on Jenelyn's bed.

Jenelyn shook her head. 'There's no way to know,' she said. 'I haven't seen the Spirits yet, so I'm not sure. I can only feel them coming.'

'Do Gretchen and Laszlo know all this?' Liesl asked.

Jenelyn nodded. 'Ja, they do. As I said, they're friends of my mother's. They know what we are.'

'This sucks,' Liesl mumbled, then added, 'But, I agree then that we should celebrate your birthday early.'

Jenelyn gave Liesl a tight, grateful hug.

'Danke, Liesl,' she whispered. 'For understanding, for being with me, and for throwing me a great birthday party.'

Liesl hugged her back.

'Don't thank me yet. I haven't done anything,' she grumbled.

'Glücklicher geburtstag!' cried Gretchen, Laszlo, Liesl, and her grandparents as they carried a large Black Forest cake covered in chocolate shavings and cherries into the dining room.

Jenelyn laughed as they set the cake down in front of her and wished her a happy birthday. The nineteen pink candles danced in celebration as Jenelyn thought about what to wish for before blowing them out.

I wish that I will love my next destination, she thought as she blew them out. It felt strange celebrating her birthday in the last week of March, but she knew it was necessary.

'Danke, everyone.' She beamed. 'It looks wunderbar!'

'What did you wish for?' Liesl asked as she sat down next to her.

'If I tell you, it may not come true,' Jenelyn teased, but she didn't believe that any more than Liesl did. 'I wished that I'll love my next destination, wherever that might be.'

Gretchen had tears in her eyes as she cut the cake. Jenelyn had warned her and Laszlo the previous week that her time might be ending. They hadn't second-guessed her. Instead, Gretchen had asked if that was why Jenelyn had wanted to go to the bank. Jenelyn knew that deep down, her subconscious must have known.

'Well, I hope you won't leave *too* soon,' Laszlo said. 'I at least want another few months.'

Jenelyn pasted a smile on her face, but she knew that Laszlo wasn't going to get his wish. A few months suddenly seemed like a very long time. She glanced around the table and was pleased to see Liesl's grandparents chatting happily with Gretchen. She was glad that Laszlo and Gretchen had friends again and that Agnes's death was becoming easier to bear. Although, she knew that it would always haunt them. Until they were sure that Agnes's spirit was happy, they would never be content.

'Do you have any ideas of where you would *want* to go?' Liesl asked her.

'Not a clue.' She shrugged. 'I mean, if it was my choice, I would stay here. It wouldn't occur to me to ever leave. But the Spirits have the last word, and that's the place I'll have to go.'

Jenelyn took a bite of her cake and moaned at the rich chocolate and cherry flavour. Liesl had been right. The cake was decadent. Gretchen gave her a warm maternal smile, and for the first time in months, it didn't give Jenelyn a creepy feeling. Instead, she knew that she would always see Gretchen as a second mother. Liesl's grandmother, Felicie, then turned to chat with her, eager to learn more about Jenelyn's strange bohemian culture now that she and Erdmann knew the real reason Jenelyn was in

Germany. She didn't mind telling them since she knew they wouldn't judge her. Explaining her culture also gave her a renewed strength, emboldening her to remember that she was following the traditional path of her family. As she spoke, she knew that one day the fear would need to be replaced with a desire for the nomadic spirit her family lived by, and that filled her with calm confidence.

April

Eleventh Month

Chapter Twenty

The freezing snow crumbled softly in Jenelyn's gloved hand. She was standing in Gretchen and Laszlo's front yard, her long black hair covered in white flakes. Tears rolled down her cheeks, and she wondered why they weren't freezing. She sniffled and shook her head. She had to stop this. Crying over spilt milk was what her mother would say. Jenelyn knew that leaving Germany was inevitable. If it didn't happen now, as she knew it would, it would happen later, and being who she was, she had to accept it.

She had woken up on this dreary April morning in a panic. For some reason, she had known that today was pivotal. Everything seemed surreal, as if it was the last time she would ever see this house, this yard, her room, everything. Gretchen's smiling face this morning had been heart breaking. Jenelyn had barely been able to stifle her tears. Therefore, she had walked outside to get a hold of herself. She knew she didn't have much time until Gretchen came after her. Gretchen knew what Jenelyn had been feeling for this past month. Jenelyn felt like Germany was her home. Not home like in Los Angeles with her parents, but her home where she had grown into an adult.

Her two sentry trees stood frozen, their limbs covered in snow. Jenelyn would miss their company dreadfully and the feeling of protection they gave her. She would miss the cheerfulness of the living room and the calm serenity of her bedroom.

Goodbyes will forever be part of your life, she scolded herself, choking back a sob. *So learn to live with it.*

'Jenelyn?' Gretchen called from the front door, 'Did you want frühstück? I'm sure you're hungry, schätzchen.'

Jenelyn couldn't help smiling. Of course, she was hungry. Her appetite had never ceased to amaze Gretchen and Laszlo even after all this time. She breathed deeply and turned, forcing her lips to turn up into a small smile.

'Ja, Gretchen,' she said, a little too brightly.

Gretchen saw right through her façade. She smiled sympathetically and walked over to her, wrapping her arms around herself to protect from the cold.

'Oh, Jenelyn,' she said. 'We're going to miss you whenever you leave. But you don't know that it will be now.'

A sharp pain stabbed her heart, and Jenelyn looked down, a lone tear falling to the frosty ground.

'But I do, Gretchen,' she murmured. 'My time is now. I don't know how I know for sure, but I do.'

'Well, we'll see.' Gretchen hugged her. 'But, for now, why don't you come eat?'

Jenelyn reluctantly agreed. They walked back into the house, where it was slightly warmer than outside. The ordinary, large breakfast spread greeted her in the kitchen, sitting out for her expectantly.

'I thought you might like to try some muesli,' Gretchen offered, her cheerful tone barely covering her concern.

She gave the bowl to Jenelyn, who looked at the mix of grains and fruits with mild interest. It looked appetising, but she felt too preoccupied to enjoy it. Thanking Gretchen, she sat down and tried to concentrate on Gretchen's cheerful chattering. Her leg started to jig under the table, and as she looked at the food, her stomach clamped – it felt like there was something she needed to do.

'Where's Laszlo?' she asked.

'He's still asleep,' Gretchen replied, her eyebrows raised. 'You know it's only seven o'clock.'

Jenelyn nodded, looking confused. 'Ja, I know that. It's just...I feel like he needs to be up.'

She looked at Gretchen, concerned, hoping she didn't think she was being rude, but Gretchen only looked apprehensive.

'Is everything alright, Jenelyn?' she asked, her tone thick with anxiety.

Jenelyn nodded, but she wasn't sure. She had the strangest feeling that she needed to get out of the house. She felt as if the walls were closing in on her.

'Excuse me, Gretchen,' she said and bolted from the kitchen and back out into the yard. A bitter north wind had picked up, swirling the frozen snow around her.

Jenelyn shivered, trembling with nerves from a persistent premonition. She felt better outside, but she still had the incessant urge to keep moving. She decided to succumb to her instincts and see where they led her. She began to run aimlessly, randomly picking a direction. The snow blinded her as she pushed through it, the flakes attacking her eyelashes and nose and making a frosty cyclone around her so dense she could barely see. Hardly aware of her movements, she ran down the street, and turned at the corner. Jenelyn had no idea where her feet were taking her, but deep down, she knew she had chosen a destination, so she wasn't surprised when she ran into the forest.

Snow blanketed the trees and ground, and it was quieter than Jenelyn had ever heard it. She could hear her heart, her breath. Puffs of steam blew from her mouth as she walked down the well-tread path to the shrine. She felt like she was on autopilot, her subconscious leading the way. In the deathly quiet of the forest, she could hear voices in her memory.

'*You have my freedom of spirit,*' her mother's voice said. '*Let the Spirits guide you.*'

'*We never say goodbye,*' she heard her father say in his gentle, gruff voice. '*It's always latcho drom, good journey.*'

Hearing her parents' voices made her feel stronger. Jenelyn stiffened her jaw and walked faster. This was her destiny. This was who she was. She wasn't going to disgrace herself by being a coward. It didn't take her long to reach the infamous shrine covered in snow, the flowers beneath it frozen and dead, and the maroon candle extinguished. A small shiver of fear slithered up her spine, but she stood firm. She listened carefully, trying to hear a muffled padded paw in the snow or hear the laboured breathing of a predator. But there was nothing, only the snow, falling heavily around her.

Jenelyn took a deep breath and spun around but could only see empty forest. She was rapidly getting nervous and knew she wasn't alone. Suddenly, her heart stopped. An enormous grey shadow was silhouetted against the snow behind the shrine. It crept towards her slowly, its features defining gradually as it came closer. It had all the appearance of a wolf, only three times larger and more alien. Its forearms were longer, rippled with muscle, and it walked with a peculiar, loping gait. Coarse grey and black hair bristled down its neck and back, standing a few inches high. Sharp pointed ears lay flat against its narrow head. Its large paws treaded silently over the snow, and its long tail swept across the ground with every measured stride. Terror choked her, making it impossible for her to breathe.

This can't be happening! Her practical voice told her, *myths aren't real!*

The deep, scarlet eyes of the werewolf pierced through her. Jenelyn could see its jagged, sharp teeth as it growled. She swallowed hard, trying to find her breath, and fought the instinct to run. She knew that it was wiser to stay still. Even though this was a much more dangerous predator than any mountain lion, she knew it was still a predator. Running would only make it attack.

To her utter shock, the werewolf stopped a few feet in front of her. It was close enough for her to feel its burning body heat and for its hot breath to wash over her face. Its smell was atrocious, like blood and sour milk combined. It simply stood there, staring at her. Jenelyn couldn't help wondering why it didn't attack her. As her fear diminished slightly, she focused on its eyes. They were blood red and menacing, yet calm. A hungry lust didn't burn in them, causing her fear to dissipate even further.

The werewolf breathed a soft growl and bared its teeth, shaking its head stiffly, fighting an internal struggle. A part of it wanted to attack, but something was stopping it. Jenelyn frowned in confusion as she watched the werewolf battle with itself. Unexpectedly, it looked straight at her again. She was quickly lost in the crimson of the werewolf's eyes, and what she saw astounded her. In her mind's eye, she could see the tall, elegant shape of the Eiffel Tower, then the majestic stone fortress of Notre Dame. Her breath shortened, and she felt faint. As she stood staring at the monstrous werewolf, she could hear a voice in her head like melodic bells singing in her ear.

'*Go, Jenelyn,*' it sang softly. '*Heed the wolf. Your true home is not here.*'

Jenelyn's eyes filled with tears. The voice was obviously her Spirits, and she knew now that the mythical creature standing before her was connected with them. Only a few minutes had passed, and then the werewolf's eyes broke away from hers. A vicious snarl ripped from its throat, making the hair on the back of Jenelyn's neck stand on end as it looked at something behind her. Jenelyn swung around in horror. Gretchen and Laszlo stood frozen in the path, matches in one hand, and a gun in the other. The werewolf gave a mighty roar and leapt nimbly over Jenelyn, rushing toward its prey.

'No!' Jenelyn screamed in anguish, feeling stupidly slow as she tried to run toward them, 'Gretchen, Laszlo!'

Before the werewolf could reach them, a bright, blinding white light intercepted from the depths of the woods, stopping the werewolf instantly. The werewolf screamed in pain and gave a high-pitched whine, backing up quickly. The light grew brighter, its radiance making everything around it turn a luminescent white. Gretchen and Laszlo had fallen to the ground in terror, clutching each other tightly. Jenelyn stood alone, frozen at the sight. The werewolf kept growling viciously, but the light was pushing it back toward the shrine. When its tail hit the granite headstone, it yelped, and the light reached forward and lit the candle. The werewolf disappeared with a mournful howl, and the light dimmed, though it was still light enough to bathe the woods in a white glow. Jenelyn squinted, trying to focus through the blinding light. It grew dimmer, until a small shape appeared, floating in the air. Jenelyn gasped. A young girl stood looking at her with playful blue eyes. Jenelyn felt a wave of understanding and relief. She knew those eyes. She knew that smile.

'Hallo, Jenelyn.' Agnes's voice sounded like a wind chime, 'Danke.'

Gretchen and Laszlo shakily crept forward, their eyes wide and watery. The spirit smiled at them, and its arms widened.

'Mama, Vati!' Agnes cried happily. 'Ich liebe sie!'

Tears streaked down Jenelyn's face as she watched Gretchen and Laszlo stare at the spirit of their daughter. When the spirit said 'I love you', she was sure that Laszlo was going to burst. His face was pleading, his eyes tortured with hope.

'Agnes, meine tochter,' he whispered, his voice cracking in sobs, 'Vergibst du mir?'

Agnes, my daughter, Jenelyn mentally repeated, *Do you forgive me*?

The spirit quivered as it laughed.

'Vater,' it assured soothingly. 'Es gibt nichts um zu verzeihen.'

Father, Jenelyn thought, *there is nothing to forgive.*

Laszlo finally exploded in a waterfall of tears, his shoulders heaving with each sob. Gretchen couldn't speak, her body wracking in sobs. Jenelyn hoped that Laszlo's pain had ended with his daughter's forgiveness. Agnes had lifted the guilt that haunted him the most. Jenelyn looked back at Agnes' spirit and smiled. The spirit waved at her and grinned. Her face was jubilant, radiant. They could all see that she was obviously happy.

'Agnes?' Jenelyn asked the light in German, 'Why didn't the werewolf attack me?'

The spirit looked puzzled for a moment, then rippled with a patient chuckle as she explained.

'Because of who your family is,' it replied in German. 'Legends cannot harm you because the Spirits protect you from them. Your Spirit used the legend to guide you to your next destination.'

A wave of confusion washed over her, leaving her stunned and unable to speak. What did Agnes mean by who her family was? Though her parents lived a free-spirited, bohemian lifestyle, they were still regular people. After being taught her family's traditions all her life, they had never admitted to seeing mythical legends. She snorted softly. Her parents could have at least warned her! Her irritation cut through the shock, and she was able to find her voice again.

'Danke, Agnes,' she said, her tone soft and hiding her irritation towards her parents. 'For protecting us.'

Agnes laughed again and flew back toward her grave. She gave them another childlike wave and then vanished. When her light was gone, the forest seemed much darker. Jenelyn walked woodenly back to Gretchen and Laszlo, who were still weeping.

'Let's go home.' Jenelyn suggested gently, helping Gretchen up. 'It's over.'

Gretchen and Laszlo stumbled next to Jenelyn on the way home, too overcome with emotion to walk steadily. When they returned to the house, they collapsed on the sofas, all lost in their own thoughts and emotionally spent between grief and terror. After an hour of heavy silence, Laszlo was the first to speak.

'She's happy,' he whispered. 'I will never have to worry for her spirit ever again.'

Gretchen beamed at him, tears in her eyes. 'I know,' she agreed, 'Isn't it wunderbar? Wittlich will forever be protected by our daughter.'

Laszlo beamed tearfully, and then held up a finger for them to wait. He ran up the stairs quickly and returned with Agnes's picture frame. A knot rose in Jenelyn's throat at the sight of the picture frame that had haunted them for years. Laszlo placed it reverently between the other two frames and turned back to them, pride lighting his face. All at once, the room seemed bright and cheerful once more, the same as the day Jenelyn arrived. She studied the soft couch beneath her, the plush carpet, the blooming flowers in the vases, and the bright yellow walls. Agnes' smile lit the room from her picture frame, her fresh face acting as a guardian to them all. The same as she was the guardian to the werewolf in the woods.

'She's here to stay,' Gretchen whispered, her voice cracking with emotion.

Jenelyn felt happy for them, but she had other thoughts on her mind. The werewolf, and her Spirit, had shown her where she needed to go, and she knew that it had to be now. However, looking at Laszlo and Gretchen's drawn faces, etched with a mixture of despair and relief, she knew it would have to wait. The rest of the evening was relatively silent, no one having much to say as they processed their emotions. Although Laszlo and Gretchen could be grateful that Agnes's spirit was happy, they had also had to endure saying goodbye to her for the last time. Jenelyn decided to give them space from her own issues and rested in her room, trying to wrap her head around her next destination.

The following day, Gretchen seemed a lot better. She was in the kitchen, as usual, preparing breakfast and acting for all the world like nothing had happened.

'Guten Morgen, Jenelyn.' She greeted, her eyes full of understanding as she smiled. 'We're much better today, danke. I'm sorry we didn't talk with you much last night.'

Jenelyn waved her hand at her. 'Don't worry, I know how hard it was for you.'

Before she could continue, Laszlo surprised them by coming into the kitchen early. The lines on his face looked deeper, but Jenelyn was happy to see that his eyes didn't seem as heavy.

'It was hard,' he agreed, echoing her words. 'But I'm glad it happened. I have a memory of my daughter again that's fresh. And you to thank for it.'

He hugged Jenelyn tightly. Tears welled in her eyes. It was time to tell them before she couldn't. She took a deep breath.

'Gretchen, Laszlo. My Spirits contacted me through the werewolf. It showed me my next destination.'

Laszlo and Gretchen gaped at her. Jenelyn almost hated burdening them with this news after the horrendous ordeal they had just gone through. Sorrow was going to replace their relief, and she felt guilty for doing it.

'I need to go to France,' she continued, her voice trembling with fear. 'As soon as possible.'

Gretchen burst into tears again and hugged Jenelyn tight. Laszlo seemed stunned. Jenelyn could tell from their faces that they weren't ready for her to leave. She had become an integral part of their lives, keeping them happy and busy once more, but she knew that she had her own life to live, and leaving them was part of it.

'So soon?' Laszlo asked, uncertain. 'But where will you live?'

'I don't know.' She shrugged and then asked, 'Do you happen to know anyone in France?'

Laszlo pondered for a moment and then nodded. 'We do, actually, though I would need to ask them if they wouldn't mind taking you in.'

'I'm sure they wouldn't mind,' Gretchen said. 'We've known them for years. We'll call them today, right after breakfast.'

Jenelyn raised her eyebrows, but felt a small wave of relief at the prospect of being able to stay with people again. Though she knew she would have to be independent one day, she didn't feel quite ready for it.

'I hope they don't mind,' she said. 'And please let them know it would only be until I could find work.'

Laszlo and Gretchen nodded reassuringly. Breakfast went by quickly, and then it was time to go upstairs to Laszlo's home office to phone their friends. Jenelyn followed behind them slowly, feeling numb. She would be on her own again, with strangers, in a different culture, and hoping that she could find a job and survive. She also knew that there was a real possibility that she may never see Gretchen or Laszlo again. Her shoulders sagged, and her steps slowed on the stairs as a wave of heavy exhaustion overcame her. She suddenly felt very old.

'Where do you need to go in France?' Laszlo asked her, popping his head outside the office door with the phone in his hand, 'Was the Spirit specific?'

Jenelyn remembered visions of the Eiffel Tower and Notre Dame, and shrugged. Her head was swimming from adrenaline and fear, making it difficult to interpret the vague message her Spirits had given.

'I guess it might have meant Paris,' she replied uncertainly. 'Or it could have been showing me obvious places that meant France. I'm really not sure.'

Laszlo grunted. 'Well, our friends live in the Poitou-Charantes region, which is in the southwest.'

'That's perfectly fine,' Jenelyn assured him. The region meant nothing to her, but she was flattered that he took her tradition so seriously. She couldn't be picky and was simply grateful if these friends allowed her to stay with them at all.

'Bonjour, Alexandre!' he said, with Gretchen repeating him since they were on speakerphone. 'It's been too long!'

Jenelyn listened curiously. It was nice to be able to hear these people before she got there. To her surprise, Laszlo had slipped into English, and she assumed it must be for her benefit.

'Bonjour!' a crackly male voice replied over the phone. 'And to you too, Gretchen.'

Gretchen greeted him, and they continued chatting for a moment, simply catching up since it had been so long. Jenelyn had to wonder how long it had been since these friends had heard from Gretchen and Laszlo after they had been socially distant for many years. These friends didn't seem too surprised though, so perhaps they kept in contact more than she realised.

'Well, there is a reason for our call,' Laszlo continued after a few moments, and Jenelyn's heart stopped for a second. 'We have an American friend that has been staying with us for the past year, and she needs a place to stay in France. Gretchen and I were wondering if perhaps you would be willing to let her stay with you until she can find work.'

A brief pause answered, followed by what sounded like snapping fingers. Jenelyn looked at Gretchen worriedly.

'I called Nathalie over to the phone, so she can talk with you too,' Alexandre answered, and to Jenelyn's relief, he didn't sound offended at the request. 'You know how she's the boss.'

Laszlo laughed as he and Alexandre enjoyed a brief moment of male banter before Nathalie came to the phone.

'Laszlo, Gretchen!' she squealed with glee. 'Bonjour, mes amies. What is this I hear about a friend from Amérique?'

Her voice was light and friendly, though her accent was much stronger than her husband's. Jenelyn thought both of them sounded like friendly people.

'She's on a kind of journey,' Gretchen explained. 'Do you remember me telling you about my bohemian friend during college? She's her daughter.'

This surprised Jenelyn. Gretchen and Laszlo must have known these friends for quite some time if Gretchen had told Nathalie about her mother. A sudden gasp of understanding from both voices over the phone made Jenelyn wonder what exactly they knew.

'Ah, bien sûr,' Nathalie said. 'That is not a problem at all. Tell the girl she is most welcome, s'il te plait.'

'It may also help her to start learning French now before she comes,' Alexandre suggested. 'She will need it to get her residence visa and for work. She will also need to get medical insurance and two photographs. Does she have her birth certificate? She will need that as well.'

'You have everything, richt?' Gretchen asked, and Jenelyn nodded woodenly.

Her heart plummeted at the thought of another language to learn and dealing with so much paperwork. Before she could become too despondent, Nathalie interrupted her husband.

'Don't worry about learning French. I will sign her up at a local class,' she assured them. 'Once they know she's taking a class, they will give her a visa.'

Gretchen shot a beaming smile at Jenelyn. She grinned tightly, but nerves were starting to overcome her. In a brief few moments, her future was taking shape before her eyes. She knew she should only be grateful, especially since she could even hear the people she was staying with. But it also sounded like another challenging transition.

'We will pick her up at the Saint-Jean-d'Angély train station.' Nathalie continued happily, 'This is nouvelles excitantes!'

Gretchen laughed. 'I'm glad you're excited,' she said. 'I know we're very thankful and relieved. She's a sweet girl and won't cause you any trouble.'

By this time, Jenelyn was starting to feel like a pet being given up for adoption. She walked over to the phone and silently asked Laszlo if she could speak to them. It was time to speak up for herself.

'Hello Alexandre, Nathalie,' she said, keeping her tone as friendly as possible through her nerves. 'I want to thank you so much for letting me stay with you. I promise I will look for work immediately and find a place as soon as possible.'

'Non, do not even worry,' Alexandre assured her. 'You're welcome for as long as you need.'

With a quick thanks, Jenelyn passed the phone back to Gretchen and Laszlo so they could discuss visas and how to obtain them. It sounded as if Alexandre knew precisely what she needed.

'How does he know so much?' Jenelyn asked Gretchen, who had quietly walked over to her, leaving Laszlo to finish the conversation.

'Alexandre works at the airport for immigration,' Gretchen said, a mischievous twinkle in her eye. 'Quite convenient, isn't it?'

Oddly convenient, in fact, Jenelyn thought. *I guess it could be a sign that this is where I'm supposed to be.*

Jenelyn was a bit daunted, though she liked that everything was set up for her. She didn't have any other options, and it certainly sounded perfect. Laszlo got off the phone with a cheerful farewell and walked over to them, his face bright.

'Alexandre gave me the website for you to apply for your visa,' he explained. 'It should take three to four weeks to be approved. Nathalie is emailing me the name of the language course and school where you'll be learning French. We can find out about medical insurance as well.'

'Wow, I guess that settles it then,' Jenelyn said, bewildered by how fast all of this had happened. 'I guess I just have to buy my plane ticket. I hope it isn't too much.'

She would only have another month in Germany to say goodbye and to pack.

'We aren't very far from Paris by train. You should be able to get a train ticket for around €100,' Gretchen explained. The price and close distance shocking Jenelyn. 'Then you will need to take a train to the Saint-Jean-d'Angély train station.'

Jenelyn nearly choked at the cheap price of the ticket, and her shoulders relaxed, knowing she wouldn't have to fly again. A train ride sounded much more manageable and certainly more economical and time-efficient since she could leave straight from Wittlich. Although the thought of having to find the next train was a bit intimidating, she focused instead on the benefits.

'That sounds perfect!' she exclaimed in relief. 'Can I book the tickets online?'

Laszlo nodded and went to the website, helping her navigate through the different prompts. In minutes, Jenelyn had them booked. The train ride from Wittlich to the Gare de Paris-Montparnasse train station would take four hours, and then for another eighty Euros, she would take a train for four hours to the Saint-Jean-d'Angély station. The thought of the long, eight-hour trip weighed heavily on her, but it was still preferable to flying.

'At least driving you to the train station will be easier than when we picked you up.' Laszlo grunted. 'A thirty-minute drive instead of five hours.'

Jenelyn chuckled and hugged him. She was going to miss him dearly. As much as she dreaded leaving, she knew the inevitable had to happen, and she wanted to take care of the necessities as soon as possible.

'Can we apply for my visa now?' she asked. 'If I only have a month, I'd better start the process.'

Laszlo agreed and went to the French embassy website. For the next hour, they filled out her visa application form. It was suddenly feeling very real to Jenelyn that she was leaving soon. She didn't feel prepared for it at all. Taking a deep breath, she shakily clicked 'submit' and sat back, her heart thumping against her chest and a knot tightening in her throat.

'Here goes nothing,' she said. 'I'll be on my way again.'

Gretchen hugged her, and Jenelyn burst into tears. Time was much too short.

Last Month

Chapter Twenty-One

Jenelyn folded her last shirt and placed it neatly into her second suitcase, laying her folder full of immigration paperwork on top for easy access. Unlike last time when she packed, she now had two suitcases thanks to Liesl and Gretchen shopping with her. Jenelyn felt her chest tighten, but didn't allow herself to sob again. She was finished crying. That was all she had been doing for the past month. It was now May, and she had been in Germany for exactly one full year. It was one of the happiest years of her life. Gretchen and Laszlo would always feel like surrogate parents, and Liesl was like the sister she never had. Edwin had been devastated when she had given him her two weeks' notice last month. He simply couldn't believe it. She had felt terrible doing it to him, but he had insisted on writing a recommendation letter for her. She had been very grateful, knowing that would help her a lot in the future.

That was a few weeks ago. Today was her last day. She snapped her suitcase shut and glanced around her room. No longer was it her room. It was only a guest bedroom. She remembered how much she loved its charm and beauty on her first day. Now she couldn't imagine not coming home to it every night. Jenelyn squared her shoulders and walked out of the room, refusing to look back. Everything was prepared, and it was time to go.

Downstairs, Gretchen, Laszlo, Liesl, and her grandparents, Erdmann and Felicie, stood waiting for her. It was nine o'clock, and Jenelyn was flattered that they had come so early in the morning to say goodbye to her. Liesl was crying, and it took all of Jenelyn's willpower not to cry as well.

'I'm going to miss you so much,' Liesl wailed, flinging her arms around Jenelyn, almost knocking her to the floor. 'I can't believe you're leaving!'

Jenelyn hugged Liesl back.

'I know,' she agreed sadly. 'I wish I could write to you, at least, but I have to be on my own.'

Liesl sniffled but nodded in understanding. Jenelyn then turned to Erdmann and Felicie.

'It was wonderful meeting you both,' she said warmly. Though they had kept her on her toes with all their questions, they were very friendly, and she had liked both of them.

'You be safe,' Felicie said, her face firm. 'It'll be all we can do to keep Liesl happy when you leave, and hearing that you had an accident won't make it easier.'

Jenelyn promised, and the old woman hugged her gently. Erdmann patted her on the back.

'Good luck, Jenelyn,' he said. 'Knowing you has been wunderbar. Thanks so much for being such a great friend to our Liesl.'

'It was no problem,' Jenelyn replied, smiling again at Liesl, who was still wailing. 'I had a lot of fun.'

Gretchen had tears in her eyes, but Jenelyn knew she and Laszlo had sworn to each other that they were not going to cry all day.

'I wish I could go with you,' Liesl managed to say, gasping between sobs. 'I'm almost jealous you get to go to France. You'll get to meet all the Frenchmen!'

She gave Jenelyn a tearful wink and chuckled. Jenelyn laughed.

'Oh, believe me, the last thing I'll be thinking about is men,' she groaned. 'I'll have bigger problems.'

It made her nervous to think about the new people that she was going to be living with. On top of that, she would need to learn a new language and new customs. No, men were the furthest problem on her mind.

After a few more hugs and well wishes, Liesl and her grandparents left, leaving Laszlo, Gretchen, and Jenelyn alone in the house for the last time. Gretchen and Laszlo were driving her to the Wittlich train station in an hour. Her train left at ten o'clock, to arrive in Paris at two o'clock in the afternoon, then arrive in perfect time to meet Alexandre and Nathalie in Saint-Jean-d'Angély at six-thirty, as they had planned.

As their friends left, she linked her arm through Gretchen's, and they walked to the living room. They sat down on the cream brocaded sofa, and Jenelyn looked around the room for the last time. Her eyes settled on Agnes's picture once more, proudly on display as it should be.

'I still think this is the happiest room I've ever seen,' she said. 'I'll never forget it.'

Gretchen squeezed her hand lovingly. 'It was made all the happier by having you here. You have helped us in so many ways.'

Laszlo nodded, grabbing Jenelyn's shoulder and giving it a tight squeeze. His voice was thick with emotion.

'We never could have guessed how much you would have changed our lives when you came,' he said gratefully. 'You brought our daughter back to us, and in doing so, brought us a peace I didn't think we would feel again. If you are ever in need, you can always call on us.'

Jenelyn gave him a tearful grin and thanked him. She felt a sense of pride that she had helped Laszlo and Gretchen transition from mourning to despair and finally, to a peaceful acceptance. The morning went far too quickly. She wished she could treasure these last precious moments for longer, but ever so steadily, the hands on the clock marched on. Before she was ready, Laszlo glanced at his wristwatch, and they all looked at one another.

'I guess it's time to go,' he stated reluctantly. 'Jenelyn, have you said your goodbyes to the house?'

Jenelyn nodded tearfully. She couldn't believe she was leaving this house forever. She had walked all the rooms the night before, memorising every crack, every wall. She had taken some pictures, but she knew that they wouldn't capture her feelings in every room.

'I'm putting a brötchen in this bag as a snack,' Gretchen said, handing her a zip-locked bag with a bun filled with meat and cheese. 'You can eat it on the train if you get hungry.'

Jenelyn gave her a grateful smile, appreciating Gretchen for always being so thoughtful to her stomach. She took the bag from her and wrapped her arms around Gretchen in a tight, silent hug. She didn't trust the knot in her throat not to betray her if she spoke.

They walked outside and piled into Laszlo's tiny car. Jenelyn felt a sense of déjà vu as she crammed herself into the backseat. Fortunately, this time, it was only for a half-hour.

As they entered the large, orange train station, Jenelyn felt her first flutters of pure panic. In a few moments, she was going to be completely alone again, without the safety and comfort of Gretchen and Laszlo.

'Gretchen,' Jenelyn said, turning to her. 'You won't forget to call my parents and let them know I'll be in France, right? I want my mom to know where I am.'

Gretchen frowned, her eyes troubled. 'You know they're not supposed to know where you are.'

Jenelyn stared firmly into Gretchen's eyes. 'Please, Gretchen,' she begged. 'It's so important to me. Remember when you said that my parents were lucky that in these present times they could know I arrived at my destination safely? Well, how is that any different than letting them know where I am? This time, they won't even know that I got there!'

Gretchen hesitantly agreed.

'Jenelyn,' Laszlo touched Jenelyn's shoulder lightly. 'It's time to go. You have your booking number, right? You'll need it to print your ticket at that kiosk over there.'

Jenelyn nodded, tears filling her eyes, as she glanced over at the kiosk Laszlo mentioned, sitting amongst a swarm of people passing by it. The train station was as busy as the airport had been with people rushing to and fro from the platforms, and she found herself just as intimidated. But she was grateful that at least this time, she had company before she left.

'Ja, I do. I'm going to miss you so much,' she sniffled. 'I love you both.'

Gretchen started crying, hugging Jenelyn. 'It's been so nice having you. It's like we had our daughter back again.'

Jenelyn tried not to cry, but it was almost impossible. Laszlo was even getting emotional, a slight tear welling in his eye.

'Well, auf Wiedersehen, Jenelyn,' he said gruffly. 'Good luck.'

Jenelyn stepped back and breathed deeply, drying her eyes. She was going to be brave. She was going to be strong. She decided that her father had had the right idea about farewells.

'We never say goodbye.' She kept her chin high as she repeated his words. 'It's always *latcho drom*. Good journey.'

Gretchen nodded and hugged her tightly, her face glistening with tears.

'Then, *latcho drom*, Jenelyn,' she cried, her voice cracked with sorrow.

With one last glance and a departing wave, Jenelyn turned around and walked toward her new life.

About The Author

Born in northern California, Erin specialized as an equestrian trainer in the Olympic disciplines, but her natural wanderlust led her to Ireland, where she currently resides with her husband and three children. Surrounded by the natural splendor of the emerald coast, she embraced her love for the sprawling landscape through hiking. With a particular interest in European culture and history, Erin moved into the world of literature to share her tales of journeys and adventures with fellow bookworms.

You can follow Erin on Facebook at
facebook.com/eebyrnesauthor

Learn more about Erin and other works on her website at
www.eebyrnes.com

Made in the USA
Middletown, DE
01 December 2021